Never Too Late

—⚡—

*A tale of love and respect binding people from
different backgrounds together*

Harold J. Fischel

This book is a work of fiction. Names, characters, places, and incidents either are products of the author's imagination or are used fictitiously. Any resemblance to actual persons, living or dead, events, or locales is entirely coincidental.

Cover Design and Production by Angelheart Design

Copyright © 2015 Harold J. Fischel
All rights reserved.

ISBN: 0692404694
ISBN 13: 9780692404690
Library of Congress Control Number: 2015936422
Moose & Buck Publishing, Howell, MI.

I dedicate this novel to all who lead the international campaign against Human Trafficking, help convict the perpetrators, and assist the victims.

The Author

Harold J. Fischel, a graduate of Washington & Lee University and the NYU School of Law, has lived and worked on four different continents. His family fled the Netherlands shortly after the Nazi invasion, moving to Curacao and Aruba before settling in the United States in 1952.

After law school, Fischel served the US Army in Germany, later retiring as a captain. Since then, he again lived in the Netherlands, before returning to the United States to work for the US subsidiary of a Chinese company.

Fischel is now retired and living in Michigan with his wife, Jan, and their beloved Labrador retriever. He has two daughters, five wonderful grandchildren, and two great sons-in-law. Since retiring, he has published three novels.

I

"What the hell are you doing here? Just getting a kick out of slumming?"

"Oh, shut up. It's my class reunion too. Did you think by turning your back on me you could cut me out of the class?"

"Turning my back on you!? Are you forgetting who left and could not be bothered by those you left behind?"

"Who are those two standing next to the punch bowl? They seem to be having a fight."

"You don't recognize them? They went to school here, same class. We called them the golden couple. That is, until their relationship shipwrecked."

"Shipwrecked? What does that mean?"

"I forgot; you weren't teaching here at the time. Let me tell you about those two."

"He is Clint Crawley. We called him C.C. He was the star athlete here at Frederick High. Captain of the basketball team, quarterback on the football team, but best known as the star pitcher on the national junior all-star baseball team. She was his pretty—nah, beautiful—girlfriend. When he graduated, he was immediately drafted by the Dodgers. In the spring he left with a lot off fanfare for training camp, and refused to take Sharleen Harjo, his girlfriend, with him. She was furious, and swore she would never speak to him again.

"Even before the regular season started, Clint threw his arm out. Apparently his elbow sort of shattered, and his career was over. He returned home, but in the meantime, Sharleen had left for Hollywood. With her good looks she had no problem getting bit parts in the movies, and soon she was a much-sought-after starlet. Clint, on the other hand, was not that lucky. Shortly after his return home his father died, and he was forced to take over the family restaurant."

"Funny, but I never heard about this Sharleen. Is she still in the movies?"

"Maybe a bit part here and there, but she is not really pursuing a movie career. Recently she became the trophy wife of Giovanni Fuentes."

"You're kidding! Really? The guy rumored to be a big-time Mafia boss?"

"Yup. That's him, and Clint better watch out."

"Why is that?"

"Well she came into town with a delegation of heavies. Presumably all 'soldiers' for the Fuentes family. It might all be a bunch of rubbish and mean nothing. But Cathleen Townsend had both of them in homeroom during their senior year; she claims Sharleen is still in love with Clint, and that Giovanni is furious that she came to this class reunion."

II

Several weeks after his class reunion, Clint Crawley received a registered letter from his bank informing him his restaurant's loan had been cancelled, and all further credit facilities were withdrawn. He knew that he was maxed out on the amount the bank had agreed to, but having them call in the entire amount caught him completely by surprise. He immediately grabbed the phone and called Jim Higgins, vice president of the bank in charge of his account. Jim was not in, but his secretary, hearing how upset Clint was, arranged for a meeting with Jim later that afternoon.

"Jim, why now? The renovation is almost complete and I am about to reopen the restaurant."

"I know, Clint. But for the last several months you have not even been able to pay the interest on the loan. That has pushed your account substantially over the amount originally agreed upon. Our financial committee made the decision. They refuse to extend any more credit. I'm sorry, but it is out of my hands."

"Okay, don't increase my credit. But can't you just let the loan continue as is until I can reopen the restaurant? You know the restaurant will have a positive cash flow once we're back in business."

"Clint, you can't even pay the interest due on the account, so the amount you owe us automatically grows each month. I am sorry. I really am, but the bank has decided to call your loan. You have two weeks to repay the entire amount, or we are forced to take action."

"Damn you! When I first came to you with the plans for the renovation, you were gung-ho to lend me the money. If I remember correctly, it was at a meeting here at the bank that one of your colleagues suggested the interior of the restaurant was getting a little worn and could use a facelift."

"I know, I totally agree with you. We encouraged you to fix up the place; but you're way over budget, and at least four months behind schedule."

"It's almost six months. How was I to know that once we started the renovation the inspectors would demand we re-do the entire kitchen and bring it up to code. If that wasn't enough, they wouldn't let us keep our license if we did not completely modernize our bathrooms. The final blow came when they made us put in an elevator so the upstairs bar would be handicapped accessible. Actually, we needed two elevators because in order to keep our liquor license, we have to offer food upstairs in the bar. A dumbwaiter was not enough. They wanted us to install a second elevator for the personnel serving the upstairs. Yes, we're over budget. It would've been cheaper to build a whole new restaurant. You guys knew damn well what was happening. Why act now? And without warning?"

"That's not fair. I spoke to you several times about your account. I warned you the amount was getting way too high."

"Fine. There is nothing I can do about it now. I think I'll just walk away from the whole mess and let the bank have the restaurant, or whatever they plan to do about collecting the money."

"That won't be so easy. Remember when we raised the original amount we agreed to lend you, you personally signed for the entire loan in order to get us to raise the limit."

"I'm surprised you did not remind me of that with, 'I'm sorry,' and sit there behind your pompous desk pretending you are a sympathetic friend. You're not sorry, and you're not going to do a damned thing to help me. You'll just hide behind that financial committee of yours. So fuck you!" With that, Clint stormed out of Jim's office.

When he left the bank building, Clint was still highly agitated. His mind was racing; what could he do to get out of this mess? He had already mortgaged his house to the hilt, and even there he was two months behind in payments. In his confused state he stepped off the curb right into oncoming traffic.

Someone grabbed his arm and pulled him back on the curb. "What the fuck do you think you're doing? You want to kill yourself or something?" It was Sharleen.

Clint quickly regained his composure. "What the hell?! Sharleen, what are you doing here? Are you stalking me or something?"

"Don't you wish. No, I'm back in town for my father's fiftieth birthday celebration. It's a big deal. His brother and sisters, all of whom still live on the reservation, have come to visit. I was in the bank arranging a payment to the caterer when you passed me in the lobby. You looked like you had just seen a ghost. I tried to get your attention, but you flew right past me. I followed to see what was wrong, and I was right behind you when like an idiot you stepped right into traffic. So what is the matter? Why were you acting so strange?"

"What do you care? I'm surprised you pulled me back instead of letting that truck hit me. I would have thought you would be happy to see me dead."

"Cut that foolish talk. I am not the enemy. Sure, I have been angry with you. When you left without me I was plenty mad. But, Clint, that's over now. You behaved like an asshole, and I reacted like a moron. But that was then; a lot has happened since. Can we just get over it and be friends?"

Sharleen stuck out her hand in a gesture to end the hostilities. Clint hesitated before accepting her handshake. For a moment he just stared at her, as if he was trying to absorb what she was saying. *Why had he turned his back on this girl? Why had he refused to let her accompany him to the Dodgers' training camp?*

"Hey, wake up. Are you going to shake my hand or not?" Slowly Clint reached for her hand. Looking at her smiling face, a wave of guilt went through him. Did he leave her behind because of his father's hang-up that her father was a day laborer at the local cement factory? Or was it his mother's concern that, because of Sharleen's mother's very dark complexion, she might have black babies?

Clint grabbed Sharleen's hand with both hands and squeezed tightly. "Sharleen, I'm sorry. It wasn't about you. It all went to my head. I was a pompous ass, and it was all about me."

"Hey, cut that shit. Enough already about the past. Like I said, this is here and now, so tell me why you're going around looking like you've seen a ghost."

"Nah, I haven't seen any ghosts. My world just fell apart, that's all."

"Want to tell me about it?"

"Don't worry about me. I'll be all right. It was some bad news I just received at the bank that hit me hard. Don't worry, I'll bounce back."

"If you ask me, you can use a drink to help settle down. Let's go over to Harry's on the corner over there, and I'll buy you a drink. Maybe you'll even tell me what's wrong."

When they walked into Harry's, a few of the people sitting at the bar waved hello to Clint, but nobody remembered Sharleen. She looked stunning. Dressed in her forest-green designer suit, she was even more beautiful than the high school girl who'd left town several years before.

They chose a booth in back of the bar. After their drinks arrived, Sharleen said, "For old-time's sake, spill it; what's wrong that has gotten you so upset?"

Clint did not feel comfortable opening up to Sharleen, but she kept pushing him, and after a few drinks he told her the whole story. After being released by the Dodgers, he had returned home. When his father passed away a few years after his return, he was forced to take over the family restaurant. As Sharleen knew, the restaurant was more or less a fixture in town; the place to go to celebrate family occasions. But the restaurant was getting dated, and was rapidly losing business to newer, more modern restaurants. On the advice of others, mostly his bank, he decided to give the restaurant a facelift. He hoped that a new look would be good for business. Unfortunately, the renovation had gotten out of hand, and the cost overrun was huge. To keep up with the ever-increasing budget, he first mortgaged his house. When that proved insufficient, he personally signed for an increase of his credit at the bank. Now he faced bankruptcy, and he would have to figure a way out.

"Why don't you go see Paul Klein at City National?" Sharleen asked.

"Are you kidding? Paul doesn't like me. Remember, I replaced him as quarterback. He was a senior, and I was just a sophomore."

"And you really think that after all these years he holds that against you?"

"Don't know, but I am willing to take a chance. I have nothing to lose. The worst that can happen is that he laughs me out the door."

III

As soon as Sharleen left Clint, she jumped into a taxi and went to see Paul Klein at City National. Without an appointment, she still managed to waltz right into his office. To her surprise, Paul recognized her immediately.

"So Clint thinks I might still be mad at him because he replaced me as quarterback? Well, that's only part of the story. Since we're all married, I can tell you the real truth now. I didn't hold it against him that he replaced me as much as I resented that he was your steady. I was incredibly jealous of him because I had a huge crush on you. Who didn't? You were by far the most beautiful girl in town, and if I may add, sexiest, too."

Sharleen blushed. "Really?"

Yes, really. But that does not mean that I can approve a loan for Clint, just because you look more beautiful than ever. Certainly not in the amount you think he may need."

"Not even if I guarantee it?"

"It would be difficult. The only way I can envision it working would be for you to have an equal amount on deposit here in our bank. "

"Okay, how can I arrange that?"

"You would open an account here and deposit the required amount. For the guarantee to be effective, we would have to block the account. You could not withdraw any funds as long as Clint's loan is not repaid. That would be ridiculous. The bank would charge interest on a loan while the same amount is on deposit here. If you have the money, why don't you loan it to Clint directly? That would be far simpler."

"No, I can't do that. He would never accept that type of help from me. Besides, it would destroy him if he ever found out he got the loan based on my guarantee. That part has to remain a secret. But didn't you just mention now that we're all married; how did you know I am married?"

"You made the gossip columns and TV shows that follow the latest in celebrity doings. 'Giovanni Fuentes Marries Young Hollywood Starlet,' made the headlines, and your name was mentioned. Is he really a big Mafia boss?"

"No comment. I don't concern myself with my husband's business."

"Fair enough. You do know Clint is married too?"

"Yes. I was told when I was in town for my high school class reunion that he married Jada Washington."

"He married Jada just about the same time he took over his father's restaurant. Did you know her?"

"Did I know her? You must be kidding! Jada was my best friend all through high school. Our families spent a lot of holidays together; her father was a co-worker of my father. Seems Clint must have something with multiracial girls; first me, and now Jada."

"If she was your best friend, you should go see her while you're in town. She's in the hospital, and I hear it is pretty serious."

"Do you know which hospital?"

"Yes, she is in Good Samaritan."

"I'll go see her as soon as I can. Can we open an account for me right now? When you tell me the amount Clint asks for, I'll wire transfer the money. Here, I'll give you my cell phone number. Call me after you have spoken to Clint. I am sure he'll visit you within the next few days."

When she left the bank, Sharleen returned to the motel she was staying at. Once back in her room she called Bennie, her husband's personal assistant. Most people referred to Bennie Cardiello as Giovanni Fuentes' favorite nephew, but he was much more; he was Giovanni's financial manager.

"Bennie, dear, I need you to do something for me."

"What's up, Sharleen, you in trouble?"

"No, not me, Bennie. But I need some money to help a friend."

"No problemo, you know Bennie can fix that for his favorite little girl. How much do you need?"

"Don't know exactly, probably a million or more."

"You crazy? That's big money! How do you expect me to arrange that? Giovanni will have my ass."

"Bull! You told me a hundred times that Giovanni has no idea about money, and that you control all of the family's financial matters. So if you really mean it when you tell me you will always take care of me, do it!"

"Calm down, my little carina. Don't be angry. You know I always help you. But this is big. It'll take time."

"Thank you. Love you, Bennie; I knew I could depend on you. I'll call you in a few days to let you know where to transfer the money to."

IV

Sharleen swept into Jada's room at the hospital in the same way she got into Paul's office at the bank. She just waved off any questions from the nurses on the intensive care corridor and simply announced that she was on her way to see Jada Washington.

To say that Jada was shocked to see her would be an understatement. "Sharleen, what the hell!?"

Before greeting Jada, Sharleen turned to the nurse on duty and asked, "Would you be so kind as to leave us alone for a while? Thank you."

Without waiting for the nurse to leave, Sharleen turned to Jada. "What's the matter? Why are you here in the hospital in the intensive care unit?"

By this time Jada had regained her composure. "Hello, Sharleen, nice to see you. No, I'm not here on vacation. If you must know, I'm pretty damned sick. Damn it all; I got stomach cancer!"

This time it was Sharleen who had to catch her breath. "Oh, God no! I'm so sorry; if I had known I would have come sooner."

"Come on, don't pretend. I know you must hate me."

"Hate you? Are you crazy? Why on earth would I hate you? We used to be best friends!"

"Yeah, but that was back in high school. Before I married Clint."

"Girl, what's the matter with you? Why would I hate you because you married Clint?"

"'Cause you two used to be lovers. I'm sure you two would have married if he hadn't left."

"Actually, *I* left. I was really mad at him. And no, I'm not mad at you. I am happy he married you; it clears up a lot."

"I'm totally confused. I was your best friend, and I married the guy you were in love with. And you're happy about it? That sounds crazy! You're just saying that because you think I might be dying from this damned cancer."

"Look, you're not going to die. So stop that type of foolish talk. Let me explain why I am glad he married you. When he left for the Dodgers' training camp and refused to take me, I was sure it was because of my race. I was fully aware of the fact his parents were opposed to our relationship. His mother was worried that because I have mixed blood, I would have black children, and his father looked down on my father. He did not think the daughter of a poor Indian day laborer was a good match for his precious little boy.

But then at our class reunion someone told me that he married you. Jada, that was great news! He did not ditch me because I'm multiracial. He didn't care about his parents' opposition, or he wouldn't have married you, a multiracial gal."

"You were at our class reunion?"

"Yes, I looked all over for you but you weren't there. By asking around I found out that you had married Clint. I wanted to look you up, but I had to leave town immediately."

"Why? Your parents live here. Couldn't you stay a few more days?"

"No, my husband…but that's a long story, let's not go there. Anyway, I came back for my father's fiftieth birthday, and today I bumped into Clint. We agreed that we were both morons, and that we would let bygones be bygones and stop blaming each other for leaving. Jada, we're friends again. Isn't that great?!"

"Yes, but why did you pack up and leave? You barely said good-bye to me."

"I couldn't cope with Clint ditching me. I was convinced it was because I am multiracial. You have no idea what that was like! All through school it bothered me. Sure, I was popular, and I had a lot of friends; but deep down I was ashamed of my family, my heritage. You have no idea what that is like, to be so popular and still be ashamed of who you really are."

"Don't know? Girl, you forget! I am you without the pretty face. Same heritage. I did not have your beautiful face, but I had the sexy butt. Ashamed? You're nuts. The boys adored us for the way we looked, and the girls were jealous as hell of our good looks. Hardly any of the girls could match our figures or our long, jet-black hair. Not to mention our bronze skin color. Girl, we didn't need a suntan to look great. And you say you were ashamed of those wonderful gifts of nature? I don't think you really mean that. You were just plain pissed off and hurt that Clint left without you."

Sharleen could not help but smile. Sick as she was, Jada was still as spunky as ever. "Okay, you had a great ass, but I had the big tits. Need I remind you that Clint really liked them?"

Jada laughed at Sharleen's reference to Clint's way-too-obvious attraction to her ample breasts. It reminded her of an incident in which their physical features got them in trouble.

"Do you remember when Mrs. Slason, a member of the school board, insisted that our cheerleader's outfits exposed too much and were much too sexy? Boy were we angry when they made us wear pants and turtlenecks just like the boys."

"Do I ever!"

"Yeah, and how out of protest we shrank our short-shorts and tops."

Sharleen burst out laughing. "Seemed like the cheering never stopped; at the next game we appeared on the field dressed in those very tight outfits."

"But we did pay a price for our protest. One-week suspension and dropped from the cheerleading squad."

"How could I forget the uproar we created by our protest, and how we finally were allowed back on the cheerleading squad during our senior year? Guess we were sort of victorious when the squad went back to wearing the original outfits that Mrs. Slason objected to."

"We were best friends. But Sharleen, I was pretty pissy with you when you refused to fix me up with that handsome cousin of yours. If I remember correctly, his name was Lakota. Boy, did I want to date that hunk."

Sharleen quickly defended herself. "Jada, I told you I would have loved to see you date him, but his father would not allow him to date any girl that was not a full-blooded Native American. I tried to make you understand that my Uncle Chayton was sort of the self-proclaimed head of his tribe, and he was grooming Lakota to be his successor."

"What about you? You're no full-blood either!"

"Yeah, but I did not ask to date him. I was family!"

Jada laughed, "I know, silly! Just pulling your chain a little. But I was annoyed when you and Lakota spoke to each other in that hogwash I could not understand."

"Oh, that. That was Indian. Lakota's father, Chayton, is a self-taught Algonquian language scholar. He told us that Algonquin is the language for which the entire Algonquian language subgroup is named. He is very proud of the fact that he is one of only two thousand or so Algonquin speakers. He did not insist that Lakota learn Algonquin, but he did insist that all of us, that included me, learn about Siouan language. That language was one of the most spoken Native American languages. The three dialects Lakota, Dakota and Nakota are all understood in much of the Sioux Nation. Uncle Chayton always stressed that language was important for us to understand our history. Lakota is fluent in our language; they spoke it at home when he was growing up. Me, I understand it. I sometimes spoke it with my dad in order to annoy my mother. But I was never really fluent."

"Okay! Enough already. I forgive you for not hooking me up with Lakota, and talking gibberish behind my back. Girl, you sure don't sound like someone who claims to have been ashamed of her heritage."

Jada was all smiles remembering their high school days. But her mood quickly changed and she said, "Sharleen, I meant it when I said I might be dying." She burst out crying. "Sharleen, I'm scared. The doctors have given up on me. I'm going to die!"

Sharleen rushed to the bed and embraced Jada, who was hysterically crying and almost yelling that she did not want to die. Holding Jada in a tight embrace and forcefully telling her over and over again that she would not die, Sharleen finally managed to calm Jada down.

"Jada, listen to me. You are not going to die! Now tell me why you think the doctors have given up."

"I heard them discussing the results of the last tests, and they agreed that there was nothing more they could do for me."

"We'll move you to another hospital; of course there is something that can be done."

"We tried, but that would cost a lot of money and we haven't got it. Clint tried everything, he really did, but we are broke, and you know my family hasn't got it."

"Don't you have insurance?"

"No. We fell behind on the premiums when Clint needed all the money for the restaurant. They cancelled the policy. They claimed it was because we had failed to make a few payments, but I'm sure it was because of my cancer."

"Those bastards! Jada, there has got to be a way. Hospitals have funds to cover cases like yours; let me dig into this."

Jada fell back into her pillows. She was exhausted from the discussion, and the pain in her stomach was getting really bad. Sharleen called the nurse back in and she gave Jada an extra injection of morphine. It did not take long for the heavy dose of morphine to take effect, and while holding Sharleen's hand, Jada fell asleep. After making sure her friend was comfortably asleep, Sharleen left the room and headed straight for the administration building. She got all the way up to the head of hospital administration, but that was as far as she got. The lady was very polite and very friendly, but she would not discuss

Jada's condition. She claimed to have to protect the patient's privacy, and Sharleen was not even family. As far as moving Jada to a specialized cancer hospital, she was adamant; there was no way unless the family could pay for it.

Sharleen stormed out of the chief administrator's office. She was not about to let her friend die because of the inaction of a stupid bunch of bureaucrats who claimed concern for their patients, but in reality only wanted money. She found a quiet place in the lobby and called Giovanni on her cell phone.

"Gianni, you have to do this for me; she's my best friend from school."

"Look, this is not our business. The lady has cancer, too bad. We can't take care of everybody. No, I'm not going to pay for her treatment in a cancer clinic."

"Gio, if you don't do this for me, you're not going to get your fat penis in between my legs when I get home."

"Boy, you must be mad. You only call your old man Gio when you're really pissed."

"You're damned right I'm pissed. If you don't make sure my friend is transferred to the very best cancer hospital and is treated by the top doctors, I'll cut you off. No more pussy for you, you stingy bastard. This is small money to you."

"Hey, watch out. This is Giovanni Fuentes you're talking to. I'll have sex with you whenever I want, and don't you forget it. I own you!"

"You only *think* you do, you bastard! I know too much; one word to the feds and you are a goner. Better yet, I give an interview to the gossip press and tell them I am leaving you because you can't keep a young girl like me satisfied."

"Shit, you little witch; you do play rough. And I love it! Okay, I'll take good care of your friend if you come home right away and pay me back with that body of yours."

V

It was six months to the day when Sharleen received an excited telephone call from Jada.

"Sharleen, great news! The doctors declared me cancer-free. I don't know what you told that hospital administrator but they found a wonderful hospital, specializing in cancer treatment that would take me for free! They treated me like a queen. And last month when I came home, this nice doctor showed up and told us the hospital had put him in charge of any further care I might need. I have been trying to contact you to thank you for intervening for us, and tell you all the good news, but you disappeared without a word. It was like you fell of the edge of the earth. We couldn't find you. Your folks had no idea how to contact you. It wasn't until you finally called your dad that they got your cell phone number from their caller ID. Why hide from all of us, even your family?"

"Oh, Jada, I'm so happy for you! That is really great news. But to be honest, I already knew. I have been keeping track of all of you. You, especially, but of course my family too."

"Why so secret? Why are you hiding from us? We contacted your husband but he would not give us any information as to where you were. What is going on?"

"Look, I'm doing fine. Please don't ask details. You know who I am married to. That should give you a clue." Without another word Sharleen hung up, leaving Jada staring at her phone and wondering why they were disconnected. Before Jada had a chance to redial, her phone rang. It was Sharleen.

"Sorry I had to hang up on you, but we can't talk safely on my phone. Gianni makes sure it is monitored at all times. I called you back on one of those pre-paid cell phones; I was told there is no way they can listen in. But to make sure, I'm only doing this one time. The family has highly sophisticated monitoring equipment, and Gianni knows everything I do."

"You're like a prisoner?"

"No, not really. He just goes berserk any time I have contact with people back home."

"What the hell is that about?"

"Before we got married, Gianni had his so-called security team vet me out. You know, no FBI contacts and all that kind of shit. Well, they found out that Clint and I went together for three years and that we were sexually active. They had the full scope on our high school senior class trip to Washington, DC. That included the part where

Alison McKenzie ratted me out and told the teachers I snuck into Clint's room every night.

"Gianni is a very jealous man, and he has been adamant that I never see Clint again. When I was in town for our class reunion and my father's fiftieth, my 'bodyguards' saw me talk to Clint and reported it to Gianni. That signaled the end of my contact with anybody back home. That even includes my parents. Gianni does stick to his promise to send over a nice amount of money to my parents each month so they can live comfortably. That was sort the inverse dowry I insisted on before I agreed to marry him. I decided not to jeopardize this arrangement by visiting or calling home."

"Girl, you really have a fucked-up life. I feel bad about it now that everything is going so well for us. Believe it or not, Clint got a big loan from another bank and the restaurant reopened almost two month ago. It's gorgeous, and we're sure it's going to be a huge success. Clint thinks he can pay back most of that loan in a couple of years. To pay back the loan will be important because Paul Klein, a guy he knew in high school, believed in him and helped him get the loan. Hey, don't know if I should ask; have you ever thought about leaving your husband?"

"Come on, things ain't that bad. I live in a mansion here on Long Island. I am chauffeured around by my bodyguard. I have all the money I want for clothes and jewelry. Best of all, I have seniority over all the other wives in our so-called family. I'm the queen bee. No, honey, even if I could, why should I leave? Besides, I knew what I was getting into when I married him. Things are fine as long as I don't kick him where it hurts, and that includes seeing Clint. Oh yes, almost forgot; never ask him how he earns his money."

"I don't know. It just doesn't sound like you. It does not sound like the 'girl talk' I always loved to have with you in high school. Sharleen, tell me honestly; are you still in love with Clint? Are you?"

"No, that ended when he left. We're friends again, but love—no. Remember, I too left, and all that was a long time ago. A lot has happened since. Besides, don't think I don't know you had a huge crush on him while he and I were going steady. I always felt a little guilty that I was blocking you. I am happy the two of you got married."

"Thanks for saying that. We may not have much, if any, contact, but I still think of you as my best friend. But the life you live now—it's not you. What on earth possessed you to marry a Mafia boss, and an older one at that?"

"Come on, you make it sound like he is a creepy old guy. Giovanni is very young for his age. He is actually quite handsome. With that gorgeous head of grey hair he looks very sophisticated, and most girls would be ready to jump in bed with him."

"Which you did?"

"Thanks! No, it did not go that fast! True, he pursued me relentlessly, but in all honesty, I did sort of have the hots for him, too. He has those muscular arms which he uses to pull you gently into his powerful chest. Just like Clint. Oops! I did not mean to go there."

"Don't worry, that's okay. But spare me any more comparisons." Jada gave a knowing chuckle, and both burst out laughing. "Sharleen, I am so glad I got hold of you on the phone. I really missed you. High school seems so long ago, and we were so close."

"Yes, Jada, I too look back with fond memories. No denying, we two were the 'belles of the ball,' and we had the pick of the crop."

Remembering their high school days made Jada perk up. "Yeah, I guess we must have caused a lot of guys to have wet dreams just fantasizing about us."

"Do you remember Timmy Housten, the kid who was always sniffing around me?"

Jada was really getting into it. "Do I ever! He just about got a hard-on when you stopped in the hall to talk to him."

Sharleen, happy to hear her friend so cheerful, continued the memories. "And what about Jack McClusky? He was always trying to get you into that flashy convertible of his."

"He wanted a lot more than just patting my ass."

"What was wrong with that?"

"Come on, Sharleen, you were going steady. That's a different situation. I was playing the field, and never committed any further than making out."

"Yes, I remember; my friend the Virgin Queen!"

"Hey, I almost forgot. Guess who Clint and I bumped into a couple of days ago."

Sharleen took a wild stab at it. "Jack McClusky we were just talking about?"

"Yeah, that would be funny, but no, we met Lakota at the movies. I recognized him immediately. He is still as handsome as ever. He introduced us to his wife, Ehawee. You know her, of course."

"Yes, they have been married for a while and live on the reservation. Did he tell you she is a real-life Sioux princess?"

"No, he did not, but looking at her, he did okay for himself. She's not as beautiful as you, but she is cute. Nice, slender body, and legs to kill for. Maybe he would not have gone for me even if you *had* fixed us up."

"Oh, stop looking for a compliment. I told you already, you were a hot chick in high school and you had the pick of the crop.

All the happy banter almost made Sharleen forget the limited minutes on her pre-paid phone. It was time to hang up.

Jada said, "Try to keep in contact please…"

"I'll try, baby. Got to go now!"

Sharleen abruptly hung up and threw the phone across the room. She flung herself on her bed and burst out crying.

VI

The car had just crossed the Triborough Bridge when two police cars pulled it over. Two uniformed policemen approached the car, one on each side. The one on the driver's side signaled for the chauffer to turn down his window. "You and your passenger, please step out of the car."

From the back seat, Sharleen instructed her driver to ask the policeman for identification. At the same time she called Giovanni on her cell phone. "I've just been stopped by some cops. Two police cars pulled us over."

"Make sure they are legit. If you think they are Lograso's goons, tell Chico to floor it and get out of there." Sharleen saw that a second policeman had joined the one talking to Chico, her driver, and when she looked to her right see saw another two policemen approach her car. They had drawn their pistols and held them pointed at Chico and her. The police had parked their cars directly in front and in back of her car, and they could not have gotten away if they tried. As Giovanni had instructed her, Sharleen called nine-one-one and gave the operator the badge number from the identification the policemen had handed Chico.

"Yes, ma'am, I checked. He is a New York City policeman, and their dispatch officer confirmed that he has stopped your car on the Westside Highway."

"Why did he stop us?"

"Don't know, ma'am. Suggest you ask him." Sharleen leaned forward and spoke to the policeman through the open driver's window.

"Why did you pull us over? My driver was not speeding or driving recklessly; you can't just pull us over like that. Do you know who I am? I'm Mrs. Fuentes, and my husband will report you for harassing me."

"Yes, we know who you are. Please step out of the car. Right now! And tell your driver to sit tight and keep his hands on the steering wheel in plain view of me and my colleagues."

"You must be kidding! You won't get away with this nonsense; when my husband hears about this there will be hell to pay." She tried to redial Giovanni but before she made the connection, the policeman smashed the rear window and grabbed the phone out of her hands. While his colleague held a pistol to Chico's head, the policeman dragged Sharleen out of the car. Another policeman came to assist him and they roughly placed her across the front fender with her hands cuffed behind her back.

"You're under arrest, so don't try to resist us. You are accused of ordering the gang-style execution of Alfredo Lograso."

"What the hell are you talking about? You're cruising for a huge suit for false arrest. You'll be on skid row looking for a job when my husband gets through with you."

"Yeah, yeah, we know you all think Giovanni and that Fuentes family of yours are untouchable. You think the Mafia can do what they like in New York City, don't you? Well, let me tell you, sister. You won't get away with this."

"What the fuck is this?!"

"So we're going to play stupid, are we? Pretend you know nothing about Alfredo Lograso being gunned down when leaving the Vroom Vroom dance club in Brooklyn? Well, Sis, we have a reliable informant who claims you ordered that shooting. We won't miss that scum, but you can't go around executing people in this here town without us catching you."

VII

Sharleen was held for several hours at the police station before being brought up before a judge. During that time she was held in isolation, and the lawyers sent by Giovanni could not see her until her arraignment before the judge. When told that there was a witness who had issued a sworn statement claiming firsthand knowledge that Sharleen had ordered the killing of Alfredo, the judge ruled that Sharleen be bound over for trial. Bail was refused, and she was immediately shipped to Rikers Island prison.

Upon arrival at Rikers Island women's detention center, Sharleen was stripped of all her possessions and told to change into prison garb. Next, she was marched with a group of new arrivals to a cell block where they intended to keep her until her trial. She was assigned to a cell with four other women.

From the moment she arrived in her cell block, Sharleen was bombarded with offensive remarks by a group of rough-looking women. The other prisoners stayed clear of this group; they appeared to be afraid of them. On the second night, this group of women surrounded Sharleen in the mess hall and forced her to follow them to an area used for recreation.

"Hello, fancy pussy, what are you in for? Turning expensive tricks for fancy businessmen?" Sharleen, who was never known as a shrinking violet, was scared out of her mind. There were five of them, and each one looked more menacing than the other.

"Hey, look at that beautiful hair. Must cost a fortune to keep it that way."

One by one they came up to her and tried to touch her. Sharleen tried to fight them off. The remarks became more and more threatening until finally, two women grabbed her and held her tight while the others pulled her clothes off. Sharleen was frantic; she tried to scream for help, but one of the women pushed a big sponge in her mouth and taped her mouth shut.

"Wow, look at that hot body. I want firsties."

"Hold on, I want that pretty face between my legs. You can have her tits."

"No way, her type only knows how to suck cock. I'll work on her pussy. Help me get her down."

The women pushed her to the floor, and two of them started sucking on her breasts. Sharleen could feel fingers exploring around her vagina. With all her might she tried to pull her legs free but she could not get them loose. The two women who held them pinned to the floor were much too strong. To her horror, she could feel her legs being pulled apart and someone bending down over her crotch. Just as she could feel cheeks rubbing against the inside of her thighs she heard....

"Get the fuck off the floor, and let her go, you stupid bitches! Hurry up, or I'll slice youse all into little pieces. Help her up and give her back her clothes, or I'll push this here knife up your cunts!"

The women jumped up and quickly pulled Sharleen to her feet. Standing in front of them was a petite woman, dressed in prison garb, holding a knife. Next to her stood a huge woman, also in prison garb, carrying what looked like a small baseball bat. All five of her accosters ran from the room, and the two new arrivals went over to console Sharleen.

"Calm down, sis, nothing serious happened. You'll recover from this, and from now on we'll protect you." They pulled the tape from her mouth and pulled out the sponge.

"Oh my God. Thank you. Thank you." Sharleen could hardly speak, tears were streaming down her face, and she stammered, "Who are you, and how did you know they got me?"

"We're friends. Well, maybe not exactly. Giovanni will take care of us, and we promised to take care of you. From now on we two, and a bunch of our sisters who share this beautiful hotel with us, will make sure no one bothers you. Not even the guards. Giovanni is a generous man, and we really appreciate his generosity."

"You mean my husband contacted you to watch out for me?"

"Don't ask questions, okay? All you need to know is that no one will bother you while you're under our protection. Oh, before I forget. Giovanni says you'll have a bail hearing the day after tomorrow. Don't worry; you'll have that big-time lawyer, Gerald O'Keeffe, representing you. From what we hear, you know him personally, and he's cleaned up behind you before. They're pretty sure he can get you out on bail."

Early the next morning, Sharleen had another surprise. The guards took her to a small conference room and handed her over to two men dressed in street clothes. They motioned for her to sit down in a big leather chair and introduced themselves.

"Mrs. Fuentes, I am FBI Agent Kenny Wilson, and with me is my colleague, Agent Raymond Lonner. We asked the warden to have you brought here so we could have a little chat with you about your pending trial. You'll probably wind up with a pretty stiff sentence unless you accept our help."

Sharleen had no idea what the man was talking about. *Why was the FBI here to talk to her?*

"This whole thing is a big mistake. I had absolutely nothing to do with the shooting of that Lograso guy. I'd like to know who the hell claims I did."

"Come on, Mrs. Fuentes; Sharleen, if I may; we have seen the indictment. The witness has been pretty clear. You had Alfredo Lograso killed because he kept on spreading rumors about you. Something about having an affair with his ex-girlfriend, who came out as being gay when he broke up with her."

"Where do you get all this nonsense? I hardly know the guy! All I know is that he is, I guess now *was*, the son of Dominick Lograso from Chicago, and that he was known as somewhat of a jerk. Why in God's name would I have him killed? I did not know that he had a girlfriend, much less that they broke up. Me having an affair with another woman? You've got to be kidding. I'm as straight as they come!"

"You don't have to plead your case with us, Sharleen. We came here to offer you our help."

"What exactly are you trying to tell me? What do you mean by offering me your help?"

"It's quite simple. You have something we need, and we in turn can help you beat this rap."

"I have something you need?"

"Like I said, it's simple. Your old man is Giovanni Fuentes, and we need some information about his operation. You can get that, and we can get the DA to drop all charges against you."

"Let's see some identification. I think you're Dominick Lograso's men trying to trick me."

To Sharleen's surprise, the two men could identify themselves as legitimate FBI agents. Her questioning mood turned to real anger. "You fucking sons of bitches. You want to use me to get at Giovanni. You don't have a chance in hell to turn me against my husband. Wait till I tell him; he'll get your asses kicked out of that stupid agency of yours!"

"Calm down. No one will ever know about this conversation. You can't prove it took place. Think it over; you're in real trouble, and we can help. No one, especially not your husband, will ever know where the information came from."

"Get out, you bastards! You probably set me up with these phony charges to get at me. No, I will not now or ever turn against my husband! Get out of here, you scum!" Sharleen got up and opened the door to call the guards to come and get her.

Before the guards arrived, the FBI agent make one last try. "Unfortunately for you, the charges against you are real. They have a reliable witness. If you change your mind our offer stands, but you have to contact us before your trial starts."

VIII

Judge Henry Matthew Bressler was known for his anti-Mafia feelings when he was appointed by the mayor of New York City to the New York City Criminal Court. It was Sharleen's bad luck to have to appear in his court for the appeal on her bond ruling.

Gerald O'Keeffe stressed the fact that Sharleen had no prior criminal history, and that she did not even have a passport. "There is no indication that my client will remove herself from the jurisdiction of the court."

Judge Bressler did not wait for the DA to respond. His ruling was swift, and clearly reflected his personal feelings. "Based on the seriousness of the charges, and that it has not escaped this court as to who the defendant's husband is, it is the ruling of this court that the defendant is a flight risk and cannot be released pending her appearance before a grand jury."

Sharleen was terrified at the prospect of being returned to Rikers Island for an extended period while waiting for the DA to present her case to a grand jury. Gerald O'Keeffe tried to calm her down by assuring her that Giovanni and he would make sure she was fully protected.

"Welcome back, pretty lady." Sharleen had to smile at the greeting. She was relieved to see that O'Keeffe had not been bluffing. On her return to Rikers Island she was assigned to another four-person cell. Two of her new cell mates turned out to be the two women who had rescued her before.

"Let me introduce you to your third bodyguard," the petite woman who had wielded the knife said. "This here is Patty. Patty takes no shit from nobody. If you don't believe that, just ask the fucking pimp who refused to give her the money he promised her." All three women burst out laughing when they remembered the self-appointed "Boss Man" squirming on the floor holding onto his severely damaged vital parts.

"While you're locked up in here, you are one of us," Patty said, "But there are a few rules you'll have to follow in order for us to continue to benefit from Giovanni's generosity. The most important rule is, never go anyplace without at least two of us at your side. The second rule is, before following any instructions from the guards, check with us. We will handle it!"

Sharleen realized that this was the same power of the Mafia that was coming to her rescue now, but had worked against her in the bail hearing.

IX

The parking lot at the main building of the Mayo Clinic was fairly crowded, but Clint Crawley spotted a space near the entrance. He had made the trip to the Mayo Clinic many times during the past month, and by now he knew the way to Jada's room without first having to stop for directions. He had been there a few days before, and Jada was not expecting him. She was surprised when he burst into the room.

He greeted her with, "Jada, I have bad news."

"Funny way to greet someone who is dying," she replied.

"I'm sorry, sweetheart, but I just found out Sharleen is in trouble."

"Oh no, what did that bastard Giovanni do to her?"

"Nothing; it's not Giovanni. She has just been indicted by a grand jury in New York City."

"What the hell for?!"

"She has been accused of ordering the gang-style execution of some mobster named Alfredo Lograso."

"No way! They must have framed her. Sharleen would never be involved in something like that. Not her. I know her too well to believe that. Sharleen wouldn't do such a thing."

"That was my first reaction." Clint looked very worried. "But the story on the news quoted someone in the DA's office. They claim to have a credible witness."

"What happens now?"

"She has to stand trial. That will be pretty soon, because her defense council asked for a speedy trial date. Seems he can't get her out on bail, so he wants the trial to start as soon as possible. The news story said that the DA's office cooperated with defense's request, and asked the judge to set the trial date as soon as possible."

"We're going. She can't go through that alone!"

"Honey, I know you want to support her, but you are in no shape to travel."

"I don't care. I'm dying anyway, and if I die a day earlier, I don't care. I must go and support my friend."

"Jada, be reasonable. You're not dying; we brought you here to the Mayo Clinic so you could have the best possible care. The doctors here are the best. They won't let you die."

"Clint, my darling, stop your denial. I escaped once, and God gave me a wonderful extra few years.

But you and I know full well that this time there won't be a miracle recovery. If you really love me, and I know you do, don't stop me. Let me go and support my friend."

"The doctors won't let you go."

"Clint, dearest; I love you and adore you, and you, as my husband, will make the decision to check me out of this place, and you'll find a way to get me to New York. Please don't let me die here while my best friend stands trial far away for something I know she could not have done."

X

Once the indictment had been issued, Sharleen's case was transferred to New York State Supreme Court, where it would be tried.

As the prosecution got ready to present their case against Sharleen, Clint Crawley pushed his wife's wheelchair along the last row in the courtroom. Up front, at the defense table, sitting next to Gerald O'Keeffe and his two co-counsels, Sharleen was oblivious as to who was sitting in the visitors' section.

"Mr. Pierro, are you ready to call your first witness?"

"Yes, Your Honor. The prosecution calls Emilia Susana Kosarek to the stand."

After Emilia was sworn in, the prosecutor proceeded to question her. "Miss Kosarek, please tell the court about what you witnessed last year on the evening of June seventh in the restaurant where you work."

"I was serving at table six, and Mrs. Sharleen Fuentes was seated with a party of eight at table eight."

"How did you know the lady you are referring to was Mrs. Sharleen Fuentes?"

"She came to the restaurant very often, and a few years ago I was introduced to her."

"Is she here in the courtroom, and can you point her out?"

"Yes, that is her, sitting at the defense table."

"Please continue. Did you hear or see anything unusual that evening?"

"Yeah, Sharleen—, I mean Mrs. Fuentes, got up from her table and went up to Piotr Bajek, who was standing in front of the hallway leading to the restrooms."

"And then what happened?"

"I saw her hand Piotr Bajek a package and she said, 'There is more when you finish the job.'"

Everybody in the visitors' section expected the defense to object, but O'Keeffe remained calmly seated. Instead it was the prosecutor who asked, "Are you sure that is exactly what you heard?"

"Yes, sir. I was on my way to the kitchen, and had to pass within several feet of them."

Sharleen looked at the witness, contempt written all over her face. If looks could kill, Emilia would have been in trouble. Sharleen leaned over to Gerald O'Keeffe, and hardly moving her lips, whispered, "That lying bitch! It's a set-up; they bought her in order to put me in jail so they could get at Giovanni."

O'Keeffe held up his hand in a gesture to calm her down. "Relax, this is going to be one of the shortest trials in history. Trust me; you're not going to be convicted. Not as long as I am defending you. Remember, Gerald O'Keeffe always cleans up after the Fuentes family. I have known Giovanni since grade school. We're like brothers!"

The prosecutor turned towards the defense table. "I have no further questions. Your witness."

O'Keeffe got up very slowly, gathering a few notes together as he approached the witness. "Miss Kosarek; may I call you Emilia?"

"Yes, sir, please do."

"Now, Emilia, how well did you know Mr. Bajek?"

"I know most people who come into our restaurant. Yeah, I know him."

"Emilia, I asked how *well* did you know Mr. Bajek? Maybe you can describe him for us?"

"Well… uh, he was pretty average-looking. You know, sort of difficult to describe."

"Okay, I understand. Will it help if I show you these three pictures, and you tell me which one is Mr. Bajek?"

With that, O'Keeffe handed Emilia three pictures.

"You seem to hesitate; what's the matter?'

"It's difficult; it's more than a year since I seen him."

"Just for the record, I'll hold up the pictures so everyone can see that they are quite different. The three men shown in the pictures don't look alike. But never mind, Emilia. Did you notice I used the past tense when asking you about Piotr Bajek? Are you aware Mr. Bajek is dead?"

The prosecutor jumped up. "That is totally irrelevant, and certainly not material to this case."

The judge disagreed. "I would like to hear what the witness has to say. Go ahead and answer, Miss Kosarek."

"Yeah, I know that."

"And you must have heard he died in a single car crash on the Long Island Express Way just about a month after Alfredo Lograso was murdered."

"Yes, I heard that."

"Now, Emilia, tell the court what else you know about Mr. Bajek's death."

"I know nothing else about it."

"I don't think that is true, Emilia. You know the police are still investigating the circumstances of the crash that killed Bajek. And you know why."

Again the prosecutor objected. "Defense is needlessly badgering the witness; the car crash has nothing to do with this case."

The judge did not agree with the prosecutor and allowed O'Keeffe to continue.

"Emilia, I put it to you that you know the police suspect Mr. Bajek was killed by members of the Lograso family as revenge for his killing of Alfredo. And Piotr killed Alfredo because he jilted him. They were lovers, and it is well know that Alfredo was bisexual. Emilia, you never knew or met Mr. Bajek!"

The prosecutor jumped to his feet, waving both arms. "Your Honor, this is preposterous! Defense is introducing some theory without any substantiating facts. I demand that this entire line of questioning be stricken from the record."

The judge ordered both defense and prosecution to approach the bench. "Mr. O'Keeffe, I will not tolerate this line of attack. If you continue this I will not only have your so-called questions stricken from the record, but I'll cite you for contempt."

"Judge, I hope you know me well enough to understand that I would not insult the court by introducing a farfetched theory unless I could later in the proceeding prove it to be true, and quite relevant to the case at hand."

"I'll accept that you acted in good faith, but I'll have to order your last line of questioning stricken from the record. I trust you'll be able to prove to me you were acting in good faith."

O'Keeffe was allowed to continue questioning Emilia. "Emilia, let's get back to some easy questions. Who owns the restaurant where you work?"

Once again the prosecutor objected. "That's irrelevant."

"Overruled. I'll let the witness answer that."

"The restaurant is owned by Federico Fuentes."

"That is Giovanni's son."

"Yes, sir."

"And of course you know Federico's wife, Felisa."

Again the prosecutor was on his feet. "All this is not relevant to the case."

"O'Keeffe, I am going to allow this, but I warn you, you are on thin ice."

"Yes, Your Honor. I'll be able to show how this relates to the witness's testimony."

Turning to the witness he asked, "How long have you known Felisa?"

"We went to school together in Rockville. I guess I've known her since grade school."

"And who got you the job in Federico's restaurant?"

"Your Honor, I must object. How is this possibly relevant to this case?"

"I have ruled before that I am willing to let defense show us why this relates to witness's testimony. Go ahead, Mr. O'Keeffe."

"I applied," Emilia said.

"Come on, Emilia. Who put in a good word for you?"

"I guess Felisa did help."

"Isn't it true she did much more than put in a good word for you? And isn't it true that Federico is not pleased with your performance on the job, but Felisa stops him from firing you?"

The prosecutor continued to object, but the judge once again overruled him and ordered Emilia to answer the question.

"That's crazy. I am a good waitress."

"That's not what I heard. Emilia, am I forced to bring in several of your colleagues from the restaurant to tell us about your run-ins with your boss?"

Emilia did not answer, but dropped her head and shook it no. As if stung by a bee, O'Keeffe jumped on the witness. Gone was his fatherly demeanor, and with his head less than three feet from Emilia he barked, "You owe everything to Felisa, don't you? And when she told you exactly what to tell the police, you could not refuse. Emilia, you never heard my client speaking to Piotr Bajek. You never even saw Bajek in the restaurant!"

Before the prosecutor could get to his feet, the judge waved him down. "Sit down, Mr. Pierro. Not now!"

Emilia bounced up. "No! No, that is not true. I did see them together, and I heard what she said!"

O'Keeffe stepped back and became his calm self again. "Emilia, please remember you are under oath. I don't think you are the type of lady who would purposely tell lies to this court. I understand you had no choice but to do what Felisa asked of you. You could lose everything if you refused. But swearing under oath because Felisa made you do it won't work. Think carefully before you answer me. Yes or no; did you see Sharleen Fuentes give Piotr Bajek a package and did you hear her say, 'There is more when you finish the job'?"

Emilia collapsed into the witness chair. She was sobbing hysterically, and the judge was about to interfere on her behalf when she stood up and screamed at Felisa, who was sitting in the front row of the visitors' gallery. "You made me do it! You always pretended to be my friend but you threatened me! You said if I did not do what you ordered me to do that I would never again work as a waitress in New York! You promised to protect me, and now see what happened!"

The judge quickly ordered the bailiff to take the witness away and see to it that she got medical care to calm her down. The visitors' gallery had become very noisy, and it was almost impossible to hear the judge order defense and prosecution to approach the bench.

"Mr. Pierro, I am sure you will agree that I have to make a directed verdict of not guilty and dismiss the defendant from further custody."

"Of course, Your Honor. Now I have a case of perjury to prosecute, and I just ordered Mrs. Felisa Fuentes arrested. Our legal department will be working on the exact wording of the warrant we have to swear out against her before the arraignment."

Through all the chaos in the courtroom, Clint carefully pushed Jada in her wheelchair to the front of the court, where he signaled to get Sharleen's attention. When Sharleen saw Jada, she pushed the journalists looking for a quote aside and rushed over to Jada.

"Jada, honey, why the hell are you in a wheelchair?"

Jada's response was typical Jada. "Hi, Sharleen, glad to see you. I've been sick with worry about this trial. Thank God it's over and that the truth came out. Now first give me a big hug, and I'll tell you why this wheelchair."

The two friends held each other for a long time in a tight embrace until Sharleen pulled back. "Okay, now tell me what is going on."

"That damned cancer. It's come back, and spread all through my body. I'm afraid this time you can't shake that magic wand of yours and get me cured."

Sharleen burst out crying. She bent over and buried her head in Jada's lap, her body shaking violently from her sobbing. "No! No, I won't let it happen. You can't leave us! Clint, we have to get her to the best possible doctors. We'll check her into Sloan Kettering Cancer Center right here in New York City. Giovanni can arrange it. He'll get her in. Today, even!"

This time it was Clint who spoke. "Sharleen, I took her to the best. She was in the Mayo Clinic when I told her about your trial. Against her doctors' advice, she insisted on leaving the hospital so we could come here and be with you."

Sharleen raised her head and looked at Jada's pale face. "Oh, honey, why did you do that? I love to have you here, but I would rather see you well. You can't leave us, really you can't. And I won't have it!"

It seemed like an awkward response, but Jada replied laughingly, "Sharleen, my dear friend, now you sound like my loving husband. Clint insisted that I was not dying, and if I stayed in the Mayo Clinic the doctors could cure my cancer. But at some point we have to face the truth. My body is worn out. I can hardly stand the pain, and morphine only helps temporarily. I can't accept another round of chemo knowing it will only prolong this agony for a couple of weeks, if that. If the two of you really love me, and in my heart I know you do, you have to let me go on my own terms."

Sharleen was uncontrollable. Her crying came out as loud shrieks. The people surrounding them in the courtroom had no idea what was going on. Here was a defendant who was acquitted, and the three of them were crying and holding onto each other as if she had been sentenced to life in prison.

Once Gerald O'Keeffe found out what was going on, he took control of the situation. Knowing the background of the various relationships involved, he made sure Giovanni did not realize who Clint was. Next he called on Bennie to arrange a limo to take Jada and Clint to the airport, where a plane he had chartered was waiting to fly them home; Jada had been adamant she did not want to return to the Mayo Clinic. Although she protested loudly that she wanted to fly home with Jada so she could take care of her, Sharleen was given a heavy sedative and packed off to the Fuentes estate on Long Island.

XI

After her arrest, Felisa was temporarily held in a holding cell behind the courtroom. While she waited to be arraigned in criminal court, she asked for Federico, her husband, to be allowed to come see her. She certainly did not expect Giovanni to accompany his son.

"Why are you here? I only asked to see Freddie."

"In case you forgot, I'm the head of the family. I am your don, and you brought shame on our family."

"She deserved to be put away. She is an imposter, and you let her get away with it."

"What does this mean, an imposter? Can you explain what you mean by that, and what possessed you to do what you did?"

"She took my place. I am the wife of your eldest son, and I deserve to be the ranking woman. I was number one until you married that knifing bitch. Who the hell does she think she is, bossing me around and always pulling rank on me? She is not even Italian; I will not accept that from that Indian with nigger blood."

Her last statement made Giovanni even angrier than he already was. "Shut your filthy mouth. As long as I run this family, no one uses words like that. Especially not you. You have always been a pretentious fool. And, once again, you have no idea what you are talking about. It is none of your business, but before I married Sharleen, my consigliere carefully vetted her. Her grandfather was Salvatore Conti, a scion of a well-known Sicilian family. At a very young age he fell in love with this older French beauty from Haiti. She was a black lady, and his family disowned him. He never recovered from that, and he wound up working on the docks in San Francisco. The couple only had one child, a girl. This mulatto girl married a full-blooded American Indian, and they are Sharleen's parents. Like it or not, there is more proud blood running through my wife's veins than you'll find in your pathetic heritage. Come, Federico, let's get out of here. This lady makes me sick!"

As an obedient Mafia son, Freddie followed his father out of the cramped holding cell. On his way home he called Gerald O'Keeffe and asked him to arrange for one of his associates to assist Felisa at her arraignment.

At her arraignment, Felisa pleaded guilty and was released on bail. A week after she returned home to their Park Avenue duplex, she tripped and fell down the stairs. She broke her neck and was pronounced dead at the scene.

Sharleen was uncomfortable with the story as to how Felisa fell down the stairs. She suspected foul play, and since it might have been on her behalf, she confronted Giovanni.

"Gianni, tell me straight. Was Felisa's fall an accident? Did you have anything to do with it?"

"Amore mio *(my love)*, you should not ask questions like that. You know that."

"Sure, I know all your rules, but I have learned that when you do not answer my questions it means yes. So, you refuse to answer?"

"Let me tell you a story and you'll understand better. When I was growing up my father, may he rest in peace, had the same position in the family as I do now. That position comes with a heavy responsibility. And as his eldest son, it was important to him that I marry the proper girl. His idea as to what constituted the proper girl was grounded in the traditions of the small village in Sicily where he grew up. So he sent word to Cefalu that he was looking for a bride for his eldest son. There were a lot of candidates and he, not I, chose a nineteen-year-old girl from a prominent family. I have to admit, the old man had good taste. She was very pretty. Mind you, not as beautiful as you, but she was pretty.

"To make a long story short, we got married and had four lovely children. Then something went very wrong. My father and a rival in another city got into a turf war about the distribution of something we no longer handle. Their family had started to operate in a part of the city long controlled by our family.

During the gang war that erupted, one of my cousins killed two of their capos. For some reason, we never quite understood why, my wife betrayed my cousin and reported him to the police. Not too long after that, my wife died. She slipped and fell under a subway train."

"Your father ordered that?"

"How would I know? I never asked!"

"But how could you accept that? She was your wife, the mother of your children!"

"Omerta! My father was a strong enforcer of omerta, and so, caroa mioa (*my dear*) am I. It is the system by which we hold the family together. And it is my duty to enforce it."

"Even if it involves the mother of your grandchildren, the wife of your own son?"

"I choose not to answer that. And now I order you to end this conversation and accept the fact that Felisa slipped and fell down the stairs."

Sharleen stared at him and walked out of the room. Over her shoulder she said, "Gio, if you don't mind, I'll sleep in the guest room tonight."

Just before leaving the room Sharleen turned around. "What about Emilia? Is she in danger too?"

"Of course not."

"Doesn't she fall under your stupid rule of revenge? She's the one who accused me."

"You don't understand, do you? Emilia is a poor soul who was taken advantage of by a vicious member of my family. Even though Felisa betrayed the family, the family is still responsible for her action.

No, Emilia is not in any danger. Gerald O'Keeffe hired a lawyer to defend her. The DA has already agreed to ask for no more than parole and extended community service. I asked Federico to transfer her to one of my restaurants here on Long Island. We introduced her to the staff as Emmy."

Sharleen stood for a while and stared at her husband. *Would she ever fully understand this complicated man?* "Goodnight, Gianni." She closed the door behind her.

XII

During the weeks that followed, Sharleen called Jada every day; sometimes twice a day. It became an obsession. For some mystical reason, Sharleen believed that as long as she kept talking to Jada, Jada would not die. But one day when she called, Jada was very weak, her voice hardly audible.

"Sharleen, it's time to say good-bye. I can't go on any longer."

"No, Jada, no. Not yet, I'm on my way... please hold on!"

Sharleen raced onto the balcony leading to the master bedroom and screamed down to the flight below. "Bennie! Bennie where are you? I need you!"

"What's the matter, Sharleen? You sound upset."

"It's Jada, I need to go. Get me on a plane as soon as possible!"

Bennie was as efficient as always, and managed to get her on a flight leaving that same evening. He apologized for the fact that first class was fully booked. Sharleen couldn't care less; all she wanted was to reach Jada before it was too late.

When Sharleen entered Jada's bedroom, Clint was sitting at her bedside, holding her hand. Her doctor was bending over the bed to check her intravenous self-administration of morphine. When he saw Sharleen enter the room he stepped aside to let her take his place. Jada's elderly parents were huddled in a corner of the room. Jada opened her eyes and recognized Sharleen; a faint smile appeared around her lips. She tried to speak.

But Sharleen bent over to kiss her and softly said, "Don't." Sharleen sat down next to the bed on the opposite side from Clint. She gently took Jada's other hand, as if to warm it between hers.

After a while, Jada summoned all her remaining energy, and in a soft voice only Clint and Sharleen could hear, said, "I have been very lucky to have had two of the best friends anybody could have wished for. You two have given me more than I deserved. Sharleen, I have always suspected that the hospital did not treat me for free." Sharleen tried to protest, but Jada shook her head. "Darling, I have been a lot of things, but not stupid. I know, thank you for that great gift, the extra years I was given to spend with the most wonderful guy in the world."

Jada squeezed Clint hand, closed her eyes and said, "Sharleen, you deserve better; it's never…" Her voice trailed off, and the rest of the sentence could not be heard. Sharleen tried to catch what she was saying and leaned further in so her face was less than ten inches from Jada's. Jada opened her eyes once more, looked straight at Sharleen and with great effort, whispered something. Her eyes closed again, and she was gone.

Tears streamed down Sharleen's face and she continued to tightly hold onto her friend's hand. Softly sobbing she kept on repeating, "Jada, Jada…" Clint was slightly more composed, but he too had tears in his eyes when he came over and tried to console Sharleen.

> "What did she say?" he asked. "I could not hear it."
> "I think she said, 'Never too late,'" Sharleen replied.

XIII

Sharleen had been despondent for months; she just could not get over Jada's death. But when Christmas arrived, she did not want to spoil it for everyone. Especially not for Giovanni. He had been very supportive while she mourned for her best friend. He had no idea that Sharleen's other best friend was Clint, his imaginary rival, whom he fought in a way that brought Don Quixote to mind.

Christmas morning, Giovanni surprised her with the diamond necklace she had been admiring at Tiffany's. "Gianni, you're crazy! That's much too expensive. I'll need a bodyguard to protect it when I wear it!" Sharleen exclaimed.

Giovanni was pleased. He loved spoiling Sharleen. Especially if it also involved showing off his wealth. "Amore mio, (*My love*) you have a bodyguard. You know I would never let anything happen to you."

Sharleen was still wearing pajamas, but she happily put the necklace on. "Your present is downstairs under the tree. You'll have to wait till we get dressed and join the others. But in the meantime, I have something that will make you happy." With that, she stretched out on their oversized king bed, opened up her pajama top, and held out her arms to him. Giovanni looked at her breasts, which she provocatively held up and pointed at him and he thought, *My God, that woman is built. How did I get so lucky?* Sharleen had to smile when she saw Giovanni's erection push against his robe. She loved seeing his reaction when he saw her body. Slowly she pushed her pajama pants down. "Get rid of that robe and show me how much you love me."

She had barely finished talking before Giovanni was on top of her. "Hey, sweetheart, slow down! I love to have you make love to me but I'm not ready. Play with me and get me nice and ready." With that, she guided his hand to where she wanted to be stroked. After a while she spread her legs, pulled him on top of her, and guided him to where he wanted to be.

The Christmas party did not start until four in the afternoon. As custom demanded, all members of Giovanni's Mafia family were invited with their spouses and children, regardless of age. The house was a madhouse, people everywhere except on the second floor, which was known to be off bounds. Giovanni himself was not there. He was out taking a test drive in an Italian sports car that his oldest grandson was trying to talk him into buying for him.

Sharleen circulated among the guests, and finally settled down in the bar where she got into an animated conversation with Bennie. Several times Bennie's hand brushed against the top of her dress. Sharleen thought nothing of it until it happened again and his hand lingered a little too long on her breasts. He was clearly trying to rub his fingers across her nipples.

"Bennie, I'd rather you don't touch me there." But his hand reached out again, and this time Sharleen demonstratively pushed it away. "Bennie, what the hell are you doing? How much have you been drinking!?"

"Come on, Sharleen, Giovanni is not here, and we can have some Christmas fun of our own."

"You must be kidding! What's the matter with you, have you been smoking pot?"

"No, no I'm serious. Come upstairs with me; we can be alone up there. No one will know."

"I think you've gone completely off your rocker. Why on earth would I want to go upstairs to be alone with you? I hope I'm wrong when I think I know what you are planning."

"Why won't you come with me? You always say how much you love me. I do everything for you, and you keep saying Bennie, I love you. All the time. Come and prove it!"

"Bennie, I do love you. I love you like a brother; but I'm not in love with you. I'm sorry if I gave you the wrong idea. I really did not mean to. I think of you as my big brother, and you are very dear to me. But no, I'm not in love with you."

"You bitch, cock teaser! You lead me on and refuse to go through with it."

"Bennie, how dare you! I am a married woman. I would never make sexual advances to you, or any other man. I will never cheat on Giovanni! And don't you ever suggest he cheats on me; I know he doesn't! Now get away from me and stay out of my sight till I cool down from this insult. You're lucky I love Giovanni too much to tell him his confidant tried to seduce me." Sharleen looked around to make sure nobody had overheard them. When she was sure nobody had, she went to join the big crowd in the main ballroom. Bennie stared after her. The look on his face was one of anger, confusion, and frustration, all rolled into one.

XIV

Giovanni Fuentes was in his library conferring with Guido Russo, his consigliere. Also present was Joseph, Big Joe Calabrese, the underboss of the Fuentes family. One of the capos of the Lograso family was involved in illegal activities that interfered with Giovanni's legal enterprises. There had been a few scuffles between local capos, but the situation was getting more serious, and threatened to break out into a full-scale war between the families. Their conversation was interrupted by a knock on the door. It was Bennie.

"Uncle, I need to speak with you."

"Can't it wait, Bennie? I have some urgent things to discuss with these two gentlemen."

"What I have to tell you is urgent too, please."

"Okay, go ahead. What's going on?"

"What I have to tell you is private. Could these two gentlemen please excuse us?"

"Come on, Bennie, you know you can speak freely in front of Guido and Big Joe."

"I would rather not, Uncle, this is private."

"Unless you messed up on some financial business, Guido and Big Joe can stay."

"Yeah, I sort of screwed up."

Giovanni signaled for Guido and Big Joe to leave the room and he turned to Bennie.

"It better be important for you to interrupt us like this, and I hope you realize you just insulted my consigliere and our underboss."

"What I have to say does not concern those two old men. Sharleen tricked me! She made me transfer a substantial sum from her trust fund to her. She claimed her family on the reservation was in serious trouble and she needed the money to help them."

"Hold it, stop there! She is not supposed to know about the trust fund!"

"She does not. She had no idea where I got the money; she just told me it was urgent."

"Okay, so she needed the money for her family. That's okay; those are good folks there on the reservation. We should treat them better. But you should not have touched her trust fund."

"It was only a loan, but she lied. It was not for her family. She used it to help that boyfriend of hers keep his restaurant."

"What in the hell are you talking about? Boyfriend?"

"Yeah, boyfriend, her lover. You remember that guy you had us check on when she went home for her high school reunion; the one who was her steady boyfriend for three years in high school. Well, turns out he is the same guy who was married to her best friend. The three of them have had this filthy love affair going on for all these years."

"What are you saying?"

"For you to understand clearly, you wife carried on an amante amore frat tre persone (*love triangle for three persons*) for all these years right under your nose. And she used your money for their restaurant!"

"If I find out mi hai mentito (*you lied to me*), I'll kill you!"

"Uncle, it's true. I swear it's true. I'm sorry I have to tell you this, but it is my duty to speak up. I was tricked; I made a mistake to transfer the money. She lied to me!"

Giovanni got up slowly. The expression on his face was like that of a man whose heart had been ripped out of his chest. In a way, it was.

"Get out. Get out of this room. Leave me alone!"

As he closed the door behind him, Bennie heard what he had always believed to be impossible; Giovanni was crying. With anguish he cried out, "Che Dio mi perdoni (*May God forgive me*) for what I have to do."

Bennie quickly ran down the stairs. On his way down he passed Guido and Big Joe, who raced up the stairs to find out what was going on. Bennie smiled to himself. *That will take care of the bitch. She thought she could dismiss me like some little boy. After all I did for her, she can't treat me like that. Did she really think I was stupid enough not to know what she needed the money for?*

XV

Sharleen had no idea why Giovanni abruptly moved out of their bedroom, and why he had totally ignored her for the last several days. Since the house had been filling up with made men and a few other Fuente soldiers; she assumed it had to do with the Lograso feud. This changed radically after she received a phone call from her father.

During Jada's funeral, she had given her dad her new cell phone number. He never called her, but she wanted him to have it anyway, in case he needed to contact her in an emergency. When she saw his number on her cell phone screen she panicked. "Dad, what's the matter? You okay?"

"Yes, dear, we're all right. But I have some bad news. Last night, Clint's restaurant burned down."

"Is he all right? How did it happen?"

"Don't worry, he's okay. Seems someone threw a fire bomb through the large picture window facing the terrace. The restaurant was closed, but a few of the staff, including Clint, were still in the kitchen cleaning up. Even though the restaurant quickly filled with smoke, they all managed to get out. But once outside, they noticed that Maja was missing. Clint went back in to get her. Due to the dense smoke, he had a hard time finding her, but he finally located her in the back hallway. She was recently hired, and not too familiar with the building. She had not been there long enough to have participated in a fire drill. She must have panicked because of the heavy smoke and run around in circles. She was unconscious when Clint found her. He picked her up and doused her in one of the kitchen sinks. Next he splashed water over himself and ran through the flames out the emergency door in the back of the building."

"Oh my God! Is the lady okay?"

"Yeah, she's doing fine. Some superficial burn wounds, but for the rest she is doing fine. Clint lost his eyebrows, and does have some first-degree burns on his face and arms. Nothing too serious. He is the town hero! Somehow they got a picture of him coming out of that back door with the girl in his arms. It's huge, on the front page of the morning paper.

"When asked why he dashed into that burning building to look for her, he just replied, 'I'm responsible for my staff'."

"Oh my gosh!" Sharleen teared up thinking about it. "Sounds like Clint."

"There is more to it than her being just a member of his staff. Maja is a very young mother of three. She has a juvenile record, and her behavior was such that she was sort of kicked off the reservation.

My brother asked Clint to give her a job, and he did more. He persuaded the hostess to take her in, and he instructed the chef to train her to become a cook. He's really a wonderful man! Maybe you should not have been so angry with him when he did not take you with him to that Dodgers' training camp."

"Daddy, I was young, very young."

When Sharleen hung up the phone, she headed straight for the library to confront Giovanni. When she flung open the door she startled Giovanni, and the men sitting around him immediately drew their guns. That did not faze Sharleen one bit. She brushed right by them and said, "Out, everybody out!"

Giovanni glared at her. "You have some nerve barging in here like that!"

"At least I don't commit criminal acts! Did you have anything to do with the fire-bombing of the restaurant?"

"Get out of here, you slut! Come hai potuto dirmi una bugia (*how could you lie to me*) like that? You were fucking another man while you pretended to love me!"

"You're wrong, totally wrong, I have never been unfaithful to you, and I did love you. Why don't you trust me?"

"Fiducia, fiducia (*trust, trust*). Who can I really trust? I loved you so much. I gave you everything you wanted. Why did you do this to me?"

"Giovanni, stop it. I did not cheat on you. Never."

"You paid for his restaurant with my money. You hid that; you never asked."

"You're right, I was wrong. I should have asked, but I was afraid you would not understand. He was my friend, and his wife was my friend, too. I had to help them. But you never really trusted me; you would have been too jealous to agree."

"You think I don't know? Well let me tell you, Ti sbagli (*you are wrong about that*)! I know you fucked him."

"Giovanni, please. That was back in high school. Sure, we had sex. For God's sake, we went steady for three years. Look, I don't ask or care who you had sex with before we were married. Why should you care about a high school affair? I have been true to you since the first day we went out."

"You're lying! I know the three of you carried on a dirty little affair behind my back."

"You stupid old man! You have no idea how much I loved you. But you, you would rather wallow in some lies someone spread about me. I can guess who it was, but after your reaction, I refuse to further argue about this with you. You would rather burn down a restaurant and endanger people's lives than listen to the truth. Giovanni, I am leaving you!"

"You're going no place unless I allow it!" He called for Big Joe Calabrese. "Bring her to the master bedroom and keep her locked up until I decide what to do with her."

XVI

There was a soft knock on her bedroom door. It was much too early for them to be bringing her dinner tray. Sharleen expected the worst, and quickly locked herself in the bathroom.

The knocking became a little louder and she could hear someone say, "Open up, Sharleen. It's me, Freddie."

Sharleen did not respond. "Sharleen, open up. I have to talk to you."

"Sure you do. Your father probably sent you to make me come peacefully to who knows where. No thank you. Go away!"

"Sharleen, I'm not the enemy. Open up, I'll explain."

Federico might be okay, she thought. *They killed his wife; maybe he is not on their side.* She decided to take a chance and opened the door to let Freddie in.

"I have to get you out of here. I don't trust what they are planning."

"Why should I believe you when it is I who caused you wife's death?"

"That's bullshit. You had nothing to do with what those old, misguided men did. They are so obsessed with their self-imposed sense of responsibility that they think they have the right to kill. I'm sick of their self-righteous way of dispensing justice. I'm sick of all the senseless killing!"

"Freddie, I always thought you fully supported your father. Don't you believe in the Mafia? Someday you'll be the Don!"

"No way in hell. I hate the fucking Mafia! Felisa did not deserve to die. Sure, she did a terrible thing by accusing you, but that is no excuse to kill her."

"Of course not. But she also took advantage of that poor Emilia."

"That's not true. She was the best thing that ever happened to that pathetic woman."

"I'm confused; what do you mean by that?"

"Let me tell you. They first met when Emelia and her family moved onto the same block where Felisa lived. Emelia was not very popular; that's putting it mildly. She was having a hard time until Felisa sort of adopted her. Felisa was probably the most popular girl in her neighborhood, and she took Emelia under her wing. She involved her in everything, and made sure no one dared mess with Emelia. Rumor has it that she agreed to make out with a guy in exchange for him taking Emelia to their senior prom. I would not be surprised if she slept with the guy to clinch the deal. When I criticized Emelia in the restaurant for messing up a guest's order, Felisa would be all over me. And I would wind up apologizing to her."

"Man! I never saw that side of her."

"No, you never really knew her."

"What did I do for her to hate me so much?"

"You did nothing. It's what happened to her after my father married you that made her hate you. She was his official hostess, and he took great pride in showing her off as his favorite daughter-in-law. She might not have been as beautiful as you, but she was pretty. At that time he was lonely, and she showered him with attention. Always making sure he was part of our activities with the kids. Then he met you, and everything changed. His life became totally centered around you. He hardly acknowledged Felisa's existence. He seemed to lose interest in our kids, and all the outrageously expensive gifts he used to buy for Felisa now went to you. It really hurt when he assigned Chico, her chauffeur, to drive your car."

"If I'd only known. Poor thing; I would have hated me, too. Why didn't you warn me?"

"You're kidding! Here was this incredibly rich and powerful man obviously in love with you. You were totally snowed. It would have been impossible for us to bring up anything negative about him. You would not have accepted it. He was like a god to you, and I know the feeling was mutual. My dad was like a college freshmen, totally smitten by you. He certainly wasn't alone in that. Most of the men in our family were under the spell of your movie-star good looks and sexy figure. Right from the start you were a powerful force in this Mafia family."

"You saw what was happening to Felisa. Did you resent me for it?"

"In all honesty, yes."

"Then why help me now?"

"Like I told you. I am sick and tired of all the killing. Mafia justice is not justice. It's criminal. It's a system to retain power that I can no longer accept. After I get you out of here, I will disappear forever. My father will never find me! As we speak, all three of my kids and their entire families are preparing to leave the country. They won't be able to use them to force me back."

"How do you plan to get me out of here? Big Joe has the place crawling with men. We'll never get out of here without them noticing."

"I have it all figured out. I called my nephew, Jessie, to come see me here at the estate. The kid is totally oblivious as to what is going on with the Lograso feud, and he is definitely not aware of what is happening to you. When he arrives at the gate, I'll make sure it creates a big commotion and we'll be able to escape through the garage and back gate."

"With a house full of people spying on me, how do you intend to get me to the garage?"

"That won't be difficult. When he arrives at the gate they'll stop him and he'll tell them that he is here to see me. They'll call me to check, and I'll get all excited. I'll be worried that the Lograso people must have spotted that fancy red sports car of his and that the kid is in danger. All those goons will run out to the gate, and I'll come up to take you to the garage. If anybody sees us, I'll say that Giovanni instructed me to take you to a safe place downstairs in the garage. I'll have my car ready to go and we'll leave through the east gate. There will be nobody there."

XVII

Their flight down the stairs to the garage seemed to take forever. Sharleen was terrified. She held onto Federico's hand for dear life. He almost had to drag her along. Once they reached the highway, she calmed down a little.

"Where are we going? Do you know a safe place where we can hide?"

"We're going to hide out in Kitty's place; we'll be safe there."

"Who's Kitty? How do you know we can trust her?"

That brought a smile to Federico's face. "I'm sure we can trust her. She's my girlfriend."

"Girlfriend? What is that all about?"

"I've known Kitty forever. We met during our sophomore year at Hofstra College here on Long Island."

"And you have kept in touch ever since?"

"It's a little more than that. Like I said, she's my girlfriend."

"Girlfriend! Freddie, I'm surprised. I never suspected anything like that from you."

"There's a lot about me you don't know. Yeah, Kitty and I have been together for a long time. You might call us lovers."

"Were you married when the two of you met?"

"Of course not. I was nineteen, a sophomore in college."

"Why didn't you marry her?"

"Oh, come on! You should know why. I'm the oldest son of a Mafia don and Kitty was not deemed suitable to be the wife of the future Godfather. What a joke! Her father was a cop in Roslyn."

Kitty Macintyre lived on her produce farm in Smithtown, and it took less than an hour to get there. The way the petite blonde woman greeted Federico made it clear that the two were more than just friends. After Federico introduced Sharleen, Kitty took her by the arm and quickly led her into the house.

"You never know who might be watching. Freddie, better put your car in the garage; we can't take any chances." Turning to Sharleen she said, "You poor thing, you must be terrified. But don't worry, Freddie will protect you." She proceeded to pour a large amount of scotch into a water glass and handed it to Sharleen. "Here, after what you've been through I am sure you could use a stiff drink."

Sharleen hesitated before she said, "Sorry, I don't drink any alcohol. But it is very sweet of you to offer. I am really very grateful that you allowed me to come here."

"Nonsense! Of course Freddie would bring you here. We wouldn't let those barbarians hold you captive, or, God forbid, even worse. Freddie told me all about you and what was going on there on the estate." She gave Sharleen an encouraging smile and her big, green eyes sparkled when she defiantly added, "If they dare put foot on my property, I'll mow them down."

A day later, her words became prophetic. The three of them were sitting around the kitchen table when Kitty noticed two cars pull up to the front of the house. "Oh shit, I think we are in trouble."

Freddie got up to take a closer look. When he saw Big Joe step out of the lead vehicle he shouted, "Sharleen! Run upstairs and lock yourself in one of the bedrooms. Hurry, they're here!"

Kitty ran to the back of the house and returned carrying two rifles. "See if you can get rid of him. I'll cover you."

Freddie opened the front door and called out, "You looking for me? What's the matter?"

Big Joe replied, "Don't be stupid, Federico! I know you got Sharleen in there. Just send her out and I'll leave you alone. I have no fight with you and I don't want to hurt you. What happens to you is between you and your father. I have been sent to bring Sharleen back, and if you don't send her out, I'm coming in to get her."

Freddie slammed the door shut. Big Joe started for the house but before he could take three steps, Freddie fired a warning shot over his head. His shot was answered with a salvo of shots from both cars. Freddie returned fire from the window, and Big Joe retreated behind the cars. For a while it was silent, but then they heard glass breaking in the back of the house. Through the narrow hallway, one of Big Joe's men came running at them, pistol in hand. Kitty aimed and fired one shot. The man fell, blood pouring out of a gaping hole in his forehead. At about the same time, the front door crashed open and four men stormed in. Freddie and Kitty opened fire and drove them back. One of the men was carrying a converted fully automatic Mac-10 pistol, and he fired a burst in the direction of Freddie. The bullets ripped him apart. Seeing Freddie fall to the floor made Kitty hysterical. She ran through the open door, firing wildly at the men crouched behind the cars. Like Freddie, she too went down in a hail of bullets.

All the bloodshed did not seem to affect Big Joe. He had a single-minded purpose. Get Sharleen! Sharleen heard him come up the stairs and enter the room next to the one in which she was hiding. She was scared out of her mind, and did not know what to do to get away from him. When he opened the door to the room she was in she crawled under the bed. He calmly searched the room until he found her. He dragged her from under the bed and slapped her hard across the face.

"So, you think you could escape from me, you fucking whore?" He roughly pulled her down the stairs and out the front door. While dragging her along, he callously stepped over the lifeless body of Kitty, and pushed Sharleen into one of the waiting cars. The two vehicles took off at full speed.

XVIII

The gang-style execution on Long Island was the lead story on every major TV network. Newspapers printed the gruesome pictures of the garish scene on their front page. The *Long Island Gazette*, in an exclusive story, reported that because one of the victims was the son of the powerful New York Mafia boss, the police suspected the Lograso gang from Chicago, with whom he had been feuding. The paper quoted an unidentified source, who claimed the two Mafia families has been feuding for some time. Under the present don, the Fuentes family had long ago switched to operating only legitimate enterprises, and the Lograsos tried to infiltrate these enterprises by the use of narcotics. The paper's source could not explain the involvement of the dead woman found on the scene. She was the owner of the farm on which the killings took place. The only possible connection the police could discover is that she was the daughter of a former police chief in a nearby town.

When Clint Crawley heard the news, he immediately called Sharleen's dad to check if Sharleen was all right. Mr. Harjo, Sharleen's dad, had not heard from her. Since the news broke, he had been trying to call her all morning, but he could not get hold of her. This worried Clint, and he contacted the police in Great Neck, Long Island, to see if they would send a car out to the Fuentes' estate in Kings Point to check on Sharleen. The Great Neck police were not very cooperative. Unless they had more definite information that something might be wrong, they saw no need to go and check. Clint called Sharleen's father back and told him he had this awful feeling that something was wrong and that Sharleen might be in danger.

"First my restaurant burns down, and now this. I have to go out there to see if she is okay."

Sharleen's father protested that if they had burned down the restaurant, they would have a reason to go after him, and if they recognized him, they might harm him.

"I've thought of that. I don't think they know my face, so there is no reason to believe they'll know who I am. I'll tell them I have come for her to sign some papers; that Sharleen is a beneficiary under Jada's will."

When Clint landed at La Guardia Airport in New York City, he rented a car. After he had bought a detailed map of Long Island, he headed for Kings Point. It took him forever to find the Fuentes estate, and when he finally located it, he could not get in. He was stopped at the gate by two men who asked what he wanted. He told them the story about Sharleen having to sign some papers for the inheritance. He was told to wait while they called the house. They came back and told him Sharleen was not home, and he had to leave. Clint consulted his map and found a road that led to the back of the estate. He thought he might be able to enter through some back gate.

He located a back gate, which was wide open, and he drove right in. He was less than two hundred yards from the gate when four men in a golf cart cut off his path. They dragged him from his car and proceeded to beat the hell out of him. When they thought he had had enough, they put him back in his car and told him to get the hell off the property. They assured him that if he returned, they would be even less hospitable.

Clint drove directly to the local police station to report the attack. To his surprise, the police told him that they had already been called to report that a trespasser had been caught on the property and, when challenged, started a fight. They were asked to be on the look-out for him and arrest him. The police sergeant Clint was talking to got a first aid kit and helped Clint clean and patch up his badly bruised face.

While applying some disinfectant ointment to the deep cuts, the sergeant said, "Do you have any idea who you were dealing with? That estate is off bounds for us. If we try to search the property, we are immediately slapped with a law suit. I don't know what you were planning, or what business you have with those folks, but for your own good, I advise you to forget it."

When Clint returned home, he went to see Sharleen's father. Mr. Harjo suggested that they go together to see his brother on the reservation and ask for help.

Chayton Harjo was an influential elder on the reservation. When he heard his niece might be in danger, he immediately called a meeting of the reservation security team. After they were all seated in his living room, he introduced them one by one.

"This is my son, Lakota. Next to him is Kangee, my sister's boy. Next to him is Oyate; his grandfather was one of our famous chiefs. Then we have Tika, Sunkwa, and Mato. All three are direct descendants of brave warriors, and we are glad that they have chosen to stay with us here on the reservation."

Clint looked around the room at the group of young men assembled around Chayton. They looked friendly enough; handsome faces with typical Indian features. But there was a sense of edginess about them, and Clint could guess that you did not want to mess with this group.

Chayton did not ask if anybody agreed with him when he laid out his plan. "The six of you will take the security van and drive non-stop to New York. You'll get Sharleen and bring her back here."

Sharleen's father gave the men some guidance. "She once told me that Giovanni and she had this huge master bedroom that looked out over the estate grounds. If they are holding her captive, she is probably held in there."

Clint objected. "It's not that easy. They won't be able to enter the estate to get her. And if they manage, how will they get her out? Those people are vicious."

Chayton stared him down. "Just because you could not gain entry, does not mean they can't. These boys are Indian! They'll know how to get her out."

Clint was the only one who protested that it was not that simple. Sharleen's father admonished him not to interfere, and the group of young men took it as an order. They did not question Chayton's authority or the wisdom of his instructions. All they wanted to know was the exact location of the estate, and how they were going to pay for the trip.

XIX

Sharleen had been back in her room for several hours when Guido entered. She quickly backed away from him but he held up his hand. "Don't worry. I won't hurt you. Sit down and hear what I have to say. Needless to say, your deceit has brought great sorrow to Giovanni and resulted in a great tragedy, the loss of his son."

"Damn you! I never cheated on him! I'm sure Bennie told him some lies about me but I swear I never cheated on him."

"Why would Bennie tell lies about you? He adores you."

"He tried to have sex with me but I refused him and he became very mad."

"And you expect me to believe that? Bennie, making a play for Giovanni's wife? You've got to be kidding. No way."

"I never expected you to believe me, but it's the God's honest truth."

"Sure, sure it is. But if we forget that story, can you think of some possible explanation why anybody would think that you had something going with your high school sweetheart? Anything at all that would satisfy Giovanni and make him accept that you never slept with the guy after high school?"

"Look, if you're not going to believe me, there is no use talking. But you can tell me how you found out where Freddie and I were hiding."

"That's simple. We knew Federico had a girlfriend. We knew all along who she was and where she lived."

"You knew Freddie had a girlfriend? How did you find that out?"

"Federico had no respect for the family. He thought we were all a bunch of stupid morons, so he was careless. We knew all along what was going on."

"Did Felisa know?

"Yes, she did."

"And she did not object?"

"She was afraid to jeopardize her marriage. She was not about to give up her position as Giovanni's daughter-in-law. She was in love with Giovanni. There wasn't anything she would not do for him; she'd jump in bed with him if he had given her the chance."

"Did Giovanni realize that?"

"Of course! But Giovanni is too much of a gentleman to take advantage of his daughter-in-law. As a matter of fact, before he met you he was a very private person. He never could justify the death of his wife. His loyalty to the family and our Mafia traditions prevented him from questioning the circumstances of her accident. He turned inward, and had little use for close friendships. That is, until he met you. From the moment he saw you, he was obsessed with you. From that moment on you were his everything. I had never witnessed someone so deeply in love."

"I loved him, too. I never cheated on him."

"Okay, okay, I heard you before. Tell me, if I somehow can straighten this mess out; will you go to him and say you are deeply sorry for all the misunderstandings and that you love him deeply?"

"No! I could never let that murderer touch me again. The thought of it makes my flesh crawl."

"Giovanni is not a murderer!"

"Oh, I see. He just orders someone's execution. Well, I call that murder!"

"You bitch! If only your personality was as beautiful as your body!" Guido got up and left the room, slamming the door shut behind him.

XX

The guard at the main gate to the Fuentes estate thought he heard a noise on the road not far from the gate. "Hey, Vito, I'm going to see what it is. Be right back." Out of precaution, he drew his sidearm and proceeded to walk in the direction from which he had heard the noise. He had not gone very far when the beam from his flashlight shone on a man lying across the road. The man was groaning, but the guard had not heard a car go by, so he wondered what had happened. When he leaned over the man, he was struck on the side of the head and he fell unconscious to the ground. Out of the bushes alongside the road, two figures emerged. Together with the man who had been lying in the road, they bound and gagged the guard and dragged him back to the gate house. Vito thought it was his fellow guard approaching and stepped out of the guardhouse. Before he knew what was happening, he too received a blow to the head and wound up bound and gagged next to his buddy. Three other men dressed in dark clothes joined the group of three standing over the bodies. After they placed the two unconscious guards back in the guardhouse, they walked quietly up to the house.

Nobody spotted them as they crawled along the outside of the house, looking for an unlocked door. Everything was locked up tight and Lakota, who seemed to be the leader, signaled the others to follow him to the balcony. Tika threw a grappling hook with a rope attached onto the balcony railing. One by one, the six men climbed up the rope and onto the balcony. Two immense sliding doors opened up from the ballroom onto the balcony, but they were both shut. Lakota pulled out a pocketknife and forced the blade between the sliding panels. By carefully working the blade up and down, he managed to pop the lock and slide the heavy glass panel open.

The men had no idea as to the layout of the house, much less where they could find Sharleen. The only thing they had to go on was Sharleen's father's suggestion that she might be held in the master bedroom, which looked onto the grounds. This didn't faze Lakota. He carefully instructed each man where to go and what to do in the event they encountered someone.

Tika and Sunkwa were paired together. They were instructed to secure the ground floor and signal if they spotted trouble. Lakota instructed all of them to place their cell phones on vibrate only so they could communicate safely.

Tika and Sunkwa slipped into the main hallway, which led to the central staircase. After carefully looking down the stairs to make sure the coast was clear, they descended and entered the first room to the left. It was the library; it was empty. They proceeded to the front of the house and spotted the lone guard just inside the front door. Not far from him, three men were playing cards. Their weapons were clearly visible. Tika and Sunkwa slid behind a massive piece of furniture that most likely was meant to serve as a coat rack for a large crowd. From their vantage point they could keep an eye on all four men. If any of them got up and headed for the stairway, they could warn Lakota of the danger.

Mato and Oyate were not that lucky. They were instructed to check out the second floor. They went down the wide, upstairs hallway to check out what looked like a set of bedrooms at the far end. They were crawling close to the wall in the dimly lit hallway when out of a door, three men appeared. Mato signaled to Oyate to quickly take cover behind one of the many ornate statues that lined the hallway. The three men paused and said goodnight. Each man entered a different bedroom. Just when they thought the coast was clear, a fourth man emerged from yet another room and headed for the stairway. Mato pointed to his own head to signal Oyate that he would take the man down. As the man passed him, he jumped from behind the statue and hit the man on his head with a blackjack. The man went down without a sound, and Oyate came over to help gag and bind the guy. Oyate noticed a big bulge under the man's shirt. He reached in and pulled out an automatic Mac-10 pistol.

He held it up and whispered to Mato, "Could come in handy when we encounter more of these creeps."

Mato shook his head no, and replied, "Remember, Chayton said that he wanted no one killed; not even badly wounded. Put it down!" The two of them lay down against the wall on opposite sides of the hallway. This gave them a clear view of the entire hallway, and they could warn Lakota if anybody came out of one of the rooms and headed for the stairway.

Meanwhile, Lakota and Kangee had gone up the stairs to the third floor. While they were surveying the outside of the house, Kangee had noticed that the lights were on in what looked to be a third-floor bedroom. In the dark he had seen the outline of a balcony. He whispered to Lakota, "I think the master bedroom must be there on the third floor. One of the rooms has a balcony. I bet we'll find Sharleen here."

Kangee had guessed right. When he and Lakota reached the third floor, they entered a wide hallway. The hallway ended in a small alcove with two loveseats and an overstuffed easy chair. Beyond that they saw a double door. Lakota did not want to take a chance and barge through the door. They had no idea who might be in there, and Sharleen might not be kept there. Worse than that, if she was not alone, she might get hurt if a scuffle ensued. Lakota saw a window in the alcove and he went over to see if it would get him onto the balcony. Sure enough, the balcony circled around. Lakota climbed out of the window, leaving Kangee to warn him if anyone appeared in the hallway. Lakota walked over to the bedroom window and saw Sharleen in her pajamas, stretched out on a couch watching television. Using his pocketknife, he carefully released the window lock and opened it less than two inches.

He pressed his face to the glass, so Sharleen could recognize him, and in their Sioux dialect said, *"It's me, Lakota. I have come to take you home."* Sharleen jumped up and recognized him instantly.

She pulled open the window and exclaimed, *"Lakota, how did you get here?"*

Lakota calmly stepped through the open window and answered, *"Father sent me to bring you home."*

Lakota held her for a short while, but then said, *"Calm down, little cousin. It's going to be okay. We won't let them hold one of us. Hurry, put on some black pants and a dark top. Do you have some good sport shoes?"* When she answered affirmatively, he told her to put them on.

"Kangee is waiting for us outside the door. We'll take you back downstairs to that big room with the sliding doors that lead to the balcony. Sorry, you'll have to slide down a rope to get down. Don't worry; we'll catch you if you fall."

Kangee met them in the dimly lit hallway, and the three of them headed for the stairway. They had almost reached the stairway when Lakota's cell phone started vibrating. He pressed the phone to his ear and heard Tika say, *"One man heading up the staircase."* He motioned for Sharleen and Kangee to take shelter behind on of the statues lining the walls.

His cell phone vibrated again. This time it was Mato, *"Man climbing stair case."* Seconds later he noticed movement at the top of the staircase. Sharleen peered out of from behind the statue she had crawled behind. She saw the figure at the top of the staircase. She thought she recognized who it was, and when the person stepped into the hallway she got a clear view of his face. It was Chico. She saw Lakota raise a club-like instrument ready to attack Chico if he came any closer.

"Don't hurt him," she whispered. But it was too loud, and Chico heard her. She jumped up and with her finger across her lips signaled him to be quiet. She startled Chico but he remained quiet and shook his head yes. He turned back to the staircase and went back down.

"Can we trust him?" Lakota whispered.

"Yes, it's Chico, my driver."

"How can we be sure he won't betray us?"

"I know Chico. As my driver, he would protect me with his life."

The three of them safely reached the second-floor landing, and carefully found their way back to the ballroom. As they disappeared through the big sliding-glass doors, through which they had entered, Kangee looked back to see if they were followed. Standing at the entrance to the ballroom was Chico, apparently guarding their escape.

When the three of them reached the ground Lakota whispered, ***"I hope you're in good condition. We have a van parked about half a mile from the gate and we'll have to run all the way."***

He waited until they reached the van to pull out his cell phone. He dialed the others. They had arranged to put their phones on vibrate only and they, unlike Lakota, would not answer. They knew that once Lakota had Sharleen safely outside he would signal them by means of a quick call and immediate hang up.

A little over ten minutes later, Mato and Oyate arrived at the van.

Twenty minutes passed, and there was no sign of Tika and Sunkwa. For the first time that night, Lakota seemed worried. "We can't leave without them. Anyone have a suggestion as to what to do?"

Oyate waved the Mac-10 in the air. "I'll go get them! I'll blast my way in with this baby! No one can stop us from leaving."

Mato reacted angrily. "What the hell are you still doing with that thing? I told you to get rid of it." Lakota was angry too, but Mato argued that it might be the only way to get Tika and Sunkwa out safely.

The argument was interrupted by a shout from Kangee, "Hey, there they are!" Totally out of breath,

Tika and Sunkwa climbed into the van. Kangee wasted no time; he jumped behind the wheel and they sped off, direction: New York City.

Lakota returned to his stoic self, and he once again reached for his cell phone to call his dad. When Chayton answered, he calmly said, *"Everything A-Okay. We're heading for the Jersey Turnpike, and we should be there way before dawn."*

As he was about to hang up, Sharleen yelled over his shoulder, "Love you, Uncle Chayton! I love all of you! These guys are unbelievable!"

She could not hear her uncle mumble, *"Just doing their duty."*

XXI

Her mom and dad were waiting for her when Sharleen arrived on the reservation. Chayton had invited them to come and stay on the reservation so he could protect them in case the Mafia wanted to get at Sharleen by using them. They had already settled into one of the many abandoned traditional Indian homes that could be found all across the reservation. Chayton had also invited Clint to come and seek shelter on the reservation. By now it was an open secret as to who was responsible for burning down the restaurant, and Chayton was sure they would not leave it at that. At first Clint refused, but he accepted after Chayton reminded him of how his face looked after the Mafia had gotten through with him when he tried to enter the estate.

Clint was scheduled to arrive the next morning. He would occupy the abandoned house next to the one Sharleen and her parents were staying in.

Not everybody on the reservation agreed with this arrangement. They pointed to the fact that neither Sharleen's mother nor Clint was even part Indian, and that they did not belong on the reservation. Having married outside the tribe, Sharleen's father was not really welcome, either. Chayton used his position to quickly put a stop to the protests. The fact that Sharleen was immensely popular among the members of the tribe also helped quell the arguments. As a young girl she had frequently come to the reservation to visit with her cousins, and most of the people remembered her as that delightful young girl. Mato remembered asking her cousin Lakota if he could help him get a date with her. He was terribly disappointed when he heard she was going steady with a boy from her school.

When Clint arrived, Sharleen greeted him exuberantly. She kissed him so passionately that her mother gave her father a knowing glance. Her father had a big smile on his face; he had always been a huge fan of Clint's. He never completely understood why Sharleen left town without waiting for him.

That night there was a tribal ceremony to give thanks for the safe return of Sharleen and the six men who rescued her. Following the party, everyone was invited to Chayton's house to continue the festivities. The party dragged on late into the night.

Clint, who was known to not shy away from a good party, got to bed very late. He had just gotten into bed when he heard some noise at the rickety entrance to the traditional house. He knew he was perfectly safe on the reservation, but he was still hesitant when he went to check what it was. To his surprise, it was Sharleen.

She looked like she had been chased by a wild animal. Her beautiful eyes were wide with fear.

"Can I come in?"

"Of course," Clint said. "You look frightened. What happened?"

"I woke up from a bad dream. They were going to slaughter me like they did Freddy and Kitty. Oh, Clint, I'm so scared!"

Clint waved her in. He looked around the bare room and continued, "I'd offer you a chair, but this place only has some old dressers and this big, king-sized bed."

"Don't worry; I can sit on the edge of the bed if you don't mind. I just want to talk for a while. That dream scared me so much I'm afraid to go back to bed. I keep thinking about it."

"I don't mind, if you don't find it awkward, since I'm only wearing pajamas."

"No, that's fine. Here, sit next to me. I want to thank you for coming to New York to look for me. You took one hell of a chance coming out there all by yourself. I started tearing up when my father told me about it. I love you very much for doing it."

Clint looked at her; he was quiet for a while, as if he was searching for the right words. "I understand how you feel. That must have been horrible to see those two people slaughtered by the same people who came after you and later held you captive. I too was scared out of my mind. When I heard what they did, and we could not contact you, I had to come looking for you. I had visions of what could be happening to you. I couldn't stand the idea of something bad happening to you. I shouldn't say this, but you've been on my mind a lot. I still love you."

There was an awkward pause. The two of them looked at each other, not sure what to say. Finally he asked, "Do you still love me? I know I shouldn't ask, but—

Sharleen interrupted him. "And maybe I shouldn't admit it, but I never stopped loving you."

"What about Jada? How do you feel about me marrying your best friend?"

"When I heard about it, I was very glad. I don't know if you can understand that."

"If you still loved me, it does sound strange."

"You marrying Jada made me feel less guilty about running away. Jada *was* me. As long as you had her, I never abandoned you. Jada was the only one who, in my mind, could take my place and make you happy. She would never let you down. I know you loved her deeply, and did not have to think back to our time together."

Clint encouraged Sharleen to talk about her dream, and her fears while she was locked up in her room. She felt good talking about it and getting it off her chest. She relaxed and stretched out on the bed.

Clint smiled at her. "Just lie there for a while and get some sleep. It will do you good after all the emotions of the past week.

"What about you? I woke you up; you haven't had much sleep, either."

"Don't worry, I'll find a place next to the bed to curl up."

"That's nonsense. You can't sleep on the floor. The bed is big enough. Come here and lie next to me."

When Clint laid next to her, Sharleen said, "I feel safe with you lying next to me. Even back in high school I felt protected when we were together."

Clint held out his hand. "And now fate has brought us together again. You know you are even more beautiful now than you were in high school?"

"That's sweet of you to say. But I am certainly not getting any younger."

"Maybe we just had to grow up."

Sharleen moved closed to Clint. When he tightened his grip on her hand he was holding, she rolled over and pressed against him and kissed him. They embraced; the belt around Clint's robe came loose. Sharleen pressed against his naked body.

"Well, we're consenting adults now," Sharleen said as she sat up. She looked at him lying on the bed, and a big smile came across her face. She dropped the robe she had been wearing to the floor; she only had on a bra and panties. She reached back and unhooked her bra. It dropped to the floor, and the panties followed. She crawled next to Clint.

Clint did not need a second invitation. As their naked bodies came together, they were mentally back in Clint's hotel room during their high school senior trip to Washington, DC.

XXII

Paul Klein had been trying to contact Clint to discuss his loan from City National Bank. Yesterday, Clint finally answered his cell phone. He told Paul that in case there would be an attempt on his life, he was temporarily staying on the Indian reservation. They agreed that it would not be good for Clint to come into town to see Paul. Paul offered to meet with Clint on the reservation.

Paul drove all over the reservation trying to locate the house in which Clint was staying. By the time he found it, it was already late in the morning. When Clint opened the door, Paul was surprised to see him still in pajamas. When he looked past Clint, he saw Sharleen quickly putting on her robe.

Paul was not really surprised. "Guess it's never too late."

"Yeah, sorry, we slept in," Clint responded.

"That's not what I meant." Paul had a big smile on his face.

Clint frowned as if he just realized something. *I wonder if Jada's last words meant the same?*

Paul did not stop to listen to Sharleen's lame excuses as to why she was there in Clint's house. "Why don't the two of you hurry up and get dressed and meet me at Chayton's house. He told me these old houses were sparsely furnished, and offered to let us meet at his house."

Sharleen was in a great mood. While they were getting dressed she jokingly asked Clint, "Are we an item again?"

Clint was more serious when he replied, "Maybe you should drop the *again*."

In stark contrast to the abandoned traditional house Clint was staying in, Chayton's house was a large, modern ranch-style house. The furniture in the den where they had their meeting was more traditional; large leather sofas and heavy wooden coffee tables dominated the room. As Indian hospitality required, Chayton made sure that there was plenty of coffee and tea, and lots of food. Chayton knew that Sharleen could be expected to arrive with Clint. The young man who had stood guard outside of Clint's house had informed him that late into the night, Sharleen had left her parents' house and gone into Clint's.

When they had gotten some coffee from the large buffet, Paul started explaining that because the restaurant had burned down, the underlying security for Clint's loan was gone, and the bank had to call the loan.

Clint started to protest but Paul waved him off. "Don't worry; we're not coming after you. I have spoken to your insurance company, and they will cover the damage. The amount they mentioned will more than cover the amount remaining on the loan. You can walk away with a little cash left over for any small outstanding claims."

He turned to Sharleen. "And you, my lady, are left with a large chunk of money."

"How so?" Sharleen asked.

Paul looked at Clint. "I'd probably have to ask you to leave the room, but my guess is you'll probably find out anyway. The truth is, Sharleen guaranteed the loan I gave you. She placed an equivalent amount on deposit at our bank. That amount is now free from any restrictions."

Clint looked at Sharleen. "You what?"

Before he could continue, Sharleen cut him off. "Shut up. I don't want to talk about it. And I did it as much for Jada as for you. By now, you know my feelings for both of you and what the two of you meant to me. So I don't want to talk about it. I had the money, and it was the right thing to do. Besides, you never used it. You recovered on your own strength, and I'm damn proud of you."

"I agree," Paul said. "You did a great job in bringing that place back to life. I too admire you for it. Let's face it. With all respect to your father and what he left you, that place was as dead as a doornail when you took over. You had the vision to see what it would take to bring it back. You only underestimated the amount it would take to complete the renovation."

Clint did not want to leave it at that, but as he turned to Sharleen, apparently to express his gratitude, she took his hand and said, "Hush, honey. Now you know, and we don't have to talk about it ever again."

Paul reverted to the money. "Sharleen, do you have any idea as to what you want to do with all that money? If it's not too presumptuous, I'd like to offer a plan."

Sharleen was still holding Clint's hand. She looked very happy, remembering how great she had felt being able to help her friends. "What did you have in mind, Paul?"

"Well, both of you sort of have a price on your head, and you can't stay here on the reservation forever. So, you have to go someplace where you can't be found, and that probably means leaving the country. I am sure the authorities will protect you, but it is best to go someplace out of the reach of the New York Mafia. A client of mine at the bank is from Bermuda. His father owns a nice restaurant there. His father is seventy, and he wants to retire. His son is helping him find a buyer. Now I was thinking, the amount Sharleen has on deposit at our bank is more than enough for a substantial deposit. Based on that, a local bank in Bermuda should have no trouble giving you a mortgage for the rest. And by the way, the restaurant has a small apartment above it, and you could live there until you find something more suitable."

"Bermuda! You're kidding? I've never even been out of the country, and you suggest moving to Bermuda?"

Paul was deadly serious. "Sharleen, there are far worse things than living in Bermuda. I've been there on vacation. It's beautiful! If I had the chance, I wouldn't think twice about moving there. It seems a perfect fit; Clint has experience running a restaurant, and I think you would be the perfect hostess. That's assuming the two of you would go together."

"I'm not that stupid to leave without her for a second time. I hope Sharleen feels the same way. If we go, we'll go together!"

Sharleen jumped up. "Yes! If we go together, I don't care where it is. I'm ready to go." She turned to Clint. "Darling, are you okay with Bermuda?"

"Like Paul says, it's a beautiful island. If Paul can arrange everything, I am more than ready to go. I don't want to rebuild the restaurant. There are too many memories here. I would love to make a new start."

Sharleen just wanted to get away from the Mafia. "I don't care what anybody says about police protection. I'm scared stiff, and I want to get far away from those bastards. I know what they'll do to me and Clint if they manage to catch up with us. I have no idea where Bermuda is, but the idea sounds great."

"Okay, I'll start the ball rolling," Paul said. "Once you own the restaurant, you can get a work permit so you can live on the island. I know they are anxious to sell as soon as possible, and I know what they are asking. All we need to do is get the two of you a passport, and you're on your way."

Clint looked at Paul. "I guess you're right, it's never too late."

Sharleen did not get it. "That's what Jada said to me when she was dying."

Clint explained, "Yes, dear, that's what she told you. She was giving you instructions and her blessing."

Sharleen burst out in tears. "Jada! Could anyone wish for a better friend? She was a saint."

XXIII

The move to Bermuda went smoothly. The gentleman who sold them the restaurant was highly respected on the island, and the restaurant had a large following. Sharleen and Clint were well received by the steady customers. Obviously, their sex appeal helped. Men could not help but be attracted to Sharleen's beauty, and the women liked her for her outgoing personality. Even though she had never done it before, Sharleen made a great hostess. The men took an immediate liking to Clint, and the women loved to flirt with him. His tall stature and manly good looks made him easily recognizable, and he was very approachable as the host.

Since business was good, Clint saw no reason to make any big changes in the restaurant. He did, however, jump at the chance to import an antique bar that had been rescued out of an Irish pub which had been demolished to make room for new buildings in downtown Dublin. With the help of an interior architect, he managed to install it in the restaurant without losing seating capacity.

After they had been in Bermuda for a year, Sharleen and Clint decided they could afford to move out of the upstairs apartment. They found a rental in a very nice section of town. Moving out of the apartment into a big house did mean Sharleen would need help with the housekeeping. She interviewed quite a few women, and finally selected Ana. When Ana told her she always brought a helper along, Sharleen told her they could not afford two people. Ana explained that her helper never got paid, and it would not cost any extra to have the two of them. Sharleen would not have any of that, and promised to pay Ana an extra thirty percent.

When Ana showed up the first day for work, Sharleen pulled back in shock when she saw Ana's helper. He was at least six foot nine and had a massive body.

"Ana, who is this?"

"This is Mikie, he's my nephew. He is really very good at cleaning. He's been helping me for years. Mikie, say hello to Miss Sharleen."

"Hullo, Missis Sharleen."

From his speech pattern, Sharleen could tell that Mikie was mentally handicapped. She was hesitant to let the two of them in and said, "Ana, we have to talk."

Ana's face betrayed her emotions and her lips trembled when she spoke. "Miss Sharleen, please let me come in and explain. Mikie is big, but he is harmless. Really he is. Please, Miss Sharleen, we need this job. I beg you to let me explain."

Sharleen felt terrible. She was embarrassed by her reaction at seeing this giant of a man. "Yes, Ana. Of course; come on in and explain."

"Thank you, Miss Sharleen, thank you so much. You'll see. Mikie is a wonderful worker. You'll be happy to have him."

"I am happy to believe you, but tell me some more. Why does Mikie come along to help you? I'm afraid I'll have to ask you to give me more details."

"Like I said, he's my nephew. My sister died right after childbirth, and I have been taking care of him."

"Didn't he have a father or something?"

"No, ma'am. My sister came to me when she was about to give birth. Before that we had very little contact. She had been working as a waitress. Anyway, that is what she said. She asked me to take care of her while she delivered the child. I called the midwife when she went into labor, but the baby did not come for hours. When the baby did come, the midwife did not know what to do. The umbilical cord was wound around the baby's neck, and she knew she had to get the baby out quickly. But the baby was too big, and she started hacking away at my sister. When she finally managed to get the baby out, he had suffered from a lack of oxygen. Later we discovered that he had brain damage. The frantic cutting had gone beyond the outside of the vagina and caused severe damage on the inside. My sister died two days later. That's why I am single. No man here on the island wants a woman who comes complete with a handicapped child."

While listening to Ana, Sharleen put her hands to her face in disbelief. She was not prepared to hear such graphic details. "You poor thing! I am so sorry you had to experience that. How good of you to have taken care of the baby. How old was he when you first noticed that he was mentally impaired?"

"It showed before he was one year; it was very clear by the time he was two."

"Couldn't you find some of his father's family to help you raise him? At least to give some financial support?"

"My sister told me she was a waitress, but we can only guess at how she supported herself. We didn't even know the baby's heritage. Look at Mikie's size and relatively light skin color. Most people think we here on the island are black. But that is not really true. We are a mixture of black people. They call us mulattos, a combination of black, Asian, Indian, British white, and American Indian."

The latter caught Sharleen's attention. "Then Mikie and I share the same blood lines."

"You do, ma'am?"

"Yes, I come from a mixture of Native American, European white, and black Haitian. Welcome to my house, Ana. I will be happy to have you and Mikie work for us."

XXIV

As if Ana's story had not been unusual enough, Clint and Sharleen continued to be a magnet for people with strange stories.

Clint was in his office going over the books when Johnny stuck his head in the door. "Hey, boss, there is a guy here to see you."

"What's he want, Johnny? I'm pretty busy right now. Maybe he can come back later."

"He's pretty insistent. Something about needing your help or he'll be deported."

"Okay, send him in."

The man Johnny brought into the office was dressed in workman's clothes. Clint thought he might be a dockworker. "You want to see me about deportation?"

"Yes, sir. I've come to ask you for a job and to help me get a work permit."

"Why come to me for that?"

"Well, you being an American, I thought you might be willing to help me out."

"What makes you think I can help?"

"You could claim you need my services, and you can't find anyone else here on the island to fill the job."

"Look, I am not about to lie for you. Besides, there are plenty of qualified people here to fill the type of jobs I need filled in the restaurant."

"I'm sure you'd be hard up finding a good financial manager."

"You look like a nice enough guy, but as I said, I am not willing to lie for you."

"You would not be lying. I spent a year and a half in the graduate finance program at Stanford. There is no way you'd find a person with my qualifications who would work for you for as little as I would be asking."

"Sounds a little farfetched, but okay, out with it. What's the story?"

"You want the whole fricking story?'

"You want my help, so tell me exactly what is going on. Why should I believe you about Stanford? I don't even know your name"

"I'm sorry, my bad. I'm Antoine Johnson from Bakersfield, California. Sit back, here comes the whole messy story.

"I was in my second year at Stanford when I met this girl. Her name was Madison, and she was taking some advanced courses in the arts and humanities. We met at a mutual friend's party, and started dating on a regular basis. During the Christmas break, she invited me to go home with her. Like an idiot,

I accepted. I should have realized that in the small southern town where she was from I would not be welcome. From the moment I arrived, there was trouble. Her family was furious with her for bringing home a black guy. The situation became really bad during the second day. That evening she and I left her house. We drove to a nearby town and discussed, over dinner, what to do. That I had to leave was obvious, but she was debating whether she should stick it out during the Christmas break or return to school immediately. During dinner she drank way too much. I should have never allowed her to drive back. But I did; my judgment was a little off because I too had a few too many. On the way back to her house, we crashed. We were not wearing seatbelts and were thrown from the car. She died instantly; I woke up in the hospital."

"I still don't understand what brought you to Bermuda."

"When I was discharged from the hospital, I was served with a summons to appear before a grand jury. They had charged me with involuntary manslaughter. Seems like the police and the local coroner decided that I had been driving."

"How did they reach that conclusion?"

"Madison died from a broken neck, the result from hitting a tree. I had broken ribs and they concluded that came from impact from hitting the steering wheel."

"The car must have airbags. They would have prevented that."

"Absolutely! But in that small town, I don't think I would have had a chance in hell not to be indicted. After that, the jury verdict would have been a slam dunk for the prosecutor. So I skipped out before they could indict me. Their small-town police department would probably not have the budget to go and find me. And based on those flimsy charges, I didn't think they'd go national. Anyway, to make sure, I skipped out of the country"

"Why were you so sure they would have indicted you?"

"Are you kidding? In that small town, her family owned the factory that was the only source of employment in town. Like I said, as an African American male, there was no way in hell I would have received a fair trial."

"Don't you think you painted our entire system of justice with a wide brush? Sure there have been terrible miscarriages of justice, but that doesn't mean all juries are prejudiced. My own parents were opposed to mixed marriages, but that did not make them bigots. They would have been able to give someone a fair trial regardless of race."

"Oh, I know. My high school was fully integrated, and I had no trouble in college. Certainly not at Stanford. But this was different. Her family hated me. I knew the extent of their hatred from their reaction when Madison brought me home with her. They were not the least bit discreet, and I could hear the word *nigger* being thrown around."

"Were you out on bail when you skipped out?"

"It never got that far. The policeman who was supposed to escort me from the court house where I was officially charged told me I would never make it alive to my trial. He said he did not agree with lynch mobs. He let me escape on the way to the local jail."

"Was he a black officer?"

"Nah, he was white. They didn't have any African Americans on the police force."

"Why did you choose Bermuda?"

"When I was growing up, my family vacationed here in Bermuda. I had no idea you needed a work permit to live here."

"Does your family know you're hiding out here?"

"No comment."

"Thanks for trusting me. You are asking me to help you, but you don't trust me?"

"Sorry, that was sort of a reflex reaction. They know I'm here, but we have very limited contact. You never know who might be watching them in the hope of locating me. They can't even send me money. If they did it could be traced through the banks. They did bring me some money a year ago."

"How did they manage that?"

"They booked one of those Caribbean cruises. When the ship docked here in Bermuda I arranged to meet them in a restaurant. But that money is all gone by now. I have been trying to support myself with some odd jobs. I heard about the need for a work permit, so I tried to lay low."

"Can't your family help clear your name?"

"My father has plenty of pull. He is head of pediatrics at St. Clare General Hospital. But escaping from custody is a crime in itself, and that complicates matters. Besides, I am scared, and would never agree to go back to the States to stand trial. I don't trust the justice system!"

"So you wound up here in Bermuda. You are sure they're not looking for you here? That could be the reason you are about to be deported."

"No, they aren't looking for me here. I'm being deported because I don't have a work permit, and they caught me working odd jobs on the docks."

"And you think I can claim you are the only person I can get to be my financial manager?"

"Without sounding too arrogant, yes. I was the valedictorian of my high school class, graduated summa cum laude from Stanford, and almost completed my master's degree in finance from there."

"Academically you've sure got me beat! I never even went to college. Let me call my friend, Jimmy. His law office has a lot to do with government agencies."

Jimmy Garretson came right over and quickly sketched out a plan of action. "First of all, Antoine has to come with me and voluntarily turn himself in. Next, he has to agree to leave the island as soon as possible. I would suggest he hang out in Aruba while I prepare the application for a work permit, which I will hand-carry to the proper authorities. I deal with those folks all the time."

Less than three weeks later, Antoine was back in Bermuda, ready to start his new job at the restaurant. On top of the money he had borrowed for the trip to Aruba, Clint gave him a hefty advance so he could move into a nice apartment. One complication remained. What to do with the girl he had been living with in a rundown apartment on the back side of downtown Hamilton? Rather than dump her, Antoine decided to ask her to move in with him in his new apartment. At first she refused, but when she realized he really liked her, she accepted.

XXV

Business was booming at the restaurant. Antoine was explaining to Clint why, rather than building their own restaurants, it would be better to lease the dining facilities in a luxury hotel on the coast. He was in the middle of showing, with detailed charts, that it would be more advantageous to expand that way. It would be quicker, require much less capital investment, and certainly reduce the risk. Right when he was about to clinch his argument, Ana burst into Clint's office.

"Help, Mr. Clint, please help! They have arrested Mikie!"

Ana was hysterical; they had trouble getting any further information out of her. They called Sharleen, and she finally succeeded in calming Ana down, enough to get the full story.

"The police came and arrested him. They say some lady has accused him of raping her. That's impossible! He has always been with me! And since he is so big and strong I have taught him, ever since he was a little boy, that if he touched a girl's vagina his penis would fall off. No way did he rape anyone. He would not know how!"

Sharleen had her arms around Ana. "Ana, it's going to be okay. Clint will go get him. Where is he now?"

"I don't know. The police dragged him away. I am so afraid he'll fight back. He won't understand what is happening."

It was Antoine who was the first to react. "I'll call all the police stations and find out who's holding him."

Clint agreed. "While you do that, I'll call Jimmy Garretson and tell him to meet us at whatever station they are holding him in. Ana, don't worry, Mikie won't resist. He's as gentle as they come. He'll just be totally confused and wonder why you did not come with him. I am sure Jimmy will get him released in no time."

When Clint called Jimmy back to tell him where to meet them, Jimmy had already located Mikie. "He's not under arrest. They took him in because they want him to be in a lineup, so the victim of the alleged rape can see if she can identify her attacker."

They raced to the police station where Mikie was scheduled to stand in the lineup. No matter how they argued, they could not get to see him until after the lineup.

The news was devastating. The woman identified Mikie as her assailant, and he was immediately taken into custody. Ana begged to see him, but was told she had to wait until they booked him. When Jimmy finally arranged for her to see him in his cell, she could not explain to him why he could not go home with her. The big guy was in tears, and so was Ana. He kept on calling out that he wanted to go home.

"I want to go home. Don't like it here. People not nice to Mikie. I go home now."

Ana tried her very best to explain why she could not take him home, but Mikie was incapable of understanding it. It was horrible to see the big man so upset. He kept on asking to go home.

"Mikie did nothing wrong. Mikie go home now."

The police constable guarding him said that he was under instructions to take him to the local jail. Ana asked to come along, but the constable said that would not be permitted. Jimmy Garretson exploded. "Don't you see this man is incapable of understanding what is going on? It is inhumane to try and separate him from this lady!"

The constable insisted that there was nothing he could do about it. He had to transport Mikie to the jailhouse, and they could not visit him until his arraignment.

Garretson turned to Ana. "Tell him it's only for a little while. Calm him down, and let him know it's only for a little while. I can't let this happen. I can't see this big guy in such agony; I promise you I will not let this happen."

Clint was not aware that his friend was capable of such emotion. Jimmy pulled out his cell phone and called the chief of police. From the way he barked into the phone, the operator knew it was very serious and she connected him through immediately. "Damn it, Rodi, you can't allow this! This man cannot be put in jail. He can't understand what is going on, and I am sure he is not even guilty."

When he did not get the response he wanted he continued, "What the hell do you mean you can't do anything about it? No, that can't be the law. If you don't intervene, I'll call Chief Justice Lawson. The hell with it, I'll call the governor!"

Jimmy's outburst had effect, and the chief came to the station to settle the situation. He determined that Mikie was certainly not a flight risk, and regardless of the seriousness of the crime with which he had been charged, they could not lock him up by himself in a jail cell. Rather than get hold of a judge to set bail, the chief agreed to let Mikie go home with Ana wearing an electronic tether. He also wanted Clint's assurance that Mikie would be available for any required court appearances.

Unfortunately, the drama did not end there. Based on the victim's positive identification, Mikie had to stand trial. Because of his mental condition, it would have been easy to have the judge determine that he was not cable of understanding the proceedings. But that might mean the court would have him institutionalized. Garretson was determined to have the case brought to trial so he could show the world that Mikie was not guilty. He had gotten to like the gentle giant and he, like Ana, was absolutely sure he was not guilty. The prosecution was hesitant to go to trial. The case had caught widespread public attention. A groundswell of supporters were calling for Mikie's release. This led to a standoff, and the case dragged on. Garretson did not care, as long as Mikie was safely at home with Ana.

The impasse came to an end when another woman was attacked in the same neighborhood. She had been walking to her car, which was parked near the back entrance of the bar which she'd just left. A man grabbed her from behind, but the woman managed to fight him off and ran, screaming, back into the bar. A group of patrons ran out the door in pursuit of the attacker. In her struggle to escape, the woman had pulled her fingernails down the man's cheek, and the pursuers had no problem identifying him. They fought him to the ground and held him until the police arrived. He was later identified as a deckhand on one of the cruise ships which came to port once a month. Since the man was rather big, and the attack took place in roughly the same area as the one of which Mikie was accused, the police asked Mikie's accuser if maybe this assailant also matched her attacker. At first, she vigorously protested that she was sure her attacker was Mikie, and that she had not made a mistake identifying him during the lineup. It was not until they pointed out that she had told them her attacker smelled of liquor, and that Ana strictly forbade Mikie from touching the stuff, that she was willing to reconsider. But she did not have to. The deckhand confessed to committing the rape. Mikie was exonerated.

This should have ended this horrible experience for Ana and Mikie, but some of it lingered on. The problem was with an elderly lady who lived next to them and who insisted that, regardless of what the police said, she was still afraid of Mikie. Having lived in the neighborhood for her entire life, she had many close friends there, and they all turned against Ana. The situation became so bad that Ana told Sharleen about it. Sharleen knew that Clint was as fond of Mikie as she was. Actually, he had grown even more attached to the big fellow with his ever-present, friendly smile. She did not hesitate to tell Ana to move into the upstairs apartment at the restaurant.

Ana protested and tried to point out, "You don't understand, ma'am. This is a fine neighborhood. People living in this area won't accept the likes of me."

"You mean because you're black and there are mostly white folks living around here?"

"No, ma'am, that is not it. You see, us poor folks live around Cedar Avenue and Victoria Street. We're not accepted in a fine area like this."

"Stop it! I don't want to hear such talk."

"Sorry, ma'am, but that is the way it is. It would cause trouble if Mikie and I moved in here. Think of what your customers would say. And it might even stop the people from the tourist ships from coming to your restaurant."

"Ana, dear, you and I grew up in a different world. My folks never had much money; my father was a day laborer in a factory, but they never had to hide in a ghetto. And I have never seen those so-called ghettos you speak of, here in Bermuda. I'm not even sure Bermuda has any slums, certainly not like those in big cities in the United States. I think you are imagining something that does not really exist. Even if it does, I don't believe in that sort of thing! You and Mikie are moving into the apartment as soon as possible. No ifs, ands, or buts about it."

"But, ma'am, we don't belong here."

"Ana, stop it! You're making me angry with that type of talk. You are moving into the apartment!"

"But what about Mr. Clint. What would he say?"

"Ana, you would hurt him deeply if he thought you could think for a moment that he would object."

"I am sorry; I would never want to hurt him. But you have to understand. I have never met people like you. You treat me like… family, and Mikie like a person. It seems like you forget that he has a problem."

"He hasn't got a problem. *We* have a problem if we don't love him. He is a kind, gentle soul, and that is more than I can say for many people I've met. Now hurry up and make arrangements for the move."

XXVI

Clint was at his computer. As he frequently did, he looked up the website of the local newspaper "back home," as he liked to call it. The first thing he saw was the story about Paul Klein.

"Sharleen, come quick! You have to see this. They are charging Paul Klein with conspiracy in a money laundering case. Here, read this."

"The local prosecutor's office announced the indictment of Paul Klein, a vice president and the chief loan officer at City National Bank. According to the indictment, Mr. Klein is suspected of facilitating the transfer of Mafia money to Bermuda. Mr. Klein is refusing to cooperate with the investigators. According to our sources, ICE initiated a program to detect weaknesses within our financial system that could be exploited by criminal organizations. HSI was formed to implement this program. Their New York Special Agent detected the transfer of a considerable amount of money from a suspected Mafia account to City National. Investigators recently discovered that the money was transferred by Mr. Klein to Bermuda and used to buy a local restaurant. The wife of a New York Mafia kingpin is listed as the co-owner of the restaurant. The transfer of the money took place quite a while ago, but the statute of limitations has not run out, and Mr. Klein can still be prosecuted for his part in this illicit activity."

"Oh no. No, no…" Sharleen was devastated. "Paul did nothing wrong. He helped us! How can they say he did anything wrong? And what are ICE and HSI?"

"ICE stands for Immigration and Customs Enforcement. Here, I looked it up on Google. HSI is ICE's office of Homeland Security Investigations. This is what I found when I Googled it:

> *ICE uses financial investigations to beat criminals at their trade. By following the money trail, law enforcement can identify and dismantle international criminal networks, seizing the networks' proceeds and related assets. ICE, along with other Department of Homeland Security component agencies, is charged with protecting the nation's borders. One way ICE does this is by investigating the illicit flow of money in and out of the United States.*

Clint looked at Sharleen, and a frown crossed his brow. "Sharleen, was that Mafia money you used to guarantee my loan?"

"Clint, I don't know. I have no idea, and I never even thought about it. I asked Bennie Cardiello, Giovanni's financial guy, to send me the money. I never for a moment thought about where it would come from. Remember, Giovanni is very rich. There was always plenty of money; he owns a lot of companies. Clint, you have to believe me, I never considered that there might be something wrong with the money. I never even thought that Giovanni might have dirty money."

Clint reached out to her. "Of course I believe you. The money might have come from legitimate sources; who knows? We have to go back home and help Paul clear this up. Even if the money was dirty, he had no way of knowing that. I don't think it was his responsibility to question the source of the funds. We'll leave as soon as possible!"

Sharleen was scared. "If Giovanni finds out that we are back in the US, he'll come after us. Clint, his thugs will kill us!"

Clint had thought of that. "We'll operate from the reservation. Chayton will be able to protect us."

"What if they arrest me? I deposited the money with Paul and he transferred it for me. Just read the article. They refer to me as Giovanni's wife. They'll think I am covering for Giovanni. That I helped launder his money."

"That's why we have to go and clear things up. I'm sure they'll believe you. Especially when they are informed about your escape from his estate."

"Clint, I'm scared!"

"I understand, but it's going to be all right. It's the US; the prosecutor will make a fair investigation and clear both you and Paul."

"Oh yeah? What about Antoine? Where was our system of justice when he needed it?"

Clint did not have a good answer for that. "That was different; this is a different type of case. Paul is well respected in town and he has a flawless reputation."

"So did Antoine, but I don't. They brand me as the wife of a Mafia boss. I'm scared of what the prosecutor will do, and even more scared of what Giovanni's men will do."

"Sharleen, it's going to be okay. I'm going to start by calling Jimmy Garretson to ask him to contact Paul's lawyer so he can persuade the prosecutor to delay the grand jury proceedings until we arrive. He'll be happy you are returning voluntarily, and he will be interested to hear what evidence you can present. If you don't mind, I'll leave it up to you to book the airline tickets. We should be ready to leave tomorrow, or at the latest, the day after tomorrow. Play it on the safe side; book for the day after tomorrow."

For the rest of the day, Sharleen was a nervous wreck. When she finally went to bed she could not sleep. She kept on tossing and turning and finally woke up Clint. "Darling, it's all my fault. I cause everybody bad luck."

Clint had not been asleep either, and he sat up. "What are you talking about?"

"It's true, I bring everybody bad luck. Your restaurant burns down, Federico and Kitty got killed, and Paul was accused of a crime, all because of me."

"Now that is pure nonsense!"

"And I should not even be living with you. No matter what Giovanni has done, I'm still a married woman."

"That's pure horseshit. He almost had you killed. Besides, I love you, and I won't let you go. So cut it out; nothing that has happened is your fault."

"Clint, I'm so scared." Sharleen rolled over and put her arms around Clint. Abruptly she sat up and pulled off her pajamas, and when she turned back to Clint she pulled his off, too. Clint realized that it was not from a sexual desire, but out of her need to find comfort and safety in the warmth of his naked body. She was sobbing softly as she buried her naked body into his. Her sobbing caused her body to make slight jerking movements and she dug deeper into his warm body. Her grip was so tight that he could hardly breathe, but he did not mind. His high school sweetheart needed him again.

It took a long time, but finally Sharleen quieted down, and her body stopped shaking. With her head still buried against his neck she whispered, "Clint, tell me you love me. I'm so scared. People think I'm so strong, but I'm not really. Darling, I need you to help me through this investigation. Tell me you'll always take care of me."

Clint raised her head so he could look into her eyes. "I love you so much it almost scares me. You know I'll never leave you." He put his arms around her and pulled her into his chest. He could feel her relax as she once again snuggled into the safety of his tight embrace.

XXVII

The next morning, Clint tried to call Antoine to tell him what was happening and to brief him on what to do in his absence. When nobody answered, he got worried; he did not expect Antoine to be out so early in the morning. Around nine o'clock Clara, Antoine's live-in girlfriend, called. Antoine was in the hospital. She told Clint what had happened.

"Last night we went out to dinner at SurfSide. You know, that nice little restaurant on the beach. When we returned to the car, two men attacked Antoine. They wanted the keys to our car, and he tried to fight them off. They beat him pretty badly and took off in our car. When I tried to stop them, they slugged me. As you can hear from my speech, I have a broken jaw."

"How is Antoine?"

"They took him off the critical list about an hour ago. He has several broken ribs and a torn spleen. At first the doctors worried about kidney damage, but thank goodness the damage in that region turned out to be mild. It will take a while, but the doctors assure me he'll make a complete recovery."

"Give me his room number. I'll be there as soon as possible."

When Clint told Sharleen what had happened to Antoine, she asked who Clint could put in charge of the restaurant while they were gone.

Clint confessed he had no idea. "With Antoine laid up in the hospital, I really have no one."

Ana had just come down from the upstairs apartment and overheard their conversation. "I can help out," she said.

"Thanks, Ana. That is very nice of you. But I'll need someone to run the entire place while I'm gone."

"I realize that, Mr. Clint. I know I'm not an educated woman, but I have watched closely as to who is supposed to do what. I know what everybody has to do, and I can make sure they do it correctly."

Clint smiled. "I'm sure you would. But at times decisions have to be made, and I will need someone with experience to handle matters."

"Yes, Mr. Clint. I know very well what you mean. I can do it! Like I said, I have no formal education, but I always watch you and Miss Sharleen very closely. I can do it. With Mr. Antoine in the hospital, you have no one else. For all you and Miss Sharleen have done for Mikie and me, I have nothing to repay you with but my loyalty. I will watch everybody working here very carefully. We will please the customers, and I will make sure you will be proud of us."

"Ana, watching is not enough. Who will be the hostess, who will seat the guests?"

"That should be young Helga. You know, the pretty one. That girl has a lot of spunk. The customers love her. I've heard them ask to be seated at a table she serves."

"And what about payments? Payroll is complicated."

"Please, sir, Antoine is not dead. I'll take everything to the hospital for him to complete. You can trust me with small amounts of cash for little things that come up. Mr. Clint, you have little choice; you have to trust me. I can do it."

Clint looked at Sharleen, who said, "I think Ana can do it. Besides, as she so candidly pointed out, we have no choice."

Clint was skeptical, but they had to leave, and he knew Ana was completely trustworthy. "Okay, Ana, come into the office and I'll explain what I want you to do."

Sharleen help up her hand. "Ho, not so fast. First, Ana and I have to make a quick visit to the beauty parlor and my favorite little clothing store."

"Okay, you two do that. I'm off to the hospital to see Antoine," Clint said as he hurried out to his car.

At the hospital, Clint found Antoine to be in fair condition. He was still hooked to the IV and some other tubes, but he was quite lucid, and managed to tell Clint in detail what the doctors had told him. He confirmed what Clara, his girlfriend, had said. They expected him to make a full recovery, but he would be laid up for quite a while. Clint told him he and Sharleen would have to leave the next day and that worried him. He was not at all sure that Ana could take care of things at the restaurant while the two of them were gone. Clint said there was little choice, they had no one else and he was willing to chance it.

When Sharleen and Ana returned several hours later, Clint did not recognize Ana at first. She looked really good. And only her hands told you that this sophisticated lady was used to manual labor.

XXVIII

Chayton Harjo and five of his security squad escorted Sharleen and Clint to the hearing. Besides the federal prosecutor, members of the HSI task force included other federal agents. Sharleen pulled back in fright when she entered the hearing room and saw all those people. The large group gathered around the conference room was not what she had expected.

Reginald Hutton jumped up from the table and came over to introduce himself. Out of earshot of the assembled group he said, "Hi, I'm Paul's lawyer. They did not want Paul to attend, and I will represent his interests here at this meeting. I can't formally represent you; it might be considered a conflict of interest. But if you are in doubt whether you should answer a question, just look at me. I'll shake my head yes or no. By the way, just call me Reggie; I hate Reginald."

Sharleen was directed to take a seat opposite a sour-faced bald man wearing outrageously large horn-rimmed glasses. Clint was seated next to her, and she squeezed his hand so hard that it started to turn blue. The bald man greeted them and introduced the ladies and gentlemen seated on the opposite side of the table. Next he made a surprising announcement. "We started this investigation following the death of your husband, Giovanni Fuentes, just about a year ago."

Sharleen let out a shriek. "What! What are you saying?" She did not wait for an answer. Her hand shot up to cover her mouth, and clearly in shock, she turned to Clint.

The bald man did not expect that reaction. "I'm so sorry, Mrs. Fuentes, I was not aware that you had not been informed of his death. If you need a moment, feel free to take a break. Can we get you a drink or something?"

Sharleen took a deep breath and closed her eyes for a moment before she responded. "I'll be all right. Let's just continue with the proceeding."

Reggie Hutton stood up and addressed the bald man. "Mr. Williams, if I may, I have important information for you."

"A little unusual at this point during our hearing, but speak up."

"Thank you. Yesterday morning I received a phone call from one Bennie Cardiello. He claims he is the one who transferred the money to Mrs. Fuentes' account at City National. He said he is Giovanni Fuentes' nephew, and that he was his financial guy. According to this Bennie Cardiello, the money came out of a trust fund legally set up by Mr. Fuentes for his wife. What's very important is his claim that the funds originally came from legitimate sources on which all taxes had been paid."

Mr. Williams asked Reggie, Clint, and Sharleen to step out of the room so he could confer with the rest of the HSI Task Force. When the three of them were called back in, Mr. Williams announced that the hearing would be recessed for five days to give Reggie the opportunity to have Bennie Cardiello come in and present his evidence.

Sharleen requested to be excused from the hearing during Bennie's testimony. She did not want to be confronted with Bennie after what she suspected him of doing. Mr. Williams understood the situation. He pointed out that Reggie, Paul, and Clint would want to be present, since the testimony by Bennie might help clear up the case against Paul and Sharleen.

Bennie arrived accompanied by Gerald O'Keeffe, the lawyer who had defended Sharleen during her trial in New York City. Between the two of them, they carried with them a ton of documents, which consisted mostly of tax returns.

The task force did not need Bennie to show the origin of the money he transferred. The Task Force had long since traced the money to Sharleen's trust fund. What was new for them was the elaborate group of perfectly legal companies owned by Giovanni. O'Keeffe brought with him all the tax returns for these enterprises. By also presenting all of Giovanni's personal tax returns, he forced the task force to conclude that there had never been a case of money laundering. Bennie made an angry plea for the HSI to leave his uncle's estate alone. He shouted at them that his uncle had never engaged in illegal business practices, and always paid taxes on all his income.

Gerald O'Keeffe further elaborated on Bennie's outburst. "I think it should be known that when Giovanni and I were young, I helped him dismantle all the illegal business practices the so-called family he inherited had been involved in. He did not want to participate in any illegal activity. And that caused many arguments between him and Big Joe Calabrese, the underboss. If it had not been for the strong support of Guido Russo, his consigliore, he might not have been able to go totally legitimate. Of course, it also helped that he had an amazing business sense, and anything he touched turned to gold."

Not long after the hearing, the task force filed their final report, and the federal prosecutor dropped all charges against Paul Klein. The case was closed, and HSI stopped investigating Giovanni's estate.

Before Clint and Sharleen returned to Bermuda, Gerald O'Keeffe came to see them on the reservation. He told them he had been searching for Sharleen ever since Giovanni's death.

Sharleen wanted to know how Giovanni died. "Was it an execution-style killing, the result of his feud with the Lograso family from Chicago?"

"No, not at all. After you left, he banned Big Joe and Bennie from the estate. They were more or less thrown out of the family. He forbade any of us, including Guido, to have any contact with them. He was very despondent, and drank way too much. When he could not sleep, he took sleeping pills. One night, he over did it. I suspect he was quite drunk when he did it. The next day they found him dead in his bed. The coroner ruled it an accidental overdose of sleeping pills. Guido thinks it might have been suicide; I strongly disagree. Anyway, I've been looking for you. He left the major part of his estate to you."

Sharleen could not believe it. "To me? Not possible! He was so angry at me that he tried to have me killed!"

O'Keeffe raised his hands in protest. "No way! The man was in love with you. He adored you; he never authorized anyone to go after you. Much less kill you. Big Joe was acting on his own. If I may, allow me an indiscreet question. Did you love him?"

Sharleen took her time to answer. "Oh my, that is very complicated. In the beginning, sure. But was I completely honest with him? I don't know! Sure, I thought I loved him. I was crazy about the man. But looking back, maybe unconsciously I used him to suppress the fact that I was still very much in love with Clint. I don't know if that is possible. He could have been a substitute, but I certainly was not aware of it. I genuinely loved him, but that changed when he ordered the restaurant burned down. I was confused; I realized I did not really know the man. Let's face it, I was afraid of him. No, stronger, I hated him."

She looked at Clint. "Who knows? If it hadn't been for Bennie's insane jealousy, I might still be married to him." Looking at Clint's handsome face made her think. *Was Jada the subconscious substitute for me? I hope not... but in my heart I do.*

Clint gave Sharleen a reassuring smile, and again the nagging thought of something she did not want to admit crossed her mind. *I hope Jada was the unconscious substitute for me.*

Sharleen turned to O'Keeffe. "I don't want the money. Can I turn it down?"

"Yes, but are you sure? The accountants are still trying to evaluate the value of all the companies he owned and of those he had a stake in. The amount is huge. Except for some amounts he bequeathed to his grandchildren and to his family back in Italy, the remainder is in the tens of millions. You are a very rich lady."

"I can't accept the money. I would perpetuate the lie I may have been living when I thought I loved him. No, I don't want the money. Can you arrange to have it distributed among charities, and also to redress any hurt he may have inflicted by that cursed omerta, and the other traditions he believed he had to uphold?"

"Very admirable. But are you very sure? You're turning down a vast amount of money. Don't you even want part of it?"

"No. We're going home to Bermuda. And if I am lucky, this wonderful guy here will do me the honor of me becoming Mrs. Clint Crawley. That's worth far more to me than all those millions of Giovanni's."

XXIX

Upon his return to Bermuda, Clint checked with the restaurant staff on how things had gone during his absence. The first one he spoke to was Joe Cedrick, the head chef. Joe had been very worried about Ana being in charge while Clint was away. Clint was happily surprised that Joe was full of compliments. He was delighted with the way Ana handled things. He could not say enough about the way she handled a difficult French-Canadian tourist.

"Clint, the way she handled it was really right on. This older guy from Quebec was giving young Helga a rough time. He made a big deal about the way the dish he had ordered was prepared. In a loud voice he told her they would never serve it that way in Quebec, and the English did not know how to cook. When Ana noticed that Helga did not know how to handle the situation, she stepped in. With a big smile she told the guy she agreed with him. It was marvelous the way they served that dish in Quebec. But maybe he would like to come with her to the kitchen to meet me, the head chef. She explained that after culinary school I had worked for more than two years in Paris in a well-known restaurant.

"When they came into the kitchen, she introduced me. She carefully went over her conversation with the gentleman so I could take it from there. I showed him the kitchen, and let him taste various items. I had several of our chefs show him what they were preparing, and made sure they let him taste what they were making. Clint, let me tell you, he was snowed. We now have our own advertising person in Quebec."

The other employees agreed with Joe; things had gone very smoothly. It was not until Clint spoke to Antoine that he heard anything negative. Antoine was furious. Clara, his girlfriend, had brought several of their friends to the restaurant for dinner and Ana had been extremely rude to her. Since this was in sharp contrast to what the others had reported, Clint hurried back to the restaurant to ask Ana what had happened.

"Ana, did you have a run-in with Clara while I was gone?"

"Yes, Mr. Clint, I did."

"You want to tell me about it?"

"I was not going to talk about it, but now that you have asked me, I guess I must tell you what happened."

"Why would you not want to tell me?"

"I didn't want to upset you, and I like Mr. Antoine a lot, so I didn't want you to know what happened."

"Now you've got me curious. Speak up. What happened?"

"It was on a Saturday night, and there was a tourist boat in town. The restaurant was very crowded. The wait for a table was over a half-hour. Clara came in with a group of five. When a table came available, she demanded that her group be seated. Jeannie was at the desk, and Clara started an argument with her. Helga went over to the desk and introduced herself as the hostess. Clara rudely cut her off with, 'Get out of here, you're just one of the waitresses.' I rushed over and agreed with Jeannie. There was no way we could let her go ahead of people who had been waiting for over a half-hour. I had to prevent a scene in front of all our other guests. I calmly waved off the two girls and offered to make room for her group at the bar. I whispered to Clara that I was sure you wouldn't mind if I offered her friends free drinks while they waited to be seated. She gave me a tongue lashing. She repeatedly asked if I had forgotten who I was, and said that she would get Antoine to put me back in my place. I did not react to that. Instead, I kept thanking her for her cooperation. The members of her group helped me persuade her to accept the seats at the bar."

"I think you handled that well, Ana. I'm sorry you had to go through that."

"Mr. Clint, that was not the end of it. She was rude to Sammy, who was serving at her table. He was trying to make their dinner as pleasant as possible. He did not deserve that type of treatment. I spoke to him in the kitchen and asked him to stay calm. We did not want a scene in front of the other guests. Sammy told me he noticed that she was making the other people in her party uncomfortable. During the dinner, Clara drank a lot. When I saw she was beyond tipsy, I instructed Sammy to stop serving her any more alcohol. This resulted in another round of nasty remarks being directed first at Sammy, and later at me. I don't know if you know it, but the lady has an alcohol problem that has gotten her into trouble many times. I was lucky; one of her friends signaled me that he would get her to leave, and he did."

"Ana, I'm so sorry. I never dreamed I would be exposing you to something like that. I really admire the way you handled it. I could not have done that well. I might have lost my temper and created a really bad incident. With all those tourists in the house, you saved our reputation. Word spreads quickly when bad things happen in a restaurant. I owe you a huge amount of thanks."

"You owe me, sir? That's almost funny. There is no way I can ever repay you for what you and Miss Sharleen have done for Mikie and me. Before Miss Sharleen gave me a job, I was destitute. I was frantic because I could not pay the rent, or afford to feed Mikie and me. When Mikie started growing up and became bigger and bigger, people stopped hiring me. They were afraid of him and would not let him in their houses. What could I do? I could not leave him home by himself; I refused to have him institutionalized. He is kind and gentle, and does not deserve that. You two accepted him. There is more. The two of you don't treat me or the others at the restaurant like employees. To you, we are real people who work with you. I never met people like you before; never knew people with money could be so nice. Never a day goes by that I don't get on my knees and thank God for letting me know and work for you."

Clint was at a loss for words. He could not find the right words to respond. Finally he said, "Ana, it works both ways. All our employees are very special to us. But you, Ana, you are extra special. Can I give you a hug?"

When Clint released her from his embrace, Ana said, "I probably should not say this, but Mikie is crazy about you. You are his guy. You must have noticed that huge smile whenever he sees you."

"I love him too, Ana. He's a joy to have around."

"Thank you, Mr. Clint. You and Miss Sharleen are the only ones who ever cared about us. Like I said, I did not know people like you existed. Bless you."

XXX

Clint intended to discuss the incident with Antoine, but he wanted to wait until Antoine came home from the hospital. Unfortunately, the situation became worse before that time.

It all started when Helga, the young waitress, asked to speak to Clint in his office.

"Mr. Clint, you know I live in the middle of town. A lot of my neighbors work in the local bars, and I have been hearing things about Mr. Antoine's girlfriend."

"You mean Clara? The one who brought a group of her friends to the restaurant?"

"Yes, sir."

"Are you still angry because she was so rude to Jeannie and you?"

"Yes, sir. But that is not the point. My neighbors seem to know her real well. They tell me she used to hang around the bars a lot before she met Mr. Antoine. They say she is hanging around the bars again, and she has been seen leaving with other men."

"Wow. That is a very serious accusation. Are you very sure we are talking about the same person?"

"My neighbors have no reason to make up stories. They work in the bars, and couldn't care less what their customers do. And I know it's her. I was with my boyfriend, and we were having a drink in the bar on the street where I live when I saw her. She did not see me, but that is when one of my neighbors told me about her."

"Thanks for telling me this. Helga, you could do me a favor by not mentioning this to anyone else."

"Of course not, Mr. Clint. Mr. Antoine is a favorite of mine, and I only came to you because I hope you'll protect him. She cheats on him, and that is not right! He is a very nice person."

"Yes, Helga. Antoine is a very nice person. I'll look into this. In the meantime, remember. This is just between us."

"I promise, Mr. Clint."

Clint discussed the situation with Sharleen, and they decided it would be best for Clint to confront Clara before he spoke to Antoine.

Antoine and Clara lived in a nice fifth-floor apartment facing the ocean. When Clint rang the bell, no one answered. He had to push it several times before he got a response. Finally Clara opened the door. From her appearance, Clint could tell that she had just woken up, and it looked like she was still very much hungover.

She greeted him with, "What the hell are you doing here? Something wrong with Antoine?"

"No, it's not about Antoine. I have come to talk to you about you."

"Oh, that bitch Ana must have complained about me. Well, tell her I don't have to take any of her shit. Who the hell does she think she is, telling me how much I can drink?"

"Clara, I think you'd better sit down and hear what I have to say."

With a slow, seductive move, Clara opened up the robe she was wearing, revealing her naked body.

"Damn it, Clara! Close your robe!"

"What's the matter? Most men love my body. Don't you like the view? I'm not insisting on only a view."

"What the hell is the matter with you? Are you drunk, or just plain crazy? I said close that damned robe! Now!" Clint was furious.

Clara pulled her robe closed. "You came here to tell me that because of me you have to fire Antoine. And I thought that if I could seduce you, I might talk you out of firing him. Sorry, I misjudged."

"Yes, you did. What an incredible thing to do! And no, I am not going to fire Antoine. Now sit down and act like a normal human being."

Clara sat down and Clint continued. "In the first place, Ana was completely right, and you are banned from the club until you apologize to her, the two girls, and Sammy. Next, what is going on while Antoine is in the hospital? Have you been hanging out in the downtown bars?"

Clara slumped in her seat but said nothing. Clint stared at her, and the look in his eyes scared her.

She pulled her robe even tighter around herself and in a very meek voice said, "You hate me, don't you?"

Clint's eyes were blazing fire. "Yes, I do. And why shouldn't I? While my friend Antoine is in the hospital, you've been acting like a whore. Why? He doesn't deserve this. He treats you like a princess, and you reward that by acting like a common slut. I don't only hate you; you disgust me."

Clara got up and moved towards a table on which stood an almost empty liquor bottle and a glass. "I need a drink," she mumbled.

"No you don't." Clint stopped her as she reached for the bottle. "The last thing you need is more liquor!"

"You don't understand, do you? I can't help it. I need the stuff."

"You can help it! You don't want to stop!"

"Don't you understand? I'm a fricking alcoholic. I can't stop!"

"Then get professional help!"

"I did. Twice I went into rehab. Twice I followed the complete fucking program. So don't stand there and tell me I can stop, but don't want to. What do you know, you righteous prick?!"

"Sit down and explain to me why, if you can't control your drinking, you also have to cheat on Antoine by sleeping with other men."

"Who says so? I don't!"

"Don't lie to me. You've been seen."

"Oh shit; fuck it all. I can't even remember. Yes, with Antoine gone I get lonely. I go out for a drink, always intending to have only one or two. But that never works. I wind up getting smashed, and there is always some guy who offers to take me home. I really don't remember what happens. I wake up here in my bed. Nude, stinking of some unknown guy's sweat. Or worse, I wake up in some stranger's bed with some guy snoring next to me. I'll swear that it will never happen again, but it always does. I can see in your face that you don't believe me, but it's true. I don't want to cheat on Antoine. I swear I don't! I love the guy, and I need him here with me. He knows about my drinking problem, and he is the only one who can help me control it. He's known for a long time that I'm an alcoholic. Together, we controlled it."

Clara let out a loud cry, "Why did he have to wind up in the hospital and leave me alone? I can't be alone! I did drugs before I met him, and he helped me stop."

Clint felt as if a switch was turned around in his brain. From a feeling of utter disgust for this woman he felt a feeling of compassion coming over him. "Clara, Dr. Seders is a friend of mine. He is head of the St. Joseph Clinic here on the island. If I call him now, will you agree to go with me to be admitted?"

"Yes, please help me. After what I have done, I can never face Antoine again."

"Let's first get you some help, and we will work on that problem later."

Clint called Dr. Seders and arranged for Clara to be admitted the next day.

He turned to Clara. "Do you want to spend the night at my house? Sharleen will be glad to have you."

Clara agreed, and they arranged that she would pack some clothes and toiletries and that Clint would be back in a few hours to pick her up.

When Sharleen and Clint arrived later that day, Clara was nowhere to be found. From the looks of things, she had not packed a bag or made any arrangements to be picked up. Clint immediately called the police and asked that they institute a search for her. He explained that she might be in a distraught condition, and advised them to check the downtown bars first.

For two days they searched the entire island, but could not find even a trace of her. Boats were sent out to dredge the harbor area, but nothing was found. They were sure she did not have a passport, but just in case, they checked all the airlines. Someone even mentioned the possibility of her being a stowaway on one of the big tourist ships.

But why would Clara want to disappear? Was she afraid of entering the clinic and being once more put through a withdrawal program? Or was she afraid of having to face Antoine? Everybody had their own theory as to what had happened to her, but they all agreed not to inform Antoine as to what was going on. When he tried to call her from the hospital, Clint made the most ridiculous excuses as to why he could not get her on the phone. Antoine started to get very worried, and finally threatened to find a way to get out of the hospital and go to the apartment to find out for himself.

Late on the third day, Clint got a call. They had found the partly disrobed body of a female, and believed it was Clara. Could Clint come down to give a positive identification? Clint was not sure he could handle seeing Clara's dead body in the condition they described her when they called him. It was Sharleen who insisted that he must go, and she volunteered to accompany him. She did not want the police transporting Antoine by ambulance to the morgue to make the identification. She put a stop to suggestions that he be shown pictures of his dead girlfriend.

After the identification, Clint and Sharleen spoke to the coroner and the two policemen who found her. They were promised a full report on the cause of death no later than the next afternoon. The report was not pretty. The coroner concluded that Clara's death was caused by a combination of alcohol and crack cocaine. Both of which were found in considerable quantities in her system.

Sharleen asked if Clara had committed suicide. The coroner was not sure. The substantial amounts of the drug combined with the alcohol could indicate that she took that combination on purpose in order to kill herself. But it was not unusual for alcoholics to use a combination of the two and accidently overdose. The police report added to the uncertainty as to the cause of death. They were not willing to rule out foul play. The body was found partly disrobed, and the coroner found heavy bruises around her thighs and upper arms. Since they had not been able to locate her for two days, they wanted to further investigate whether she had been sexually assaulted and held for those days.

XXXI

Antoine was not listed as next of kin. And because there was no formal connection between him and Clara, it fell to Clint to inform him of her death. He asked Jimmy Garretson, Antoine's best friend, to go with him to the hospital to see Antoine. Sharleen wanted to come along, but Clint felt it would be best if only he and Jimmy went.

When they broke the news to him, Antoine remained fairly calm. He was sad, but relatively composed. He thanked his two friends for coming and said, "I was expecting bad news. Maybe not of her death, but I knew something bad must have happened when I couldn't reach her on the phone."

Clint responded, "Yeah, I could tell you were not buying any of my lame excuses."

"I appreciate what you were doing. Thanks for trying to protect me, but I should have known something like this was coming."

Jimmy and Clint looked at each other, wondering what Antoine meant by that remark. Jimmy went ahead and asked, "What's that supposed to mean?"

"I have kept a lot from you guys. I never told you much about my relationship with Clara."

Clint could tell his friend had a need to talk about Clara, so he went ahead and asked Antoine to explain.

"It was kind of weird how we met. I had not been on the island very long, and was living in a cheap hotel near the docks. I was rapidly running out of money, and considered calling my parents for help. I was sitting in a bar mulling over the situation when a woman came over to talk to me. She was a hell of a good-looking dame, and I eagerly started a conversation with her. We seemed to click; after quite a few drinks, she asked if I wanted to come home with her. That one night turned into two nights, and eventually she invited me to move in with her. She introduced me to her friends, and they helped me get odd jobs in the harbor."

"Doesn't sound that weird to me," Jimmy said.

"Maybe not, but let me tell you the rest. It didn't take me long to realize she had an alcohol problem, and we fought about it a lot. Each time when I threatened to move out she would beg me to stay, and she would promise to stop drinking. She promised, but she could not keep her promises. She was an alcoholic. Even though she sort of controlled it, the problem persisted, even after we moved to the new apartment I rented when Clint hired me.

"One day I came home from the restaurant, and she was smashed. I have no idea where she found the alcohol. We purposefully kept none in the apartment. We had one hell of a fight, and the next day when I came home she was gone. She was gone for three days, but returned to plead with me to take her back. I refused, but she used sex to get me to agree. I should have known better. She was full of demons. Physically she had been given great gifts, but mentally she was a mess. She once told me about her childhood.

"At the age of ten, she went to live with her aunt. I never understood why, but I think it had something to do with finances. When she was fourteen, her aunt's husband raped her. Her aunt did not believe her, or chose not to believe her. According to what she told me, he continued to sexually abuse her until she finally confided in her eighth-grade teacher. Nobody believed her, even though doctors determined that she had had sexual intercourse. Her aunt's husband was a well-respected policeman, and Clara was accused of trying to cover up having had sex with some of her classmates. Her aunt kicked her out. She wound up living in some sort of a girls' reformatory school until she was eighteen."

Jimmy was used to a lot, but Clara's story really got to him. "Boy, she was really mentally scarred. Besides her alcohol dependency, did she exhibit any other problems?"

"She probably did, but I liked her a lot so I put up with her problems. Except for the alcohol. It always got in the way of things. The night I got mugged, we had gone out to dinner at SurfSide. The people at the tables around us were having drinks, and she begged me to order her just one. I refused, and she became more and more agitated. When we went to get our car, some men approached us and asked for money. Clara was very rude to them. When they persisted, she became belligerent. They took it out on me and fled in our car. I was furious with her!"

Jimmy wanted to know if they ever made up.

"Yes, we did. She came to the hospital, and it was the same old story. Looking back, I really don't know how much I loved her, or whether I liked how dependent she was on me. Sexual attraction also played a big part in our relationship. As I said before, emotionally she might have been deprived, but physically she had been given the best."

XXXII

Emotions surrounding Clara's death had not yet had a chance to die down when tragedy struck again. The restaurant was booked solid for a heavily advertised "Night in Paris" dinner when Ana was struck with severe chest pains. During the chaos that followed, Jeannie, who was at the reception desk, stayed calm and called an ambulance. The ambulance arrived within minutes. Sharleen insisted on staying by Ana's side and riding with her in the ambulance. Clint quickly found Mikie, and the two of them raced at break-neck speed to the hospital, arriving just as Ana was wheeled into the emergency room. From the emergency room, Ana was immediately sent through to an operating room.

While on the gurney, she continued to hold onto Sharleen's hand and whispered, "Mikie loves Clint and you. He trusts you. Please take care of him." Sharleen wanted to assure her they would, but she was stopped at the emergency room doors and never got a chance to respond.

The wait seemed endless, but finally one of the doctors came into the waiting room. He signaled to Clint to come over to him so they could talk. From their whispers, Sharleen could guess that the news was bad. Mikie only partly understood what was happening, but from Clint's reaction, he realized something bad had happened to Ana.

Sharleen held him firmly by the hand but he broke loose and ran towards the direction of the operating room, screaming, "Ana! Mikie wants Ana!"

Clint ran after him and managed to catch up to him before he reached the end of the hall. Mikie was frantically crying out for Ana, and Clint threw his arms around the big fellow. Together they sank to the floor. Clint cradled Mikie's head in his arms. By this time, both of them were crying, and Sharleen bent over the two of them.

Clint lovingly stroked the big man's hair. "We are not leaving you. Mikie, Ana wants you to stay with us. Do you understand? Ana wants you to stay with us." Then in between his own sobs, Sharleen heard him whisper into Mikie's ear. "Mikie, we love you. We'll always take care of you. The three of us will never forget Ana. I promise."

That same day, Clint and Sharleen moved Mikie into their big house to stay with them. At first he did not understand. Sharleen was very patient with him. She kept showing him around the large guest room and repeated over and over again, "This is all for Mikie. This is Mikie's room. Mikie will stay here, Ana said Mikie should stay." She showered him with gifts. Over and over she told him that Ana did not want to leave him, but she was happy he was now with Clint and her.

Eventually Mikie settled down, and Sharleen was thrilled to see how he took to Clint. Clint treated him like a handicapped younger brother who had come to live with them. The two were inseparable; Clint started teaching Mikie things he had never been exposed to. Together with Antoine, he took him fishing. Mikie loved it, and Clint was ecstatic because Mikie caught on so quickly. By the second trip, Mikie was fishing without Clint's step-by-step directions.

Clint was aware that Mikie had not reached his full potential. He arranged for a private teacher to help Mikie increase his vocabulary and his ability to express himself. Although his speech remained rather limited, Mikie became much better at understanding basic concepts. He developed far enough that Clint could 'promote' him to assistant doorman at the restaurant. He even got his very own uniform with gold shoulder boards. The customers loved the big man with the infectious smile. Mikie had himself a real job.

XXXIII

Sharleen had no idea what Clint was up to when he arranged for Antoine to come stay with Mikie. He had booked a weekend getaway for the two of them in one of the finest beachfront hotels on the island, and only told Sharleen that it was time for them to have some time off from their busy schedule at the restaurant.

On their second night, Clint said that he did not really like the hotel's big, rather noisy restaurant. Rather than go to one of the smaller restaurants near the hotel, he had room service arrange an elaborate, candlelit dinner in their suite. They had just finished eating when he held up his wine glass and nonchalantly said, "Oh, by the way, will you marry me?"

Sharleen let out a shriek, jumped up, and flew around his neck. "Yes! Yes, and yes." While kissing him, she dragged him to the big, king-sized bed and pushed him down onto it.

Laughing she said, "You bastard! I had no idea what you were up to. Yes, yes I'll marry you! I've been wondering if you'd ever ask. Who could have dreamed that we would finally get this far? This is so great! You probably don't remember. We talked about it in eleventh grade; two kids who thought it was inevitable that they would get married."

She was still laughing and kissing him when her cell phone rang. It was her uncle, Chayton Harjo. Chayton's greeting was short and his message was urgent. "Big Joe, that Mafia guy you told us about, has been snooping around the reservation. Lakota checked it out. He is looking for you. Apparently that whole damned ICE investigation about the money gave him the information he needed to find you. From what he did when you escaped with your friend Federico, I know you are in danger. If he snoops around town he'll find out that you are in Bermuda, and he might come after you. I am sending Tika and Mato out to protect you."

Sharleen was trembling when she responded, "Hold on a sec. I want to tell Clint what you told me." She turned to Clint and relayed what her uncle had told her.

Clint took Sharleen's phone and spoke to Chayton. "I have a pretty good connection with the police here on the island. I am sure I can get them to notify us if he lands here. Can you get a picture or detailed description of Big Joe, so I can give it to the police?"

Chayton had nothing like that, and he pointed out that it was Sharleen who could provide a detailed description of the man. Clint told Chayton to hold back on sending Tika and Mato. They had never seen Big Joe, and they were not familiar with the island. It would be best to rely on the Bermuda police for protection. Clint said he would go speak to the police chief in the morning.

When Clint hung up he said, "Big Joe's timing is great. He found the perfect way to break up a romantic evening."

"That's not funny," Sharleen said. "I'm scared out of my mind. I told you what that man did to Freddie and Kitty."

"I know." Clint took a deep breath. "I was only trying to calm you a little. Yes, I know he is very dangerous. I was trying not to show it, but I am as worried as you are. But the Bermuda police are excellent. They pretty much control who arrives and who leaves. If we give them a detailed description, they'll catch him at the airport. They control the boat traffic, too; I'm sure they'll take protecting you very seriously. That we have become a high-profile couple is good and bad. It's bad in that if he manages to get onto the island, he will have no trouble locating you. The good part is that the police will take us seriously, and go out of their way to protect us. After I speak to the police chief, I'll go see the minister. Knowing a cabinet member never hurts."

Before she received her uncle's call, Sharleen had been in a great mood. "Damn it all. Everything was so great until that phone call."

Clint agreed. "Yeah, that certainly is enough to take anyone out of a romantic mood."

Sharleen pulled Clint close. "Not so fast, darling. I need you to hold me tight now more than ever. And maybe while you hold me, you can find a way to distract me."

Clint could not answer. Sharleen's lips were in the way.

XXXIV

Clint had left very early to buy fresh fish for the restaurant at the market, and Mikie was still asleep in his room. Sharleen was in the kitchen enjoying her first cup of coffee when she thought she heard something at the door. Agnita, the new cleaning lady, usually did not arrive until eight thirty, but maybe she wanted to make an early start today.

When Sharleen opened the door, she stood face to face with Big Joe. Her scream was silenced by his big hand, pushed across her mouth. Holding his hand tightly in place, he shoved her back through the door, all the way against the kitchen wall. Desperately, Sharleen tried to wriggle free, but Big Joe held her pinned against the wall, his hand across her mouth pushing her head back, and his knee pushing hard into her abdomen. With his right hand he produced a switchblade. His thumb pushed a button on the side of the knife; the six-inch blade sprang out.

He had a horrible grin on this face when he leaned in closely and said, "So I finally caught up to you Puttana (*whore*), and now you're gonna die. But not before I cut up that pretty face of yours and slice those tits you used to get Giovanni. No, you won't have a pretty corpse. Che te pozzino ammazzaa! (*you shall be butchered*). I'll even slice your fica (*cunt*) to pieces."

Sharleen closed her eyes, waiting for the pain and ensuing death. She never saw the arm coming from behind Big Joe's back. The arm shot around his neck and pulled him back in a horse-collar. The knife fell to the floor, and Big Joe made gurgling sounds as the chokehold tightened even more.

Sharleen opened her eyes and all she could say was, "Mikie! Mikie!"

Mikie was holding Big Joe tightly in a chokehold. The man's face was turning blue.

Mikie did not seem to notice. He held on while he said, "Man bad. Tried to hurt Sharleen. Mikie mad. No hurt my Sharleen. Man bad, very bad."

By this time, Sharleen had recovered enough to realize that Big Joe could no longer hurt her and she said, "Mikie good. Mikie very, very good. Now let the man go."

But it was too late for Big Joe, and when Mikie let go, his dead body fell in a crumpled heap on the floor. Sharleen grabbed her cell phone to call Clint. Clint told her to call the police.

Clint, the police, an ambulance, and the fire department all arrived at about the same time.

Mikie ran to Clint and shouted, "Man bad! Man try to hurt Sharleen. Mikie don't like that. Clint not here, Mikie take care of Sharleen. Okay? Okay?"

Clint put his hand on the big man's shoulder. "Yes, Mikie. You did good. Clint is very proud of you. We are all very proud of you."

Clint went over to comfort Sharleen, but the two ambulance attendants were already tending to her. To prevent her from going into shock, they gave her a strong sedative and kept talking to her, making sure she could handle the panic that had taken hold of her.

Her trembling stopped and she turned to Clint for comfort. "Clint, he tried to kill me! If it wasn't for Mikie, I'd be dead by now!" Clint was quite shaken up, too. His initial calm had covered how upset he was.

By this time, Sharleen had gotten over the worst of her fear. Ignoring the policeman who was asking her a question, she raced over to Mikie and threw her arms around his neck.

"Mikie, you saved me! Will you ever truly understand what a great thing you did? Just let me hold you for a while. I don't want anyone to ever again say you're slow. Nobody could have done better. Mikie, do you understand? You saved my life!" Mikie just smiled. He was so happy that he had done well and made Sharleen happy.

The policemen made quite a fuss over Mikie. Judging by the size of the body lying on the floor, they were impressed by the strength Mikie must have had to bring Big Joe down before he could injure Sharleen. One of them playfully put his police hat on Mikie, and they all posed with him for the news photographer who had arrived at the scene.

That picture made the front page of all the local papers, and Mikie became a hero on the island. The story as to what happened spread quickly. As it was passed on from mouth to mouth, Mikie's action became more and more heroic.

Clint asked Antoine to take charge of the restaurant for the day, since he wanted to stay home with Sharleen. That night Sharleen could not sleep. She tossed and turned, and when she noticed that Clint was also awake, she reached over to touch him. Clint rolled over and held her.

Sharleen needed more. "No, I want you, not your clothes." Without a word they both stripped, and Sharleen settled against Clint's warm body. With his arms around her, she finally fell asleep. Clint lay awake for a long time wondering whether he should have taken better care to prevent Big Joe from reaching Sharleen without his being there to protect her. All he could think was *thank God for Mikie*.

XXXV

Clint's self-recrimination about not protecting Sharleen turned into anger at the police for not notifying him that Big Joe had arrived in Bermuda, and their failure to offer sufficient protection. He asked Jimmy Garretson to arrange a meeting with the premier and the police commissioner to discuss why Big Joe had not been identified upon entering Bermuda. Even though Clint knew both men personally, Jimmy pointed out that they were not the right persons to speak to. The governor was in charge of internal security and police, and the minister of public safety should carry the ultimate responsibility for any failure of the police. Before the meeting, Clint had also complained in a newspaper article about what he called a flagrant error on the part of the authorities.

Having read the article, the governor and the minister of public safety were prepared to respond to Clint's complaint. The minister produced a report from the airport police station about the measures that had been taken to be on the lookout for Big Joe. The report concluded that he could not have slipped through customs without being detained. The unit charged with maritime policing also reported that all passengers arriving by boat had been checked. This left the question open as to how Big Joe managed to get through unnoticed and attack Sharleen. The governor promised a full investigation.

It was not until three weeks later that the police came up with the first clue. The captain of a small fishing boat was arrested for smuggling a wide variety of goods. During questioning, he admitted to having smuggled people ashore. Subjected to further interrogation, he revealed that he was part of a network of people operating out of Cape Hatteras, North Carolina. From there, wanted persons often sought refuge on one of the islands in the Caribbean. He was paid well to ferry people across the six hundred forty miles to Bermuda. When given the description of Big Joe, he admitted he had brought him to Bermuda.

XXXVI

It was Monday morning. Clint, Antoine, and Mikie had gone fishing. The restaurant was closed, and Sharleen had decided to sleep in. She had just gotten up when she heard a noise in the back of the house. She was still jittery from the attack by Big Joe, and as Rodi Knowles, their good friend, had told her to do, she called the police. Rodi was the chief of police, and the response was instant. Two squad cars raced up, and the policemen quickly cornered the intruder.

The intruder turned out to be Alfonzo Fundo, who had come to finish a project he was working on for Clint in their backyard. Alfonso was the less successful son of the Fundo family, well known on the island for their agricultural enterprises. To say that Sharleen and the police were embarrassed by Alfonzo's apprehension would be putting it mildly.

Luckily for all concerned, Alfonzo was a good-natured, happy-go-lucky fellow who thought the entire incident was funny. He teased Sharleen that he was really out to kidnap her, and he poked fun at the arresting officers. He asked if they had ever captured a more dangerous criminal. Everyone wound up laughing, but it did show the effect Big Joe's assault on Sharleen had had on her and the police department.

This explained why, when two weeks later Bennie Cardiello arrived on the island and asked for directions to Sharleen's house, the police detained him. Bennie explained that he meant Sharleen no harm. On the contrary, he had come to ask her to forgive him for the lies he told about her. The police contacted Sharleen, but she resolutely turned down Bennie's request to come see her. Eventually, Bennie got to speak to Clint, and begged to get to speak to Sharleen. He said that since he had been helpful in explaining that the funds he transferred were from legally earned funds, and all the taxes had been duly paid on the profits, she should have no fear that he would now try to hurt her.

Sharleen told Clint she was not afraid of Bennie. She did not want to see him because she hated him. Bennie kept on insisting. Finally, Clint persuaded Sharleen to let him come out to the house to talk to her.

When Bennie entered the house, the first thing he said was, "Forgive me. Sharleen, please forgive me for what I did." This took the wind out of Sharleen's intent to greet him with a flood of invectives.

Bennie continued, "I told Giovanni the truth. I told both him and Guido that I lied about you. That I made up the whole story because I was mad that you rejected me. I did not go and see him personally; I was sure he would kill me. Instead, I wrote a letter to him and Guido explaining what I did. Later, I was surprised to hear he did not order me killed. He just banned me from his house and expelled me from the family."

Sharleen interrupted him. "You mean Giovanni knew before he died that I did not cheat on him?"

"For sure. Like I said, I wrote him a letter explaining everything. I told him I was in love with you. And because you always called me your darling, and said I was your favorite, I thought you were in love with me. Each time you said, 'my dearest Bennie,' to me, I thought you really loved me. We were about the same age, and Giovanni could have been our father, so I thought you would want me to make love to you. I always fantasized sleeping with you. I was shocked and hurt when you rejected me. Sharleen, I wrote Giovanni that you loved him, and the only reason you did not tell him about what I did was because you did not want to hurt him by exposing my betrayal."

It took a while for Sharleen to digest what Bennie was saying. To assure she understood correctly, she had him repeat several times that Giovanni knew the truth before he died.

This new information made Sharleen want to know more about Giovanni. Had she ever really known the real Giovanni? Had she loved and slept with a man capable of having her killed? She was happy now that she knew Giovanni was told she had never cheated on him, but she was not sure what he intended to do when he was mad at her. Had she ever been in danger of being killed? Gerald O'Keeffe had said she was not. But what about the fact that Big Joe came after her? Was Big Joe really acting on his own, without any instructions from Giovanni? O'Keeffe had been Giovanni's friend forever. Maybe he could not admit to himself that his good friend was capable of ordering her killed.

Bennie tried to explain. "Giovanni never tried to have you killed. He was mad at you. There is no doubt about that. But I think he had you locked away to protect you from Big Joe. Giovanni never ordered anybody killed. It was always Big Joe who wanted revenge. He is the one who had people killed. He was very powerful within the family. The important capos were on his side. Giovanni never had much control over Big Joe. But Big Joe made a big mistake in killing Federico. Freddie was hugely popular with the younger members of the family. When Freddie was killed, the family rapidly fell apart. Finally, Giovanni, as the don, was able to ban Big Joe from the estate, and oust him from his position of underboss. Guido the consigliore fully supported his don, and further guided the complete break-up of the family."

Sharleen was flabbergasted. "You mean to tell me the Fuentes Mafia family is no more? Are you saying Giovanni died as a legitimate businessman?"

"Yes! Sounds crazy. But as his nephew, I always thought of him as a legitimate business man. I managed the money, and it always came from legal enterprises. He inherited the position of Mafia don. But he never lived it. Much was done in his name, and his failure was not to stop that. His belief in tradition was his crime."

Sharleen was more confused than ever. "I don't know what to think. At first I really loved Giovanni, and you were my pal; both of you were always taking care of me. He was my husband, and you were my brother. But during the last couple of years I have hated both of you. Yes, I really despised the both of you. Now I don't know what to think."

Bennie did not forget why he had come. "Can you forgive me for what I did to you? I should be, and I am grateful, that you stopped me from cheating on my uncle. I adored the man, and I could not have lived with myself if I had slept with his wife. Those must be hollow words to you after I tried to cover my sin by lying about you. What I did to you ruined my life; I have been under psychiatric care for years. It won't change the fact that I hate myself, but it might soften that feeling a little if you tell me you forgive me for what I did."

Sharleen could not help herself. She reached out to Bennie. "Oh, Bennie, we were such fools! All of us. You took good care of me, and I forgive you for having your strong emotions run away with you. Don't hate yourself. Just sever the past. I did, and found happiness."

Before Bennie left, Sharleen asked about Chico. "Do you know where Chico is? Is he okay?"

"Yeah, he's fine. He lives in Jersey and is taking care of Guido."

"What happened to Guido?"

"He had a stroke. Even though he took part in breaking up the family, all the events leading up to the collapse of the family structure were too much for him. Chico is running the trucking company he owned."

Sharleen was glad to hear that Chico had safely survived all the turmoil and was doing okay. "When you see Chico, ask him to write me. I'd love to hear from him."

After Bennie left, Clint lashed out at Sharleen. "How in the hell could you forgive that swine for making up that terrible story about us?"

Unlike Clint, Sharleen was calm and she replied, "Because it was partly my fault."

Clint became even more agitated. "No way! He wants to go to bed with you, and because you rightly reject his advances you are partly responsible for his making up all that shit? The bastard was covering his own ass. You had nothing to do with that!"

"Calm down, honey. I think I am starting to understand. Remember I once said that I bring bad luck to people I meet? You pooh-poohed it, but there is some truth to it. I never took responsibility for the effect I had on people. I have always been told I have a nice body and face, but I never considered how it affected people. Take Bennie; I believe him when he says he was in love with me. Maybe I helped lead him on. Mind you, I did not mean to, but I always sort of flirted with him to get him to do things for me. It was, 'Bennie, my dear,' this, and 'Benny, darling,' that.

I sort of looked at it like talking to my brother. He felt I was coming on to him, and I guess he had the hots for me. I never stopped to think about it.

"I liked him a lot, but now that I think about it, I used him to get what I wanted. And now it's clear I used my looks on him. In a way I did the same with Giovanni. I really loved the man, but did I use my body to get him to love me? Don't forget Felisa, Federico's wife. I should have realized that my looks posed a threat to her. If I had stopped and looked at things from her standpoint, I could have been a friend to her rather than her enemy. I could have made sure she was included in all activities, and watched out for signs that Giovanni was ignoring her."

Clint was not ready to buy Sharleen's mea culpa speech. "The only thing I accept is that you are the most beautiful woman I know, and that it would be easy for those guys to fall in love with you. But they are responsible for what they did. Just because you're beautiful does not make you responsible for the way they acted. That is nonsense!"

"I think I should have been more aware of their feelings and acted accordingly."

"Yes, Saint Sharleen. And I am not responsible if I go lusting after every beautiful woman I meet. After all, it's their responsibility to guard me from my feelings. Sharleen, next you'll tell me that women who get raped are responsible because they led the poor guy on. Come on, let's get real! You are not responsible for what Bennie did! Stop trying to blame yourself."

Sharleen tried to calm Clint down. "Easy, let's not fight about this. Do you realize it's the first disagreement we've had since our class reunion? We're together, and that's what I always wished for. The irony is that Bennie made it happen. Without his lies I might still be married to Giovanni. I got my man, who happens to be the kindest, most wonderful guy in the world. So how could I be angry with Bennie?"

Clint could not help but laugh. "You have a screwy way of looking at things, but that is one of the many things that make me love you so much. Okay, if you say so, Bennie helped bring us back together."

Sharleen had one of her naughty smiles. "You don't have to agree if you don't want to. All you have to do is say again how much you love me, and come over here and repeat it and prove it."

XXXVII

Clint started to worry about what would happen to Mikie if anything ever happened to him and Sharleen. He discussed it with Jimmy Garretson. Jimmy explained that he could start a trust fund for Mikie, but that it would be far simpler if Clint and Sharleen went ahead and adopted Mikie. He also pointed out that there would be an obstacle. They could not adopt Mikie together because they were not married. Clint assured him that they would take care of that in a hurry.

Sharleen chose to keep the wedding small. Most of the people on the island had always assumed that they were married when they arrived, and she thought a big wedding would not be appropriate. They followed Jimmy's instructions, and filled in the required notice of intended marriage. Sharleen insisted that they hold hands when they went to pick up the wedding license. As she said, "We're still young enough to be romantic about this day."

The wedding ceremony itself was not too romantic. It was a civil ceremony in the registry general's marriage room. They were required to bring two witnesses. They asked Antoine and Joanna Jennings. Joanna was an associate in Jimmy Garretson's law office. She could not stand the name Joanna, and everybody called her J. J.

Over the years, J. J. had become Sharleen's closest friend, and she was more of a maid of honor than a witness. The day of the wedding, Sharleen arranged a dinner in a private room of one of the beachfront hotels. She thought it would have been tacky to have it in their own restaurant. She invited J. J., Antoine, Jimmy, his wife, and Rodi Knowles and his wife. The party was joined later that evening by the premier and his wife. They'd had to attend an official function earlier in the evening.

When the dinner was coming to an end, Jimmy Garretson asked for everybody's attention, he had an announcement to make. "For me this is a very special day. Not only did I have the honor of being at the wedding of two of my very best friends . . . yes, that really makes me happy. I have come to love them both, and dare proclaim that one plus one does not mean two. In this case, it means perfection." This was greeted with loud applause. Jimmy held up his hand, "There is more wonderful news. I have the honor to announce that Joanna Jennings, affectionately known as J. J., has been unanimously elected to be a partner in the law firm of Garretson, Clements, Davis, and Munson."

J. J. let out a shriek. She jumped up and ran over to Jimmy. "Jimmy, really, really, I'm a partner?"

Jimmy could narrowly keep his balance, J. J. was hanging around his neck. "Yes, dear. You are a full partner. And well deserved, I might add."

One by one the other diners went over to J. J. to hug and congratulate her. Sharleen noticed that Antoine hugged J. J. in a very intimate way, and his embrace lingered for quite a while. *That's more than just a polite congratulation*, she thought. Her thoughts were interrupted by the premier.

He stood up and tapped his knife against his glass for attention. "And well deserved it is. I have nothing but praise for this young lady. Let me tell you a little-known story about J. J. I think Jimmy is the only one among you who knows about this. Several years ago, while I was still what they call a back bencher, J. J. came to see me. She told me that the opposing party was spreading rumors that I had conspired with a powerful businessman to manipulate the election. In exchange for his assistance I would have promised to take the lead in passing some legislation that would help his enterprises. Mind you, I was very much in favor of the legislation in question; it was one of my main projects. But I had met this businessman, Jeffrey Bloch, only once. I doubt that he even knew my name.

"J. J., who always was, and still is, very active in recruiting grassroots support for our party, had picked up bits and pieces of rumors about me conspiring to fix the election. When she came to see me, she really grilled me about the election. After she had assured herself that the rumors were pure fabrication, she dug down to get at the truth. Turns out they had been started by Leon Kramer, the son-in-law of John Robbins, the CEO of Star Ocean Ferries, a company that stood to lose their monopoly position if this legislation passed. Leon Kramer was at that time a powerful force in the opposing party.

"J. J. discovered that my opponent, who opposed the legislation, had been secretly receiving a lot of financial support from Star Ocean Ferries. John Robbins used bribes in an attempt to influence the election. Armed with this information, J. J. went to Spencer Miller, the investigating reporter for our local TV station. When Spencer Miller broke the story on the air it meant the end of the political career of Leon Kramer. John Robbins had to resign as CEO of Star Ocean Ferries. I won by a landslide, and got the nickname Mr. Clean. Believe me, that image did not hurt in my ascent in the ranks of my party."

After the dinner broke up, Antoine walked J. J. to her car, and the two of them were still chatting when Sharleen and Clint came out of the restaurant.

During the dinner, it had not only become obvious to Sharleen that Antoine liked J. J., but she also had known for quite some time that J. J. had a crush on Antoine. Later that week during lunch with J. J., she brought up the subject. "If you like the guy, why don't you let him know it?"

"That's funny. You want me to go up to Antoine and announce 'I really like you.' That should go over well."

"Don't be ridiculous! I don't mean for you to do it that way. But there are plenty of more subtle ways a girl can let a man know she likes him."

"Oh, he knows I like him as a friend. And I think he likes me as a friend, but certainly not in a romantic way."

"How do you know that? And why not?"

"Guys don't go for fat girls like me. They like a jolly, fat girl as a friend, but not as a girlfriend. And, in case you haven't noticed, I'm beyond plump."

"Okay, so you're heavy; but why are you so sure he won't look beyond that? You have a good head on your shoulders, are his intellectual equal, and have a great personality. For goodness' sake, girl, you are a partner in the best law firm in Bermuda! Why wouldn't he go for you?"

"Honey, with your figure, you have no idea what it is like to be as fat as me. Besides, with his past experience in the US, he stays away from any romantic entanglements with white girls. For him, I'm too white."

"I'm sorry to disappoint you. You might think you can pass for white, but you are a light-skinned black girl. I am multiracial, and you're black. Here in Bermuda they might call you a mulatto, but back in the States you are considered black. Don't worry; Antoine won't be afraid to date you. So that's not a problem. We're both very proud of our heritage. So what is your excuse now?"

"Like I said, men don't like very fat girls like me."

"You keep saying that; what makes you so sure of that?"

"Fine! If you want to embarrass me, I'll tell you. When I was younger, I was really hungry for romance. I wanted a guy to love me. I finally got a chance to go out with this fellow, and I thought I would grab my chance. After the date, I asked to go home with him. When we were in his apartment I was all over him. I got him excited by rubbing against his private parts. We went into the bedroom, and when I undressed, I saw his desire for me physically fade."

Sharleen did not catch on right away, so J. J. explained, "His hard-on shrunk away, and he told me to get dressed while he waited in the living room. When I came out of the bedroom, he handed me money and ordered a cab to take me home."

J. J. looked away. She had tears in her eyes, and Sharleen felt awful.

Rather than comfort J. J. and pity her, Sharleen slammed her hand on the table. "If it's all about a few extra pounds, we'll take care of that. No friend of mine is going to let a guy she likes slip through her fingers just because she thinks she is too fat. We start your exercises and diet tomorrow morning; I'm your coach."

J. J. tried to protest. "I've tried before, but it's no use. I was born to be the jolly fat girl."

Sharleen's response was short and sweet. "This is not optional. You will cooperate, and Antoine will become your man. I like both of you too much to listen to your protests."

XXXVIII

As J. J. had predicted, it was not easy. In the beginning, the pounds just would not come off. But Sharleen was a hardnosed coach. No matter how discouraged J. J. became, she pushed her through the moments of self-pity. Eventually success did come. First in the form of a few pounds, but the weight loss had started, and from then on it went faster and faster.

A major setback was narrowly averted when Sharleen thought J. J. had lost enough weight to join a health club. They signed up together and were excited to start. They had bought new gym outfits and looked pretty good. Disaster struck the moment they came out of the dressing room. Like a bunch of bees swarming around honey, the men, young and old, could not keep their eyes off Sharleen. Some even went so far as to whistle and make suggestive remarks. This was the last thing Sharleen had expected. She felt terrible for J. J., who did not get any attention at all. She turned on her heels and headed back for the locker room.

Before she had taken more than five steps a loud voice called out, "Hey, J. J., Sharleen, over here! Come on over and I'll show you how to operate these treadmills." It was Antoine. He quickly walked over to them, and his demeanor clearly showed the other men that he was not pleased by the way they greeted his friends.

As if he had been instructed to do so, he ignored Sharleen and turned to J. J. "You look really great. I have been aware that you were losing weight for some time. Wow, now you look better than ever. Come to show off a little? Just kidding! I did not know you two were working out together."

When J. J. responded that she and Sharleen had been going at it real hard during the last year, he remembered to also compliment Sharleen. "As usual, you look splendid. No wonder Clint doesn't look at other women. You two should have told me you were interested in training. You do know I'm a workout freak, right? I'm in this club at least four times a week, but I've never managed to get Clint to join me. I'm excited the two of you joined. Now I have two buddies to work out with."

Sharleen had never know J. J. to be shy. But when her friend hung back, she knew she had to carry on the conversation. "We'd love to join you on a regular basis. J. J. tells me she is not finished, and wants to lose a few more pounds."

Antoine was not pretending, he was genuinely interested in J. J. He worked with her on the treadmills, then took her over to the free weights and held her up when she could not reach the bar to practice her pull-ups. Sharleen watched the two of them and thought *my work is done*.

It turned out to be *almost* done. Antoine was not the problem; he was not afraid to show that he liked J. J., and kept asking her on dates. It was J. J. who, at times, made things difficult. She was so unsure of herself that she found it hard to throw herself completely into the relationship. When Antoine showered her with attention, J. J.'s response was not that of the jovial, outgoing gal Sharleen knew.

Sharleen jumped all over her. "What's the matter with you? The guy keeps asking you out. He showers you with attention. He clearly likes you, and you respond like a cold fish. You changed your mind; you don't like him?"

"I'm afraid it won't last. I love him so much that I won't be able to take it if all this turns out to not be for real. Why would this incredible guy want me? I dread the day will come when he cools down and we stop dating. I am so afraid this won't last, so I don't want to get too close to him."

Sharleen wanted to get mad at her friend, but then she realized that with J. J.'s past, she had all the right to feel the way she did. "J. J., please listen to me. Do you really think I would lead you into a situation where I knew you could get hurt?"

J. J. was surprised. "Why do you ask such a silly thing? I trust you. You are my friend, and you would never hurt me on purpose."

"Then you have to trust me when I tell you Antoine's feeling for you is sincere. He's starting to like you more and more. And why wouldn't he? You are a wonderful person. Where is he going to meet someone as funny, intelligent, and successful as you? And I almost forgot, with a figure that is becoming more and more sexy by the day. It might be crude to say, but you've become quite a piece. Turn around and let me look at you. Your backside reminds me of my friend Jada's rear. We used to joke that she had the ass and I had the tits. Gal, looking at you, I see you got both. You're hot! "

J. J. looked at Sharleen. "You really mean all that?"

"I certainly do. Now stop the crap and go for it."

When J. J. gave Sharleen a big hug, Sharleen whispered into her ear. "Not for me to decide, but the time might be ripe to go beyond a goodnight kiss."

J. J. took Sharleen's advice to heart. She threw herself into the relationship with Antoine, and was not afraid to show her excitement each time he asked her out. One day she decided it was time to take their relationship one step further.

When Antoine brought her home after a dinner date and kissed her goodnight at the door, she asked him in for a nightcap. Antoine had been to her apartment many times before, but always with a group, never alone in the evening. She had carefully planned the whole thing. First she would serve him his favorite drink. Next she would excuse herself and change into the very sexy negligée she had bought for the occasion. Then she'd seduce him!

Things turned out differently. When she handed Antoine his drink he said, "J. J., I'm scared to ask, but do you love me?"

J. J. was stunned but recovered quickly. "Honey, do I love you? I'm crazy about you."

"How come you took so long to show it?"

"When I was carrying all that weight I was sure you could not be interested in me. No guy would go for a fatty like me."

"You're wrong, baby. Very wrong. I liked you from the first day we met. You sparkled, and you were full of witty stories. I thought you were delightful."

"What about physically? Didn't my fat body put you off?"

"Yes, you were heavy, but you were never grossly obese. Anyway, that did not matter. Compared to some of the women I was dating you were a breath of fresh air. Their personalities were very much like a somber, rainy day. You came across as a bright, summer day. Being with you made me forget my bitterness about what happened to me in the US, and the bad things that happened to poor Clara. I was more than a little interested in you, but you held me at arm's length. I backed off, thinking you did not much care for me, or maybe you had a boyfriend you did not talk about."

J. J. could not believe what she was hearing. She had worked so hard to make this wonderful man like her, and now he had just told her he liked her all along. She literally jumped into Antoine's arms.

Smothering him with kisses, she asked, "You asked if I love you. How about if I tell you that you are all I ever wanted. At times all I could think about is how I wanted you to love me." She completely forgot about the expensive negligée meant to help seduce him. Resolutely she grabbed his hand and led him into the bedroom. After a long, passionate kiss they helped each other strip. She was not the least bit afraid that his passion would fade away.

They went over to the king-sized bed with its soft fluffy mattress and he gently lowered himself onto her naked body. J. J. remembered that she had bought a box of condoms in anticipation of what she hoped would happen. Reaching for the box she asked, "Do you want to use protection?"

"Not if you promise to marry me."

This was more than J. J. had dared dream. "Oh my God!" She slung her legs around him and shouted so loud the neighbors could have heard. "Yes, yes, and one more yes! I think I'm going to explode I'm so happy. Yes, I'll marry you!"

Early the next morning the phone rang. It was Sharleen. "Do you want to go jogging today?"

J. J.'s sleepy response was, "No, not today."

"Why not?" Sharleen asked.

"Antoine is here."

"Halleluiah!" Sharleen shouted, and quickly hung up the phone.

XXXIX

Getting engaged was not the only big event in J. J.'s life that year. The political party, for which she had tirelessly campaigned, won a landslide victory. His Excellency the Governor appointed her to the Senate. Five members of the eleven-member Senate are appointed on the recommendation of the premier and represent the governing party. It helped that she was a personal friend of the premier, but critics could not deny that, as a partner in one of the leading law firms in Bermuda, she was a highly qualified candidate.

Sharleen decided that all the exciting things that were happening called for a huge celebration. It was hard to decide which event should take the spotlight. For Sharleen there was no question about it. Their official adoption of Mikie was very high on her list!

But besides the official adoption of Mikie, J. J.'s and Antoine's engagement, and J. J.'s appointment to Parliament, there was more going on to be excited about. A few years back, Antoine had advised Clint to, instead of building a new restaurant, open a branch in one of the oceanfront hotels. Their small, intimate restaurant was doing fine, but an old beachfront hotel came up for sale. Antoine organized a consortium to buy the hotel, with the objective of completely renovating and expanding the property. He and Clint formed a partnership that retained fifteen percent ownership of the project. In addition, they assured themselves of the right to own and manage the two specialty restaurants planned for the newly renovated hotel. The hotel, renamed The Ocean View, had just opened, and was one of the showplaces on the island. Opened by His Excellency the Governor, it was considered a major tourist attraction. The two restaurants own by Antoine and Clint were a big success. Both featured well-known head chefs. One had been lured away from a restaurant in New York, and the other from a four-star restaurant in Chicago.

At first, Sharleen had planned to have the reception in their original restaurant. But the guest list kept growing and growing, and the party was moved to the main ballroom of The Ocean View. She started by inviting their friends. Next, she added the staff of their original restaurant. This was followed by a list of government officials and political allies of J. J. Soon the tourist bureau handed in a list of important travel agencies in the US and Europe that should be asked to send a representative to help promote the new hotel. It was no longer a personal affair. It became a public relations event. Sharleen cleverly solved that problem. The night before the official reception she arranged a dinner party, for family and close friends, in one of their own restaurants in the hotel. She flew her parents in from the US to be part of the festivities.

The fact that Sharleen's parents were coming made J. J. jealous. She kept on telling Sharleen, "I so want to meet Antoine's parents. He talks about them a lot, but is still desperately afraid of having them come over. He is so sure the authorities are keeping an eye on them in the hope of tracking him down. I try to tell him that the chances of that happening are very remote. I try to assure him that they have long forgotten about him, and besides, someone who skips out of a grand jury trial in Cisaro, Mississippi, is not important enough to be on the radar of the national authorities. But he is not to be moved. When I beg him to have his parents come by on a cruise ship to see us, he tells me that his father is not well enough to do that."

The reception was a huge success. The Ocean View was hugely popular, and Clint and Antoine became part of the movers and shakers in Bermuda. Together with Jimmy Garretson, they appeared on everyone's A-list for official receptions and parties. Besides being Antoine's fiancée, J. J., as a member of the Senate, was a well-known personality in her own right. Her stature shot up when the premier asked her to be the new minister of public safety.

Sharleen just about burst with joy when she heard about J. J.'s appointment as the new minister of public safety. "J. J., this is unbelievable! You are a fricking big deal! I'm going to address you as Madame Minister! Oh man, this is so great. You deserve this; you work so hard, and you are so smart they had to choose you. You're the best thing that has happened to this government since they won the election."

J. J. was happy with her appointment, but she could not join in Sharleen's enthusiasm.

"Why aren't you celebrating?" Sharleen asked, "This is a great day!"

"It should be. I've dreamt about something like this. But Antoine and I are sad that his parents can't be here to celebrate with us. His dad's health is slipping, and he misses them terribly."

As she did with the weight issue of her friend, Sharleen tore into her. "If this is a big deal for both of you, do something about it!"

"Come on. What do you expect me to do about it?"

"You're a damned minister now. That makes you an important person! Bermuda might not be a world power, but you are a member of our government. That should give you enough clout to get something done."

"Like what?"

"To go to that small, stupid town and bang the heads together of those prejudiced bastards. Honey, let me tell you, they do not represent the US I grew up in. Sure, there was prejudice around me. I'm multiracial. But the prejudice was limited. The majority of people were not like that. If they were, they did not bother me. For God's sake, I was homecoming queen my senior year. I had a lily-white boyfriend! Clint's parents were not comfortable with non-whites, but they would never stand for something like what happened to Antoine. I really believe what happened to him was extreme. Those people might not have wanted a black man for their daughter, but to send him to jail for something they knew she did? That we can't allow. And you, sister, are now in a position to do something about it."

XL

As she had done many times before, J. J. took Sharleen's word to heart. She decided to travel to Cisaro, Mississippi, to see if she could use her position as a government official to correct what had happened years before to Antoine. In case her mission failed, she decided to keep Antoine in the dark, and not tell him why she was going to the US. Not to make him suspicious, she told him she had been invited to an international conference on tourist safety and the jurisdiction of local governments.

The first thing J. J. did upon arrival in the US was to hire a lawyer in Jackson, Mississippi. Together with that lawyer, Stewart Kagan, she went to Cisaro. The two of them started collecting official reports from around the time of Antoine's car accident and arrest. They were stopped cold when they tried to get copies of the police investigation of the accident. An arrogant clerk simply told them those were dead files buried somewhere in the archives. J. J. asked to speak to a supervisor. When the clerk finally relented, Jeb

Florey came out of his office to speak to them. J. J. explained why they wanted to see the reports.

When Jeb heard the purpose of their investigation, he expressed his displeasure in no uncertain terms. Addressing J. J. he said, "You black folks think you can come barging into town and think we will overturn a perfectly legitimate conviction of some nigger? Well, let me tell you. That might work for you in some places, but not here in Cisaro."

J. J. stayed perfectly calm and produced her passport. Shoving it under Jeb's face she asked, "Do you know what this is?"

Jeb studied the document. "Congratulations, you have a passport. Looks foreign to me. Don't know if it's valid here in America, but why show it to me?"

J. J. had to laugh at the man's ignorance. "Yes, it's a passport. It is a diplomatic passport, valid in the United States. Even here in Cisaro. And if you don't want the feds swarming all over your office, you'd better hurry and produce those reports I requested."

Jeb realized that J. J. meant business, and that further refusal could get him in a heap of trouble. Grudgingly, he told the clerk to search for the reports and give copies to J. J.

J. J. and Stewart Kagan thought the reports were very significant, especially the report made by the state police which appeared to have been ignored by the office of the local DA. This report contradicted the findings of the local police that Antoine had been driving.

J. J. and Stewart Kagan had to go through a similar scenario to get copies of the original coroner's report. That report far from proved the DA's contention that Antoine was the driver. It showed how drunk the girl had been, and could be used to show that she might have been the driver. Pieces of glass found imbedded in her head and upper torso came from the driver's side window.

Securing a copy of the hospital records proved to be impossible without a court order. J. J. approached a local judge, but she denied her request to see the hospital records. More complicated than getting all these reports was trying to trace witnesses who had actual knowledge of the events surrounding the accident.

They finally found a retired police officer who was willing to talk freely. He remembered the night of the accident. The accident occurred not far from town. He and another officer were sent out to investigate. The state police were on the scene. But the Cisaro Chief of Police ordered them to disregard the report made by the state troopers, and only file their own report. The chief had been pretty specific in stating that he expected their report to show that in his words, "that black fellow had been driving." This ex-cop also told them that, although he had not seen this personally, his buddy on the force told him that the hospital, in a later report, had increased Antoine's blood alcohol level above what it had actually been measured to be on his arrival.

Their excitement in finding this witness was quickly tempered when he refused to give them a signed affidavit relating what he had told them. He said he felt bad about it, but he feared for his life if he testified against the authorities. He pointed out that, after they left, he would still be living in Cisaro.

J. J. decided it was time to call in the help of the federal authorities. She made a visit to the FBI office in Jackson. To get to talk to the bureau chief, she once again used her status as an official of a foreign government. As luck would have it, the bureau chief, Agent Thomson, loved Bermuda. He had been there twice on vacation, and hoped to visit there again after he got through paying for his kids' college education.

After Agent Thomson got through reading the reports J. J. had brought with her, he said, "We've had our eye on that town for a long time. Over the years we've been told of many civil rights violations that have occurred and are occurring there, but we have never been able to prove a thing. These reports give us a nice basis for a new investigation. Although the statute of limitation has run out on the violations that witness you found describes, we can still use his testimony. Don't worry, he'll have all the protection he'll need. I would love to have those bastards threaten him. I'd have a brand-new case!"

J. J. thought she was ready to have Antoine cleared of any charges, but then came the big surprise. She discovered that Antoine had been convicted in absentia for fleeing while under arrest pending his grand jury trial. Stewart Kagan confirmed that in absentia trials are very rare. Most judges would not allow it.

J. J. asked Stewart to get a copy of the proceedings, and she checked to see whether the presiding judge was still alive. After a little digging, she found out that Joshua Summers had been the judge who allowed the DA to proceed, even though the case was in conflict with the right to due process. Justice Summers was retired, and was living in a senior retirement community in Florida. J. J. decided to go to Florida to ask the judge on what basis he had allowed the proceedings to continue. When J. J. confronted him, he was very belligerent.

"Who the hell are you to come here and question my ruling? Of course I was correct. The defendant's absence was clearly voluntary, so we had every right to try that bastard."

J. J. remained icy calm. "And who the hell do you think *you* are, addressing me with such disrespect? To you I might appear as any old black gal you can stomp on. Sorry, mister, not this time! In the first place, you will address me as Your Excellency. I am a cabinet minister in my country. Previous to my appointment I was a partner in one of the leading law offices in my country. As a member of the New York State and the Federal Bar, I am familiar with US law."

The old judge looked at J. J. as if he had seen a ghost. How could this young black woman have achieved all that? When he regained his composure, he was crude enough to ask.

He handed her the opening, so J. J. gladly gave him a piece of her mind. "Under your rule I could never have been anything but a cleaning lady. Thank goodness I did not grow up under the thumb of old, prejudiced despots like you and your whole corrupt bunch of oppressors. No, I was not told that I was not intelligent enough to be an equal to you pompous bastards. As a high school graduate, I received a scholarship to go study in England. After graduating from Cambridge, I had the opportunity to stay on and study law.

"When I finished, I returned to my native Bermuda and joined the law firm of Garretson, Clements, Davis, and Munson. After a year, they selected me to go New York University School of Law to get an American law degree. Upon my return, I was the youngest associate to head a section. Now I am a partner in the law firm. I bet that you, with your flimsy law degree from some Podunk college and your small-town judgeship, can't come close to matching all that. So let me teach you the law of this great country. In 1993 in the case of *Crosby v. United States,* the US Supreme Court ruled that federal law, and I quote 'prohibits the trial in absentia of a defendant who is not present at the beginning of trial.' So you were incompetent, and used the wrong case law."

Not waiting for a response from the old man, J. J. turned and left the room. She felt great having had the opportunity to yell at one of the people who had hurt her Antoine. She was still boiling at the thought of what they had done to him.

XLI

J. J. returned to Jackson to meet with Stewart Kagan. She asked Stewart to start proceedings to have a higher court set aside Antoine's conviction. Stewart pointed out that it could entail a long, dragged-out procedure.

He recommended a much quicker way. "Why don't we apply to the governor for clemency? The governor has the power to change the decision of a trial court. He can issue a pardon, which amounts to total forgiveness of all criminal penalties. I realize you would prefer having the whole thing set aside and clean his record completely, but this is much faster. The end result might not be perfect, but the effect is the same, and your fiancé would be free to come home."

In preparing the application for clemency, Stewart made good use of J. J.'s position as cabinet minister of a sovereign country. The governor's chief of staff was impressed by her position, and helped rush the application through official channels. Things went better than Stewart had hoped for. The governor invited J. J. to his office, and offered an official apology for the miscarriage of justice that had occurred. He did not go so far as to condemn the responsible officials in Cisaro, but he did use the words 'flagrant miscarriage of justice' several times. J. J. left his office with an official document, bearing the governor's seal, proclaiming that, "Antoine Johnson, formerly residing in Bakersfield, California, and presently a resident of Bermuda, is released from any and all penalties resulting from his conviction...."

J. J. could not wait to get home and tell Antoine the good news. Before she boarded the plane for Bermuda, she called Sharleen and triumphantly declared, "Mission accomplished."

Sharleen had always been convinced that J. J. could accomplish anything she set her mind to, but this was over and beyond. "Girl, you are Wonder Woman! I know you're smart, but this is it! I am so happy for you. Have you called Antoine?"

"No, I want to tell him in person. So mum is the word. Don't breathe a word about it till I get a chance to tell him."

When J. J. arrived home, she said nothing about it. She waited until she and Antoine sat down to dinner when she said, "I really think it's time to go see your parents."

Antoine looked annoyed. "You know that's impossible, so stop it. It hurts enough that I can't go, so I don't need you to remind me."

J. J. pulled out the document with the pardon and slid it in front of Antoine. He looked at it, skimming it quickly and asked, "Is this for real?"

"Yes, baby, it is. We are going home!"

Antoine jumped up, nearly upsetting the dinner table. He flew into J. J.'s arms, tears streaming down his face. "Honey, you're incredible. Are we really going to see Mom and Dad?"

By this time he was crying like a baby, and he buried his head in J. J's lap. "Oh my God, we're going home. You'll meet Mom and Dad! How did you do it? How did you get the governor to sign this?"

"Honey, you never did anything wrong. They were wrong, and it had to be corrected. It was unfair to keep you from your parents, and it was terrible that you could not introduce me to them. From what you told me about them, I already love them."

Antoine was like a little boy. Once the tears dried up, he wanted to call his parents right away.

J. J. stopped him. She had another surprise he could tell them. "Sharleen booked airline tickets for all of us about an hour ago. The five of us are going to meet your folks. Me, you, Clint, Sharleen, and their son Mikie. We're leaving for Los Angeles in two days. I would love to get married while we are there."

XLII

Antoine's homecoming was even more emotional than everyone had expected. He had been warned that his father would be in a wheelchair; their passionate embrace showed the bond between father and son. Both men were overcome by their feelings. It revealed the deep respect Antoine had for his father, and the pride the doctor had in his son.

J. J. freely displayed her emotions when she embraced Dr. Johnson. Antoine had often talked about his father, and she loved the man even before meeting him. She was more hesitant in embracing Antoine's mother. She watched how this stately lady squeezed her son to her chest and prayed that she would do the same to her. She had lost her own mother when she was twelve, and yearned to have this woman love her.

Antoine's younger sister could not get enough of J. J. She adored her older brother, and this was the girl who had made him happy. She kept hugging J. J., and made a point of calling her "Sis." Antoine had only met his sister's husband once before, and that was at a hastily arranged meeting on a cruise ship docked for the day in Bermuda. His sister's three sons had never been kissed by a man they had never met before, but were okay with it when they saw how happy their mom was to have her brother back home.

The most spontaneous greeting came from Mikie. In his wheelchair, Dr. Johnson was no longer the overpowering presence he had been in his prime, but he still dominated the room. Mikie had no problem stepping up to him and giving him a big hug. He was really the star of the show when he proceeded to say, "Clint, my father. Sharleen, my mother. Antoine, your son. J. J., your daughter?"

Dr. Johnson burst out laughing. "Yes, Mikie. We love J. J., and we are happy to have her become our daughter. Mikie, we love you, too. In my practice it was always a joy to see the openness and honesty of persons society labels as handicapped. You had no problem asking what was on everyone's mind, but no one dared to ask. Yes, Mikie, I can give you a resounding, yes! Mrs. Johnson and I love J. J., and we are very happy."

Mikie gave the doctor one of his engaging smiles and went over to Mrs. Johnson.

Sharleen saw him hesitate and understood why. "It's okay, Mikie, you may hug Antoine's mother.

For J. J., the proof that Antoine's family fully accepted her was not only in the heartwarming welcome she had received. She was totally convinced when she heard of the preparations Antoine's mother and sister had made for their wedding. The moment they were told that Antoine and J. J. planned to get married while in the US, the two of them had set out to make all the arrangements.

The day after her arrival, J. J. got a full briefing. She was told that Bakersfield was in Kern County, and that they had called the Kern County Clerk's Office to make an appointment to get a marriage license. Luckily, they did not have to be residents of Kern County to apply for a marriage license. Kern County does not require blood tests, and there is no waiting period. They would be required to bring a picture ID. J. J. could present her passport; Antoine would be allowed to show the document in lieu of passport issued by the consulate in Bermuda. He had applied for this document in order to enter the US because his passport had been revoked when he was listed as a fugitive.

To perform the ceremony, Mrs. Johnson had asked their dear family friend, retired judge Sumner Friedman to do the honors. The wedding was to take place at the Johnson home. She had invited all their friends to a catered, sit-down dinner.

After the official ceremony, Judge Friedman deviated from the usual procedure. Rather than address the new couple himself, he invited Antoine's father to say a few words. The doctor gladly accepted.

"J. J., Antoine, this is the day we could only dream of. To have you, Antoine, return home is a dream come true. And to have you bring us this woman is a gift so wonderful it makes us wonder what we did to deserve such a blessing. Son, let the hurt and hate of what was done to you flow away in the knowledge that it also led to you meeting this one-in-a-million girl. Any girl you love would always be welcomed by us, but J. J. has truly stolen our hearts. J. J., Antoine is our only son, and we have always wished the best for him. You, my dear, are the best.

"If you had merely paved the way for him to come home to us, that would have been more than enough. But we can see how deeply you love him, and how much he loves you in return. That is what every parent wishes for their child, and you two have made that wish come true.

"Clint and Sharleen, we want to express our deep affection for you. You took our son in during his most difficult time. You got to know him for the wonderful person he is, and, to top that, you introduced him to the love of his life. I hereby declare you two to be the guardian angels of the Johnson family.

"And by the way, I love your son. His smile could brighten anyone's day.

"And to you, our friends, it is our privilege to have you with us to share this wonderful event. Without you, the dark days of our son's exile would have been even darker. Your support has meant a lot us. Thank you."

When the almost two hundred guests stopped applauding, Judge Friedman raised his hand to ask once more for their attention. "As an officer of the court, I was sworn to uphold the constitution of this great country. You can't imagine how it hurt that I was unable to help Antoine, whom I have known since he was a teenager. I could not step in to prevent the hurt done to my dear friends, his parents. Multiple times I petitioned the courts to reverse his unlawful conviction. Each time they refused to hear our case. Enter this wonderful young lady from Bermuda, and she singlehandedly did what I and some very famous lawyers could not get done. Please join me in a toast to this special woman."

He raised his glass, "J. J., to you. I speak for all of us when I say, thank you for having taken away the hurt, and for restoring our faith in our system of justice. My admiration for you knows no bounds."

When the cheers died down for the second time, the retired judge continued. "In deference to the rich mixture of religions of the family members and their guests, I was asked to conduct a non-religious wedding. However, I ask your indulgence of an old man who feels poetry enhances the significance of this day. I read to you two of my favorite poems:

Where There Is Love (by Helen Rice)

Where there is love the heart is light
Where there is love the day is bright
Where there is love there is a song
To help when things are going wrong
Where there is love there is a smile
To make all things seem more worthwhile
Where there is love there's a quiet peace
A tranquil place where turmoil cease

Harold J. Fischel

Love changes darkness into light
And makes the heart take wingless flight
Oh, blessed are those who walk in love-
They also walk with God above.

The Day
(Author unknown)

May this be the start of a happy new life
That's full of special moments to share
May this be the first of your dreams come true
And of hope that will always be there…
May this be the start of a lifetime of trust
And of caring that's just now begun…
May today be a day that you'll always remember
the day when your hearts become one…

XLIII

Sharleen thoroughly enjoyed the wedding. She was J. J's matron of honor, and Clint had been asked by Antoine to be his best man. But in her heart, she was just a little jealous. Her own wedding had been a small, informal affair. In the hope of having a big wedding in the US, she had invited her whole family to come join her in Bakersfield. To her regret, she learned on arrival that Kern County would not issue a marriage license if you were already married. At most they could renew their vows, but that was not what she had hoped for.

Clint was aware of her plans to have a joint wedding with J. J. He secretly spoke to Sharleen's uncle Chayton about the possibility of arranging an Indian wedding. Chayton explained that the Native American wedding ceremony varies from region to region. Music forms the major part of the ceremony, and singing is the dominant form of musical expression. Instruments are only used for rhythmic accompaniment. With the small group of family members present, it would be hard to arrange a ceremony of any significance, but Chayton had a plan.

While serving on a national committee of Indian affairs, he had met Duane Martinez, who represented the Tule River Tribe. Duane lived on the Tule River Indian Reservation, which was about seventy miles from Bakersfield. Chayton contacted him. They discussed the fact that Sharleen was only fifty percent Indian because only her father was a Native American, and Clint had no Indian blood at all. Despite this, Duane offered to arrange a full-fledged Indian ceremony on the Tule River Reservation.

When Clint revealed the plans for a full-fledged wedding ceremony for Sharleen and himself to be held on the Tule River Indian Reservation, everybody loved the idea. Sharleen and her dad were very excited.

Clint hired a big tour bus to take the whole group to the reservation. The trip along the South Fork of the Tule River took almost two hours. The winding road into the foothills of the Sierra Nevada Mountains was perfect to create an authentic setting for an Indian wedding.

The wedding party was welcomed onto the reservation by Joseph Dermott, the head of the Tule River Tribal Council. He explained that Sharleen would be asked to accompany several of the older Indian women to prepare for the ceremony. The rest of the party was invited to join tribe members in the large reception center, which had been closed to tourists for the day.

The Indian ladies took Sharleen to a private residence where she was asked to bathe herself in water which had been brought in from a nearby river. The ladies explained that this was in order to receive the blessing of the Spirit of the Earth. Next, they dressed her in a simple white dress, and gave her moccasins to wear on her feet. They took great care in fixing her hair, which flowed loose over her shoulders, adorned only by a single red flower on the side. When she was ready, they accompanied her to an open field, where all the wedding guests had gathered. In the middle of the field there was a large fire, and a group of men sitting around a large, double-headed drum. They were singing in unison and drumming with sticks.

Joseph Dermott asked Clint and Sharleen to come stand beside him and he explained, "Because of the diverse cultures of the Native American tribes, there are many different versions of Native American wedding ceremonies. I have chosen parts of the most common practices.

"First, I will ask Sharleen's father to recite the Ten Commandments:

Native American Ten Commandments

Treat the Earth and all that dwell thereon with respect.
Remain close to the Great Spirit.
Show great respect for your fellow beings.
Work together for the benefit of all Mankind.

Give assistance and kindness wherever needed.

Do what you know to be right.

Look after the wellbeing of mind and body.

Dedicate a share of your efforts to the greater good.

Be truthful and honest at all times.

Take full responsibility for your actions.

Next, Joseph instructed Clint and Sharleen to take seven steps clockwise around the fire. Clint had to go first, followed by Sharleen. He handed them each a sheet of paper, and told them to read the appropriate vows out loud.

The Rite of Seven Steps
Groom, Step 1:

O, my beloved, our love has become firm by your walking as one with me. Together we will share the responsibilities of the lodge, food, and children. May the Creator bless us, and give us many noble children to share. May they live long.

Bride, Step 1:

This is my commitment to you, my husband. Together we will share the responsibility of the home, food, and children. I promise that I shall discharge all my share of the responsibilities for the welfare of the family and the children.

Groom, Step 2:
O, my beloved, now you have walked with me the second step. May the Creator bless you. I will love you and you alone as my wife. I will fill your heart with strength and courage: this is my commitment and my pledge to you. May God protect the lodge and children.

Bride, Step 2:
My husband, at all times I shall fill your heart with courage and strength. In your happiness I shall rejoice. May God bless you and our honorable lodge.

Groom, Step 3:
O, my beloved, now since you have walked three steps with me, our wealth and prosperity will grow. May God bless us. May we educate our children and may they live long.

Bride, Step 3:
My husband, I love you with single-minded devotion as my husband. I will treat all other men as my brothers. My devotion to you is pure, and you are my joy. This is my commitment and pledge to you.

Groom, Step 4:
O, my beloved, it is a great blessing that you have now walked four steps with me. May the

Creator bless you. You have brought favor and sacredness into my life.

Bride, Step 4:
O, my husband, in all acts of righteousness, in material prosperity, in every form of enjoyment, and in those divine acts such as fire sacrifice, worship, and charity, I promise you that I shall participate, and I will always be with you.

Groom, Step 5:
O, my beloved, now you have walked five steps with me. May the Creator make us prosperous. May the Creator bless us.

Bride, Step 5:
O, my husband, I will share both in your joys and sorrows. Your love will make me very happy.

Groom, Step 6:
O, my beloved, by walking six steps with me, you have filled my heart with happiness. May I fill your heart with great joy and peace, time and time again. May the Creator bless you.

Bride, Step 6:
My husband, the Creator blesses you. May I fill your heart with great joy and peace. I promise that I will always be with you.

Groom, Step 7:
O, my beloved goddess, as you have walked the seven steps with me, our love and friendship have become inseparable and firm. We have experienced spiritual union in God. Now you have become completely mine. I offer my total self to you. May our marriage last forever.

Bride, Step 7:
My husband, by the law of the Creator, and the spirits of our honorable ancestors, I have become your wife. Whatever promises I gave you I have spoken them with a pure heart. All the spirits are witnesses to this fact. I shall never deceive you, nor will I let you down. I shall love you forever.

When they finished their Native American wedding vows, Joseph tuned to Clint. "Now you can act like a modern American and kiss you lovely bride. You're a very lucky man; she really looks like an Indian princess. She is one of us. We will hold you to your promise to take good care of her."

Next Joseph called on Chayton to read a blessing that was written for the movie *Broken Arrow*. Although it is not based on Apache tradition, it is commonly used at weddings:

Apache Blessing - 1
Now you will feel no rain,
for each of you will be shelter for the other.

Now you will feel no cold,
for each of you will be warmth to the other.
Now there will be no loneliness,
for each of you will be companion to the other.
Now you are two persons,
but there is only one life before you.
May beauty surround you both in the
journey ahead and through all the years,
May happiness be your companion and
your days together be good and long upon the earth.

Apache Blessing - 2

Treat yourselves and each other with respect, and
remind yourselves often of what brought you together.
Give the highest priority to the tenderness,
gentleness, and kindness that your connection deserves.
When frustration, difficulties, and fear assail your relationship,
as they threaten all relationships at one time or another,
remember to focus on what is right between you,
not only the part which seems wrong.
In this way, you can ride out the storms when clouds hide the face of the sun in your lives—remembering that

even if you lose sight of it for a moment, the
sun is still there.
And if each of you takes responsibility for
the quality of your
life together, it will be marked by abundance
and delight.

During most of the ceremony, Sharleen had kept her emotions intact; but when her mom and dad came forward to kiss and congratulate her, she could no longer hold back her tears of joy. She was still clutching Clint's hand, and once more she flung herself around his neck. "Darling, what a gift! Nothing in the world could have been better."

All Clint could answer was, "Are you finally as proud of your Indian heritage as I am?"

That was the moment J. J. came flying up to them. She too had tears streaming down her face. "Beautiful! That was so beautiful. I can't get over it." As if J. J. had given the signal, all the guests came forward to congratulate the "newlyweds."

Mikie had not completely followed what was happening. Initially the drumming had scared him, but Dr. Johnson put his arm around the big fellow and told him it was a fun game to show how much Clint and Sharleen loved each other. That pleased Mikie, and he enjoyed the rest of the ceremony. He liked the part when Clint got to kiss Sharleen.

He pointed at Sharleen and said, "Pretty. My mother pretty."

The ceremony was not completed until the members of the tribe distributed presents to all the guests. They were symbols of what the tribe wished for Clint and Sharleen. Corn represented fertility; feathers represented loyalty; stones represented strength.

When the wedding party was about to board the bus for the trip back to Bakersfield, Joseph Dermott approached Dr. Johnson. "Do you remember me?"

Dr. Johnson looked puzzled. "Help me. Where did we meet?"

"A long time ago. Before we got the reservation financially on its feet, you were instrumental in treating our kids free of charge in your hospital."

Dr. Johnson remembered. "Yes, I remember. My staff called you Indian Joe. You fought like a tiger for those kids. I remember your outrage when an intern said that the Indian kids were prone to illnesses because of your lifestyle."

Joseph laughed as he tenderly put his hand on the doctor's shoulder. "And I remember the dressing down you gave anyone who treated our kids differently from the full-paying patients. I am happy we now own forty acres in the Airport Industrial Park, and an additional eighty in the development along Highway 190. It's been our privilege to pay back by donating to the children's ward of the hospital. Now you know why the playroom with the TVs and video games is called the TRT *(Tule River Tribe)* Room."

XLIV

A few days before all five of them were scheduled to return to Bermuda, J. J. took Antoine aside and told him she had a serious issue to discuss. Antoine looked worried, but she told him to just sit down and listen.

"Antoine, I have been watching your interaction with your family, and it is obvious you are very close. I can see your folks are going to miss you terribly when you return to Bermuda. I want a truthful answer from you. If I offer to stay here in the US with you, would that make you happy?"

Antoine did not take any time to answer. "No way. Bermuda is my home. I love my family dearly, but I definitely do not want to live here. Having said that, it's awfully sweet of you to offer. Do you fully realize what you just offered to do?"

"Yes, I have thought about it for a long time. If you'd chosen to stay here, I would too."

"Look, I am not staying here, but sweetheart, if we stayed here, you would have to give up everything you've worked for. You're a Cabinet member now!"

"My offer stands. Being your wife means a lot more to me than being Minister of Public Safety. I am offering 'Wherever thou goest I will go'."

Antoine was really touched by J. J's offer. "J. J., that is profound. Your offer to sacrifice everything for my happiness is incredible. You know I love you, but now the word love does not go far enough to express my feelings for you. But I have to repeat myself. Bermuda is my home, and I fully intend to return with my beautiful bride."

"Did you ever consider staying here with your family? If you were still single, would you try to rebuild your life here?"

"No. After what happened in Cisaro, I would never feel comfortable living here."

"Cisaro is not America. Look at your parents. They never had any trouble."

"Cisaro may not be America, but my parents are not typical, either."

"What do you mean? They are African Americans living here. Why are they different?"

"They have heard the word discrimination, but for them it never came close to home until my experience in Cisaro. My dad was a high school football star who chose not to follow a professional career. As the valedictorian of his class, he got a scholarship to medical school. He was a damned good surgeon, and was sought after by some of the best hospitals in the country. He loved the California weather, and finally settled here as head of pediatrics at St. Clare General. My mom was famous in her own right. If you pick up a copy of fifty-year-old fashion magazines, chances are you will find her on the cover. She was one of the few black models who got national assignments. They and their close friend Judge Friedman could afford to ignore discrimination. They simply refused to have anything to do with the few who did not respect them for who they are."

"Wow, I've married into royalty! But seriously, Antoine, are you really afraid to live here?"

"Yes. I tried not to show it, but I was apprehensive about coming here. Being around my folks and their many friends, black and white, helped relax me. But living here? No, that's not for me. Besides, I really love Bermuda, and the work Clint and I are involved in. If I hadn't met Clint at a critical time, who knows if I would ever have come to love Bermuda. And, by the way, if I hadn't met Sharleen, I wouldn't have met the love of my life."

J. J. and Sharleen had few if any secrets between them, and J. J. discussed the conversation she had with Antoine about his fear of discrimination with her. "Did you feel this way when you lived in America?"

"I was more worried about being multiracial than I should have been. But if you want to hear about discrimination, talk to my mom. A biracial girl marrying an Indian, that's asking for it! But let's be honest, discrimination exists in every country. America is certainly not the worst. Ask Antoine. Had he been a poor black man working odd jobs on the docks in Bermuda, would he not have felt any discrimination? Maybe it would have been mostly economic, but skin color would also count in certain white circles in Bermuda."

J. J. and Sharleen continued their discussion about discrimination and the times they had been afraid to go someplace out of fear of not being accepted. At the same time, they both had to admit to instances where they had discriminated against a person because of his or her race or religion. They agreed that it was easy to be dragged along when you were with members of your own group. The group could be persons from the same race, religion, or even country.

Sharleen laughed and went to the extreme. "We even hated kids from the rival high school, and none of us was brave enough to disagree."

Later that night, the two of them were sitting by themselves in the cozy library of the Johnson home. It was time to relax after the hectic last days, and they were enjoying recalling the best parts of their stay.

J. J. was in a sentimental mood and said to Sharleen, "I'm so lucky to have you as my friend. I can always rely on you to have my back, and you always encourage me. And I don't mean only to go after the man I love."

Sharleen said that it was she who was lucky. That she needed J. J.'s friendship.

"What makes you say that?" J. J. asked.

"Well, I need a girlfriend to discuss things with, and tell her about my feelings. Clint is my soul mate, but that is different. I rely on you for what they call 'girl talk'. In high school there was Jada; we did everything together, and I could tell her things others would not understand. You and I have the same relationship. Not that you are another Jada. She was very different from you, but the bond is the same. I rely on you to listen to me and share things with me. I hope you feel the same about me."

J. J. had to admit that she had never had a close friend. "Having a close friend like you is a totally new experience for me. Emotionally, it's done wonders. Mind you, I did have friends. But I was always the bright one, the career girl, the one they could not really relate to. With you I'm very comfortable. I don't mind if you think of me as a substitute for Jada. If what I heard about her is true, it's an honor to be in the same league."

"It's never good to compare. You are you, and Jada was Jada. Both great people, and I am blessed to have had both of you as my best friend. I'm very happy with my life, but it would not be the same without you. I love having you as my best friend."

J. J. had to have the last word. "That makes two of us. I think our husbands have a similar bond."

"Nah, men are more private. It's hard for them to share their true emotions."

Clint came into the library. "It's getting late, Sharleen, time to get back to the motel."

Antoine and J. J. had been staying at the home of his parents. Clint and Sharleen and the rest of the wedding party were staying at a motel about a half-hour away.

XLV

When they arrived at the motel, Clint was dead-tired and wanted to go to sleep right away. But Sharleen wanted to make love before she fell asleep. She did not have to twist Clint's arm to get him in the mood. They had the room to themselves; Mikie was fast asleep in his own room down the hall.

After they made love, they fell asleep. Sharleen was safely tucked in Clint's arms when a cry coming from the room next to them woke her up. "Clint, honey, wake up. Something is wrong in the room next door."

Clint sat up. "Who is staying in that room? Are they one of our group?"

"Yes, it's Lakota and Ehawee's room. I'll go see what is wrong."

Sharleen threw on her robe and rushed next door. She knocked on the door but no one answered. She knocked again and said, "It's me, Sharleen, open up!"

Slowly the door opened. Ehawee was standing in the doorway, fully dressed, blood dripping from the side of her mouth.

Sharleen was shocked. "Oh my God. Ehawee! What happened?"

Ehawee was crying. "He hit me. Lakota hit me!"

Sharleen put her arms around Ehawee. "You poor thing! Why, what happened? Why would he hit you?" She pulled Ehawee into the bathroom and wiped her mouth with a towel. She continued to question her.

Ehawee could not stop crying. In bits and pieces, she told Sharleen what happened. "After we left the Johnson's house, we went to a bar in town. We had quite a few drinks, and started arguing about how much he drinks. On the way to the motel he stopped and bought a bottle of vodka to take to our room. When we got into our room he continued drinking, and I got mad at him, calling him a drunk. You know he's got a few DUIs back home? He's driving on a suspended license!"

Sharleen was surprised. She had never heard about Lakota's drinking problem. "I never heard he had a problem. Where is he now?"

"Just before you knocked on the door, he went stomping out. I'm afraid he is driving around in our rental car. We rented it in my name because of his suspended license. He's quite high; I hope he doesn't hit someone and kill them. Oh, why can't I stop him from drinking so much?"

Never Too Late

By this time Clint had entered the room. When Sharleen briefed him on what had happened, he called Antoine. After they conferred with Doctor Johnson, they decided to call the police to ask for assistance. They knew the police might arrest him for drunk driving, but they decided that was better than taking a chance that Lakota could get into a bad accident and kill himself, or someone else.

It did not take long for them to get a call back from the police. Lakota had already been stopped by a patrol car and arrested. He had blown a 1.5% blood alcohol level, almost twice the legal limit, and was being held at the downtown police station. Clint and Antoine went down to the police station, while Doctor Johnson made a few telephone calls to see if he could get Lakota released. Even though it was late at night, Doctor Johnson reached a friend of his who could arrange for Lakota to be released on bail. Clint took Lakota back to the motel, where he put him to bed in his room. Sharleen had moved in with Ehawee.

The next day, Clint took Lakota to Doctor Johnson's house, where they sat down with Antoine and his father to discuss the situation. Lakota was very defensive. He explained that he could not help his drinking; that Native Americans were prone to alcoholism. That it was something in his DNA that made him drink.

The argument irritated Doctor Johnson and he pushed it aside. "As a surgeon I have never studied the subject, but nobody makes you drink. It is you who decides to keep drinking, even though you believe it is your heritage that makes you addicted to alcohol. There are many people who get addicted to alcohol, and only a small percentage are Native American. They have to decide for themselves that they want to stop drinking; then we can help them in rehab."

Lakota's attitude changed. "It's not that easy. I've tried to stop, but each time I start back up. It doesn't work!"

Antoine joined the conversation. "Have you tried rehab?"

Lakota had not. He explained that he was ashamed of his weakness, and of the fact that he was weak because he was Indian.

Clint wanted no part of that. "That is fucking bullshit. Sharleen never touches a drink. Her father never drinks, and I know your father never drinks. I do not know if that is because they think they could get addicted to the stuff. I never asked; but they are Indian and don't drink! So you don't have to drink!"

Doctor Johnson quickly took back the conversation. "Lakota, something got you started. Do you mind being very honest with us and telling us what made you feel unhappy, uncomfortable with your life? In other words, what made you start drinking, even though those around you had decided not to?"

Lakota hemmed and hawed. The directness of the question made him uncomfortable, but he wanted to talk about it.

"It's my dad. He wants me to be like him. It's what the tribe expects of me. I'm expected to live on the reservation and help preserve our traditions. They want me to be Chayton's son in the traditional way. I went to high school in town, and I always wanted the freedom that my classmates had. They were not tied down by strict rules of behavior. They could do their own thing."

Antoine laughed. "That's what you think! Try being the son of a famous doctor and deciding not to go to college. Let me tell you, any old college would not be good enough. You are expected to be at the top of your class and go to the very best university. Mind you, there is nothing wrong with it. I'm grateful to have had such a background. Why do you feel you could not be a proud Indian and still achieve what was important to you?"

"The way you explain things, it sounds easy. But I always felt this tremendous pressure. If I did not follow and uphold our tribal traditions, I would fail my people. I personally would be responsible for the disappearance of the Indian Nation. Of a proud people."

Clint shook his head. "Sounds a little egotistic to me. But I do understand some of it. Your father is a great man. An overpowering personality. I admire the man, but I would hate to be placed in a position to follow in his footsteps. That would be a very big order to fill! I think you are proud of being an Indian. You do not hate your traditions. You are just afraid of having to be a second Chayton!

Lakota, there is nothing wrong with that. I would be too."

Lakota opened up even more now that he felt some understanding for his position. "That's only part of it. As Chayton's son, I had to marry the right girl. Never mind my high school sweetheart, with whom I was secretly going steady. No, the tribe had to find the right girl for me. They found Ehawee, a certified Sioux princess. I have nothing against Ehawee. She is nice enough, and she too had no choice in the matter. It was decided that we would make the perfect couple, and I gave in. I tried to explain things to my high school sweetheart, but she could not understand why I did not resist. She became very angry, and never spoke to me again. I know I deeply hurt her, and she did not deserve that."

It was Doctor Johnson who once again brought the conversation back to the problem at hand. "Lakota, we can discuss your marriage at a later date, but now we have to decide if you're ready to enter rehab. I can get you into the very best program here in California. But you have to want to stop drinking, or it won't be very successful. I expect we can get you a suspended sentence based on your willingness to enter a rehab program."

Clint asked if he could take Lakota aside for a minute. When they were away from the others, Clint told Lakota about Clara. "I did not want go over the details in front of Antoine, but I want to impress on you what it was like to see her when the police finally found her. Lakota, alcohol can do that to a person.

Don't let that happen to you. You are better than that. Don't stop being the guy all of us admire for the heroic rescue of Sharleen. You're strong enough to stop drinking!"

The two of them returned from their private talk and Lakota said, "I think I am more than ready to enter rehab. I hate this drinking, I really do. I'll have to enter into a deep discussion with my father once I lick this problem. If he is really the man you think he is, he will understand how I feel. As for my marriage; an Indian wedding does not recognize the possibility of divorce. I am enough Indian to agree with that. I am afraid I might have ruined one girl's life; I am not about to do that to another."

While Lakota was talking to the men, the girls had circled the wagons around Ehawee. Ehawee had been brought up even more strictly than Lakota. As an Indian princess, she had been raised to carry on the traditions of the Indian nation, even if that meant marrying into another tribe. Unlike Lakota, she had never dated; she considered it normal that her tribe would select her husband. Actually, she had been very happy to marry Lakota. He was very handsome, and treated her like the princess she was. Until his drinking got the best of him, she considered herself a lucky girl.

Sharleen felt terrible for Ehawee. She looked across at the girl who sat slumped on the couch between J. J. and Sharleen's mother. She really liked this young girl, and had always admired how erectly she proudly carried her tall, bony frame. She hated to see her sitting there, holding her head down and compulsively wringing her hands together.

Ehawee kept saying over and over, "You don't understand. It's not his fault. He did not mean to hurt me. He loves me; he really does."

This made the other women angry. J. J., especially, did not want hear that it was not his fault. "Damn it, Ehawee, next you are going to tell us that you deserve it, that it is your fault!"

Ehawee sat up. "No I'm not stupid like that. Of course he should not have hit me. And yes, it has happened before. It's always the liquor. He goes out of control when he drinks. I try to make him stop, but he has demons I do not understand. When he is not drinking, he is a great guy. I love him, and I am happy they chose him for me. So don't start in with me about divorce. Besides our civil ceremony, we too had an Indian wedding, and divorce does not exist. I'm staying with him no matter what."

This little outburst from the usually timid Ehawee surprised the women.

J. J. took back a little of what she had said. "Okay, you love him, and I have to admit, until tonight I considered him a charming man. I never expected anything like this from him. But you have to face it, he is an alcoholic. They are always sorry when they are sober, and they promise never to do it again. So, where do we go from here?"

Sharleen tried to explain. "My father was very strict about alcohol. He never allowed it in the house. I was given a lot of free rein while growing up, but drinking alcohol was not part of the deal. Since none of my family drank, it was easy to follow their example. I am really shocked that Lakota of all people is the one who developed a drinking problem. He was always the perfect one. The cousin I looked up to. It was sort of a given that if anyone could rescue me from the Mafia it would be he. I wonder what happened."

Again Ehawee repeated, "He's got demons, and we have to help him. I don't want to lose him. I really love him."

J. J. put her arm around Ehawee. "I have to respect that you won't give up. Even after what happened tonight, you are willing to fight for him. The men have taken him aside, and my father-in-law is planning to get him to commit to going into rehab. Let's wait and see what they agreed on."

XLVI

On her return to Bermuda, Sharleen found a letter waiting for her. She did not recognize the return address and quickly opened it. It was from Chico.

The first thing that came out of the envelope was a picture of Chico's family. The plump redhead standing next to him was almost a foot shorter than he. The two boys standing in front of them were almost identical. With their long, dark-blond hair and freckled faces, they did not look like either parent. Greedily, Sharleen started reading.

> Dear Sharleen,
>
> I got your address from Bennie. It took a long time for him to give it to me. We don't see each other very often, and initially he forgot he promised to give me your address. Sorry to report, he is not doing very well. I think it is more mentally than physically. I don't know if he told you when he was

out there, but he was recently divorced. Now his second wife is divorcing him, and he is living with a new girlfriend. I've been married for seven years. Victoria (Vicky) is from England. She is a nurse, and I met her when Guido was in the hospital. We have five-year-old twin boys. If you look at the picture, you can see we are a pretty diverse family. Guido made me go to night school to get a degree in accounting so I could eventually run his trucking firm. He retired three years ago, but is still living with us. He won't hear about a retirement home, and we love to have him. The boys think of him as their grandfather. That is nice, since Vicky's father lives in London, and her mother died even before she emigrated to the United States. As you know, both my parents are deceased.

Guido and I talk about you often. I keep telling him your arrival was the beginning of the break-up of the Fuentes Family. I am sure it set in motion events that allowed Giovanni to disband the family. I think he always wanted to do that, but because he clung to some old-fashioned traditions, he dared not do it. Guido strongly disagrees, but he has come around and speaks of you with respect. I myself am very happy you arrived.

I hated the Mafia, and am grateful to you for causing the break-up of the family.

Giovanni knew I did not like the Mafia, that's why he assigned me as your driver. He felt I was the only one who would guard you with my life, regardless of what happened within the family. And I was loyal to him because he took me in after my parents died. I was only fifteen when both my parents and my four sisters died in a house fire. The fire was set by an opposing family as retribution for the supposed role my father had played in the killing of a member of their family. I felt our family was just as bad. Men like Big Joe killed for the slightest provocation, and Giovanni was never strong enough to stop him. I am glad I am finally able to tell you all this. As your driver, I liked you a lot, but I was always a little afraid of you. After all, as Giovanni's wife you were my absolute boss, and I could never guess your true feelings about the family.

On the night you saw me in the hallway, I was on my way to check that no one had harmed you. Believe it or not, Giovanni made me do that every night. It was impossible for me to arrange your escape, and I was glad some men had come to get you.

Our trucking company is doing very well, and we recently signed some very profitable contracts. If business stays good I would love to take my family to visit you in Bermuda. I have told Vicky all about you, and she would

love to meet you. I hope you're doing well,
and that you think about me once in a while.
Sincerely,
Chico

When Sharleen put down the letter, she sat quietly for a while. How could everything be so different from what she had thought to be reality? Giovanni was never the man she thought he was. Clearly he was never that strong, debonair tycoon she fell in love with. But on the other hand, he was not as bad or as cruel as she had thought when she fled.

Sharleen kept thinking about how different things were from what she thought them to be. Take Lakota, for instance. She had always thought of him as her strong cousin, fiercely proud of his heritage while in reality he was crumbling under the yoke of the image she had of him. She was so glad that, in the end, everything had turned out all right for him.

One of the therapists in Lakota's rehab program confronted Lakota's guilt about abandoning his high school girlfriend. She explained that it is quite common for girls to get jilted at least once while still in high school. Almost all of them get over the heartbreak. Usually, by the time they fall in love with the next guy. But with Lakota's girlfriend, she suspected something else. She pointed out that the girl seemed quite okay with the fact they kept their relationship a secret. Was that because she also wanted it to be a secret from her family? How would her family have reacted if they had known she was going with a Native American boy? Lakota had never thought of it in that way. When the therapist asked him if she had ever introduced him to her folks, he had to admit she had not. She always kept him carefully away, under the pretext she was helping him keep their relation a secret.

After Lakota had been in the rehab program for three weeks, he returned to the reservation. Ehawee thought he had things under control and his drinking was a thing of the past. Less than two weeks later, she found out it wasn't.

She woke up in the middle of the night and heard Lakota stumbling around in the kitchen. When she got up to find out what he was doing, she found him sitting at the kitchen table with a bottle of vodka in front of him.

"Where the hell did you get that?" she yelled in their Sioux dialect. *"Damn you! Why are you doing this?"*

Lakota just stared at her and did not answer. Ehawee ran over to the table and took a swipe at the bottle of vodka. It fell over, and its contents flowed all over the table. Lakota jumped up and tried to right the bottle. Ehawee pushed him back and started beating on his chest with both her fists.

"I can't help it!" Lakota cried. *"I can't sleep. My insides keep turning around; I'm scared."*

"Don't do this! Don't spoil everything! We were doing so well. You have to stop!"

"I tried, I can't. I can't do it!"

"I love you, but if you don't stop drinking, I'll leave you."

Lakota burst out in tears. ***"No, please don't leave me! I'm trying to stop... help me!"***

He fell to the ground, crying. Ehawee threw herself on top of him. ***"We can do it together. We can do it! I love you, I'll never leave you. We will win."***

Ehawee smothered Lokota's cries with her kisses. She tightened her long legs around him and kissed him even harder. Lokota's arms went around her, and the two of them rolled around the floor in a tight embrace. Spontaneously they started pulling at each other's clothes, and soon they were locked in a naked embrace. Their emotions poured out, and neither of them held back when they made love.

Totally exhausted, they lay naked on the cold kitchen floor. For a long while, neither spoke. Finally Lakota said that if Ehawee would bear with him, he would return to rehab. This time he was determined to succeed.

Once Lakota successfully completed the rehab program, he was urged to sit down with his father and explain his feelings. Rather than fight his son's feelings, Chayton understood what his son was trying to convey. He showed a great deal of insight when he explained himself to Lakota.

"Being a Native American represents who I am. Our family did not come from very impressive forefathers, but I worked myself up to become the leader on our reservation. The unofficial chief of our tribe.

I am who I am because of my Indian heritage. I believe in our traditions, and I feel called upon to help preserve as much as possible of our culture. I am the tribe, and the tribe is me. But you are my son, and if I have to choose, I will always choose you! You are my son. I will not let my feelings for the tribe destroy you. Lakota, go where your heart leads you. You have my blessing. You were not born to save the tribe!"

Lakota felt as if a huge weight had fallen from his shoulders. He gladly accepted Chayton's offer to pay for the honeymoon he and Ehawee never had. Rather than a cruise or a trip to Hawaii, Ehawee chose to go to Bermuda to visit Sharleen and Clint. Her choice proved to be the gateway to a whole new life for the two of them.

During their two-week stay in Bermuda, Ehawee fell in love with the island. Besides the natural beauty, it was the lifestyle that attracted her. She was amazed that J. J. could retain an identity of her own, even though Antoine had become extremely successful. Actually J. J., as a Cabinet member, was much better known than Antoine, but that did not affect the relationship within their marriage. The more Ehawee talked with Sharleen and J. J., the more she wanted to live in Bermuda. She longed for the freedom these two had. The freedom they enjoyed to live their lives unencumbered by family tradition or cultural boundaries. She discussed the possibility of moving to Bermuda with Lakota, and he decided to talk to Clint about it.

Lakota approached Clint about the possibility of settling in Bermuda. He never intended to ask Clint for a job. He just wanted to know the legal ramifications and the job possibilities on the island. He was caught totally off guard when Clint started talking very enthusiastically about his coming to work with Antoine and him.

"We really need someone like you. The company has grown so fast, we have trouble keeping up with the daily operation. Antoine is the finance man, but by his own admission, stinks as far as daily operations are concerned. I am totally involved in the kitchen operation of the three restaurants. Sharleen desperately needs help in running the daily stuff. Man, can we use you!"

Lakota said he was surprised that Clint would trust him, given his history with alcoholism.

Clint brushed that aside in a hurry. "That was just a temporary divergence. That was not the real you. I know the real Lakota. Lakota to me is the man who managed to rescue Sharleen after I had failed. I could not pull off the operation; you did. Man, you're my hero! Whatever I said that night about alcoholism, that was not about you. I would love to have you join us!"

By this time Lakota was in tears. "Getting Sharleen out of that damned mansion was the normal thing to do. She is my cousin, and those guys had to keep their hands off her. But to step in when the situation is not obvious, that is a gift. Many people think that when you successfully complete rehab, the battle is won. But that is far from true. Yes, to get through rehab is hard, very hard. To stay on the right track is even harder! For a guy like me, without any real prospects, it's impossible without the support of people who care about you. Ehawee and I have talked about you and Sharleen a lot. To us, you two are the perfect couple, living the ideal life. And now you're asking us to join you. If you think of me as rescuing Sharleen, what do you think you are doing to us as a couple right now? You are my cousin; you are my family, coming to rescue me. Ehawee won't believe what you just offered."

Sharleen felt all warm and fuzzy thinking of how well things had turned out. Lakota and Ehawee went to the States to get their things in order and returned to Bermuda to settle there for good. Clint went way out to pave the way for them. Even before they returned he saw an adorable little house in a great neighborhood near the beach. He bought it and had it furnished for Lakota and Ehawee.

When Sharleen pointed out that what he did was a little extravagant, his response was, "Look, we can afford it. We've made a lot of money lately, and what good is success if you can't share it with those you love? I really, really like those two."

Now Sharleen had two bosom friends; J. J. and Ehawee. At first J. J. thought Ehawee was too submissive. But that was not true at all. Ehawee knew what she wanted, and was not afraid to fight for it. She had proved that by refusing to give up on Lakota. Sharleen admired the inner toughness of the girl. She

271

knew who she was, and was proud of her heritage, something Sharleen had to learn later in life.

It did not take long for Ehawee to carve out a place for herself in the personnel department of the company. She was a competent judge of people. She did not presume to have any expertise in hiring kitchen help. But she was a great judge as to who would make a good waiter/waitress or bellhop. Sharleen started relying on her to make the final choice on new hires.

The very best part for Sharleen was seeing the relationship between Lakota and Ehawee grow. From the beginning, Ehawee had told her she loved Lakota, and her actions showed it. But Sharleen was not too sure about Lakota's feelings for Ehawee. She could see that he liked her very much. That was obvious. But did he love her, or was he only true to his marriage vows?

Sharleen did not get a clear answer until one day when the seven of them went for a long walk along the beach. They had been out for several hours, and the sun was just starting to set. They walked along slowly, admiring the color of the water and the sky. Ehawee leaned on Lakota's shoulder, and Sharleen watched him take her hand and lovingly gaze at her. He looked into Ehawee's eyes, and his look told Sharleen the truth. He did not need any wedding vows to stay true to this girl. He loved her.

XLVII

Sharleen sat at her desk in her office in The Ocean View. She was deep in thought, staring at the ocean when J. J. came barging in.

"Wait till you hear this! Some creeps approached me about allowing a casino here in Bermuda. I told them no way! We don't want to become a Batista-like island, conveniently located close to the United States. But they persisted. Even offered to make it worth my while if I promised to propose it in a Cabinet meeting!"

"I'm not surprised they approached you. They know you are Antoine's wife, which indirectly connects you to The Ocean View. Clint told me a while ago that some syndicate, closely linked to gambling casinos in Asia, was trying to buy this hotel. Apparently they repeatedly approached Raffi Nussbaum, our main shareholder."

"Is he willing to sell?"

"Hell no! He thinks Antoine is a genius, and regularly consults with him on financial matters. The way Antoine constructed our limited partnership fascinated Raffi, and he made it possible for us to raise the money needed to go ahead with the plans to build. Antoine invited him to come to Bermuda to look over the plans. He met Clint, and the two clicked. They became real good buddies. Raffi introduced Antoine to several investors with deep pockets. Raffi remained the major investor, and he controls the general partner of our limited partnership. Antoine isolated Raffi's personal fortune from liability by making one of the many corporations he controls the general partner, not Raffi himself. Next time he is in Bermuda you should ask Antoine to introduce him."

"Have you ever met him?"

"Yeah, way back when we first got started. Lately he only comes for one-day visits, and the three of them only discuss business. I'll ask Clint to urge him to stay over for a day. We could all have dinner together. You'll love the guy. He's all personality, talks a mile a minute, and has enough stories to tell about strange people he has met to keep you amused all night. He's young for a person who has done so much. They tell me he started with nothing and is worth several billion."

"Should I tell the prime minister that I was approached about allowing casinos?"

"Of course! To protect yourself you should be very open about it. Who knows what they might say to put you in a bad position. You should also let the prime minister know they tried to get control of The

Ocean View. Do you know who is behind the group that approached you?"

"Haven't got the slightest."

"Well, we'd better find out. It's best to know who we're dealing with before they make any further moves. I bet it's the same people who approached Clint about the hotel."

After discussing it some more, Sharleen decided it would be best if they asked Clint and Antoine their opinion as to what to do.

Clint suggested the first thing they should do would be to check if the people who approached J. J. were the same as those who had approached him. He asked if J. J. had any way of getting back to the person who approached her. J. J. said that she was sure they would try again in a few days.

Sure enough, three days later, while J. J. was leaving Government House, the same two men approached her. She told them she did not want to talk on the street and directed them to a nearby café.

J. J. took a seat in the back and the two men quickly joined her. "Have you thought about what we asked you to do?" one of the men asked. He appeared to be the leader.

"Look, I'm not going to discuss anything with you till I know who you are. I smell a rat. I think you were hired by our opposing political party to get some dirt on me."

The man laughed. "That's funny, really funny. No, we don't have time for games like that. We need your cooperation to get your government to allow us to open a casino here in Bermuda."

J. J. tried to get more information out of them by developing a discussion. "We have plenty of opportunity here to gamble. Why do we need a casino?

"Nah, you don't have any *real* gambling."

"Yes we do," J. J. responded. "We play our dice game Crown & Anchor in the summer. And several places in Hamilton show games on TV on which people bet. And there is the Internet. It gives access to online casinos and poker. Besides all that there are private clubs where one can play bingo or tombola. So why would we need a casino?"

Now the second man spoke up. "We know that your government is looking to allow casinos in the near future in order to boost tourism."

The spokesman cut in, "Licenses will be given to new hotels that still have to be built. We plan to take over an existing hotel and secure a license before any new hotel is completed. With your cooperation we can do this, and hopefully secure a monopoly position. If you and your husband cooperate with us, we'll make it very rewarding for you."

J. J. pretended to be indignant. "And you expect me to talk to you about that without knowing who you are!?"

The spokesman replied. "You're right. Okay then, I'm Roger Chen, and this is Jimmy Kelly. We are the contact men for our group."

"And what group is that?" J. J. quickly asked.

Jimmy looked at Roger with a questioning look. He was not sure they could answer, but Roger had no trouble answering. "We are part of one of Asia's foremost casino operators. You have probably never heard of us because we do not promote our name to the general public, but most people have heard of our casinos."

J. J. laughed. "Good for you. I'm glad for you that you are a big casino operator, but that tells me nothing. Who are you? Who's the big guy behind your operation?"

The two men looked at each other and Roger went ahead to explain. "Our group is called EurAsia Partners. We do have more interests besides casinos, but the division which operates the casinos is called Kejayaan Besar (*great success*). We report to Mike Sundaram. Sorry, we don't have any contact with upper management. The group is too big for that. But Mike is empowered to make a deal with you, and we will put you in contact with him."

J. J. knew she was hitting pay dirt. "He will come here to Bermuda to meet with me? And why did you mention my husband? Do you think I need his permission to make a deal?"

Roger was quick to assure her that was not the case. "Oh, no. We know you are an independent lady. Sorry, we did not mean to give you the impression that you needed his approval. No, we mentioned we wanted to take over an existing hotel, and he is part owner of The Ocean View, the biggest and newest. That is the hotel we are aiming for."

"I'll discuss all this with my husband. But I have to warn you, we are quite well off, and it will take a lot of money to make my husband part with his interest in our hotel."

"Don't worry, we know that. Our group has plenty of cash; you deliver, we pay."

J. J. got up. "Meet me here next Monday at three in the afternoon, and I'll give you our answer at that time."

XLVIII

The first thing Clint did was to call Raffi to inquire about Kejayaan Besar. Raffi told Clint that he had heard of the group. If he remembered correctly, it was a bad bunch. He promised to call back as soon as he had the full scoop on their operation.

Raffi called back in four days and reported, "It really is a bad bunch. They do operate a few casinos, but that it not the major part of their operation. Their funds come from money laundering and narcotics. Lately they have also been engaged in the sex trade. Rumor has it they buy kidnapped women and girls from the ex-soviet satellite states and sell them, mostly to Europe, but also to North and South America. The leading figures are Kai Sambanthan, the leader. They call him Harris. The second in command is Haikal Vasudevan. He goes by Richard. Their number one hatchet man is Ameer Suppiah who calls himself Andrew. Mike Sundaram and Devan Priya seem to be related to Vasudevan, and those two are their contacts to their so-called legitimate operations. All four leaders are wanted in several countries, and Interpol is looking for them. If they get caught they'll most likely be put to death in some countries. The saying goes, 'You kill the snake by cutting off the head.' Mike and Devan are like Teflon. No one can pin anything on them. They've been arrested, but there is always a complete lack of evidence, and no country has been able to convict them."

Raffi went on to warn Clint that this was a highly dangerous group and not to mess with them. "If you cross them, they'll kill you just as soon as shake your hand. I'll contact Servans Te *(Keeping you safe)* and hire them to protect all of you in case they want to play rough."

Clint objected. "That won't be necessary. We have adequate protection here. I have already contacted my friend, Rodi Knowles, the chief of police. They're keeping an eye out for us to ensure they don't try anything."

Clint's nonchalant attitude annoyed Raffi. "Damn it, Clint! You live happily on your safe little island. You have no idea what happens in the real world. Servans Te has been protecting me for years. Guys like me face the constant threat of being kidnapped for ransom. Servans Te has a worldwide network and protects me wherever I go. Like it or not, I'll hire them immediately, and ask them to send at least two of their Latin American agents to watch over your group on the island."

As Raffi had ordered, two agents of Servans Te arrived within two days. But discussions as to what J. J. had to do and say during her meeting with Roger and Jimmy were interrupted by what happened at the country club.

Ehawee had been taking golf lessons at the country club when, during a lunch break, the new general manager came over to introduce himself. During their conversation, he referred to Mikie as "that big freak they use at the hotel as the official greeter." Ehawee was outraged, and punched the man in the face. It was not quite clear if she knocked him out or if he hit his head against a table when her punch knocked him backwards. In any case, he was out cold when the staff rushed over to help.

The incident caused quite a commotion, and the staff called the police. When Rodi Knowles arrived, he immediately blamed the general manager for the incident. Being new, the man had no idea that Mikie was a national icon on the island, and that it was not acceptable to say anything derogatory about the gentle giant. The whole affair was shushed when the American holding company, which owned the country club, agreed to transfer the man to one of their properties in Jamaica.

XLIX

The agents from Servans Te insisted that J. J. would not be allowed to meet by herself with Roger and Jimmy. Sharleen volunteered to go along; everybody agreed that she was the logical choice, since she could be introduced as representing an important part of the ownership of The Ocean View.

During the meeting, J. J. carefully outlined the demands which Antoine had endlessly rehearsed with her. She explained that they were willing to sell their interest in the hotel for fair market value. In addition, for persuading Raffi Nussbaum and other shareholders to sell, and the government of Bermuda to grant an exclusive casino license, they wanted twenty million dollars. The way the twenty million had to be paid took J. J. more than ten minutes to explain. An additional sum had to be available in the off chance someone had to be bribed.

During the meeting, J. J. noticed that Roger was fascinated by Sharleen. He could not keep his eyes off her; it was Jimmy who took careful notes so he could accurately relay J. J.'s demands. When the meeting broke up, the two men promised to contact their bosses and get back to them within the next two or three weeks.

On the way home, J. J. said to Sharleen, "Boy, that Roger fellow really went for you. He was drooling over you. He just about had his tongue hanging out. Girl, you really make men's heads spin! It was almost like going with you to the beach when you wear that cute red bikini of yours. Maybe next time we should take Mikie along to protect you."

The plan was for Sharleen to wear a wire during their next meeting. Authorities in several countries had tried but failed to get some hard evidence against Roger and Mike. If Sharleen could record the conversation, during which they probably would incriminate themselves, then Interpol could arrest them and use them to get at their bosses.

It took four weeks before they heard from Roger and Jimmy. They arrived on a huge private yacht which was flying the Panamanian flag. They sent word that they wanted to meet on the yacht because it was best suited for a private conversation.

While they were preparing to go and meet with the two men, Ehawee announced that she was coming along. She was not going to let her two friends do this without her. "Look, I'm a lot stronger than either of you two. You'll need me in case of an emergency. Besides, I'll carry an extra mic in case Sharleen's fails. They are so small, I don't see how they can possibly work."

Clint explained the logistical plan to the girls. He, Antoine, Lakota, and the two agents from Servans Te would be on his boat to record the conversation coming from Sharleen's wire. Since Ehawee would also be wired, they would take a second receiver. The meeting had been arranged for late in the evening, so he could take advantage of the darkness to maneuver his boat close enough to pick up the signals. He had arranged with Rodi Knowles that several squad cars would be parked out of sight, not too far from the dock. He had asked that a minimum of eight policemen be available in case he signaled that the girls were in danger.

When Clint saw the way Sharleen was dressed he said, "No you don't. You're not going like that."

"What's wrong with the way I'm dressed?" Sharleen asked.

"That cleavage is way too much. I can damn near see your nipples!"

"Don't be such a prude. I have to distract those guys by giving them something to look at. If I don't, they might spot these microphones under my armpits and that sender strapped to my back. Boy, these things are uncomfortable."

"From what J. J. tells us, you distract them enough already. Do me a favor; put on another blouse. And you, Ehawee, what are you doing? You normally don't have that much up front."

Ehawee laughed. "Thanks for the compliment! You don't have to rub it in. I know I'm flat as a board, but now it's an advantage. I can hide twice

285

as much as Sharleen. I'm wearing falsies. They are specially made for spying; complements of Servans Te. One side has the mic built in, and the other the sender and a small battery. I'm a virtual broadcasting powerhouse. They can hear me all the way back in the States. Hello, Daddy Chayton, can you hear me?"

Everybody had to laugh and Lakota said, "If Dad knew what we are about to do he would kill me! He would never condone exposing you girls to this risk."

At nine that evening, the three girls boarded the sleek yacht to meet with Roger and Jimmy.

At the top of the gangplank they were stopped by a nicely dressed man. "Sorry, ladies. I must check you over before you can board."

Spontaneously Ehawee turned, and while going back down the gangplank she said, "I've not come here to be felt up by you! If you are looking for a cheap thrill, go to a whorehouse downtown."

Out of nowhere Roger appeared. "Let them pass, Ameer. Kai wants to talk to them, and he is not going to like it if you delay them."

On Clint's boat the men clearly heard what Roger said. Antoine whispered, "Bingo! The big bosses are aboard the boat. We have the big fish right here in Bermuda."

Clint immediately notified Rodi to be on the alert, but not to approach the yacht until he was told the girls were out of harm's way.

Roger took the three ladies into a very nicely appointed lounge and started to introduce them to the three men standing at the bar. "This is Mr. Sambanthan; call him Harris."

Harris came over to shake their hands. With a heavy accent he said, "So nice to meet you. Please sit down and be comfortable. May I offer you a drink?"

Roger did not wait for the girls to answer, and continued to introduce Haikal Vasudevan and Devan Priya. They had already run into Ameer Suppiah at the top of the gangplank.

The three girls refused the offer of drinks, and Sharleen got right to business. "Have you considered our offer?" She was scared stiff. They had not expected to be confronted by the very top of the group. She had fully expected only to record Roger and Jimmy and quickly leave the yacht. Now she hoped that her signal was being picked up, and somehow they would get word to her as to what to do.

The moment they heard the ringleaders were aboard the yacht, Clint maneuvered his boat even closer to the yacht, and carefully placed his bow against the stern. Lakota and the two Servans Te agents jumped on the tiny space on the lower deck right behind the engine room. Lakota threw a rope around the railing of the deck above him and climbed up. He dropped the rope ladder, which he had taken from Clint's boat, to allow the two agents to join him on the top deck. Clint and Antoine covered the operation with rifles they had gotten from Rodi. When the three men had taken a defensive position on the top deck, Clint secured his boat to the yacht, and he and Antoine joined the men on the top deck.

J. J. knew she had to keep the conversation going, so nothing would look suspicious, and they could leave after having made the deal. She drew on all the knowledge she had absorbed from the briefings Antoine had given her while studying how to present their offer. Devan Priya kept staring at Sharleen. He got up slowly and approached her. Before Sharleen could avoid his outstretched hand he ripped off her blouse, revealing the wires leading to the microphone under her arms, and the sender on her back. All the men jumped up and started shouting at the same time. Ameer quickly ripped the wires loose.

Nobody noticed Ehawee, who carefully kept aiming her falsies in the direction of what was happening. She did not realize how successful she was. Her signal was loud and clear, and Lakota had a receiver tuned to a tiny mic in his ear.

Kai Sambanthan grabbed the intercom and shouted into it for the captain to immediately start the engines and get the yacht on the way. He forgot that the intercom was set to only be heard on the bridge and in the engine room. Nobody was in either place.

Ehawee pulled a ten-inch dagger out of her right boot and told Sharleen in Sioux, *"Grab J. J. and get behind me."* She waved the dagger at the men and shouted, "If anyone comes near us I'll cut his balls off." She continued in Sioux, *"If you can hear me we are in the main lounge to the right of the foyer which faces the gangplank. Hurry if you hear this. Watch out, it looks like one man has a pistol."*

Lakota heard her loud and clear. Without hesitation he mouthed, "Follow me!" and raced in the direction of the gangplank. In front of the foyer there was a lone guard smoking a cigarette. Lakota dropped to the deck and crawled behind the guard. With a swift stroke of his blackjack he knocked the man out cold. He signaled to the others to join him. They entered the foyer and turned right. When they reached the lounge, they burst through the door. Ameer was quick and drew his pistol. The two Servans Te agents were quicker. Both of them fired, and Ameer went down before he could release a shot. None of the other men were carrying weapons.

Clint signaled on his cell phone for Rodi and the police to storm the yacht. The gunshots coming from the lounge had alerted the crew, and they came storming out of their rooms. Lakota tried to barricade the door to the lounge. Before he could get the door secured, a crew member armed with an automatic rifle tried to enter. Lakota kicked him in the groin and quickly snatched the automatic rifle before he slammed the door shut.

Before long, they heard gunshots as the police boarded the yacht and started disarming the crew. By now, the girls were safely huddled in the arms of their husbands. Clint took off his shirt and put it around Sharleen to replace her tattered blouse. Gratefully Sharleen pressed against his bare chest. He was still as strong and well cut as he had been in high school.

There was a loud knock on the lounge door. "It's me, Rodi. Open up! It's all clear. The entire crew is in custody. You'll never guess what we found!"

What they found was amazing! In a room tucked away in the bowels of the yacht, they released fourteen women ranging from about seventeen to middle thirties. They were terrified, and had trouble understanding what was happening. Only one of them spoke English. Rodi called an ambulance to take away Ameer. He was dead. The rest of the men who had been captured in the lounge were carted off by the police. The crew had already been taken away in paddy wagons.

Rodi thought Sharleen, J. J., and Ehawee would be better able to calm down the women they had found than he and his men. He led the three of them downstairs to where the women were huddled together. Sharleen ran towards the women and threw her arms around one who looked like she was in shock.

As she embraced the woman she gently rocked her back and forth, repeating over and over, "It's okay. It's okay, don't be afraid; we're here to help." The woman looked up at her. She could not have been more than seventeen. Sharleen kissed her on the cheek and repeated again, "It's okay, no one will hurt you. I'll hold you." Gratefully the young girl put both her arms around Sharleen's neck and buried her head in her shoulder.

J. J. was less emotional, and instantly knew what to do. She sat on the floor and motioned to the women to join her. They formed a circle around her and she signaled for them to hold hands. Using words from the many languages she spoke, she signaled the women to join her in a Russian lullaby she had learned as a child in boarding school. The effect was amazing. One by one the women joined in, and those who did not know the words hummed along. The crying stopped, and the group seemed to relax slightly.

One of the girls spoke up. She was the only one who could speak English. "How did you know we were kept on this boat? Who sent you to free us? Are we really free, or are you going to sell us to another group?"

J. J. started to explain very carefully. She paused frequently to let the English-speaking woman translate in one of the languages she spoke. There were still a few who only understood from sign language what was happening. One of the women, who appeared to be the oldest of the group, came over to sit next to J. J. She took both her hands and repeatedly bowed her head while saying several short phrases J. J. did not understand.

The English-speaking woman who had been translating said she believed the woman was saying, "I owe you my life."

"Tell her that is not true," J. J. said. "Tell her that for us it is just as great a gift that God let us find you as it is for you that you were found." She pulled the woman over to her and kissed her on both cheeks.

The women were brought to the Ocean View Hotel. Sharleen wanted them placed in the luxury suites, only four of which were unoccupied. She also wanted them to room only two to a suite. Six women were brought to a nearby hotel, which made three of their best suites available. The government cooperated by making good medical care available. The government further ensured that no journalists were allowed to approach the women for a week, and then only after the medical staff gave their okay.

L

The capture of Kai Sambanthan and his gang was headline news all over the world. People who had never heard of Kai's criminal gang could still relate to the freeing of the fourteen women who had been held captive on his yacht. Interpol rolled up the rest of the gang on information they squeezed out of the men captured in Bermuda. Many countries wanted to try them, but the authorities made sure they wound up in countries that would lock them up for good.

For a while there was some squabbling over jurisdiction. The reason Kai had been so elusive was that he had been living on his yacht for many years. Even his casinos could not be directly connected to him. They were officially controlled by several companies operating out of Malaysia and Singapore. His narcotics dealings were all through a loosely connected network of small-time freelancers.

His human trafficking operation was set up like the old slave trade. He would buy women kidnapped by gangs. These gangs operated mostly in Romania, Ukraine, Belarus, Kazakhstan, and Uzbekistan. The women would then be auctioned off to invited guests while his yacht was sailing on the high seas, out of sight of any law enforcement officials. The guest lists which Interpol impounded on the yacht revealed many interesting names. Some were well-respected political as well as business leaders.

Two days after the arrests and the impoundment of the yacht, Raffi Nussbaum arrived on his private plane. On the one hand, he was delighted that Kai and his cronies had been arrested, and delirious about the women being freed. But on the other hand, he was angry with Clint and Antoine because they had exposed their wives to such danger. He wanted to meet each of the women found on the yacht to hand them a cashier's check for fifty thousand dollars to help resettle them, and as an apology for the world letting this terrible thing happen to them. He cried when he heard that several of the women had been sexually abused while held captive on the yacht. He promised each one of them to pay for their trip back home. If they wished to escape all the publicity, they could choose to travel on his private plane.

When he came to a dark-haired seventeen-year-old girl, she thanked him using several Hebrew words. Raffi promptly answered in fluent Hebrew. When all the women had been introduced, he took the young girl aside. Her name was Lital, and she was from Uzbekistan. Raffi asked her to tell him more about herself and how she was kidnapped.

Never Too Late

Lital admitted that she had run away from home when she was seventeen. Her family had tried to force her into an arranged marriage, but she could not stand the boy they had selected for her. She was to marry the boy as soon as she turned eighteen. One afternoon, she met Igor at the local disco. It was the place in town where young people gathered, but her parents had strictly forbidden her to go there. About a month after she met Igor, the two of them took off for Kazakhstan, hoping her family could not trace her in that big country. They found jobs waiting on tables in a small restaurant. One night, two men came in and talked to Igor for quite a while. Igor asked her to step outside with him. The next thing she knew, she was dragged into a car, and someone injected something into her arm. After that, the only thing she knew for sure was that they brought her via the Black Sea to the Mediterranean, where she was smuggled onto the yacht.

She had been on the yacht for a week, and had heard rumors she and the rest of the women would be auctioned off in a few days. Instead, the yacht traveled full speed for several days. She had no idea they had docked in Bermuda when they were all locked up together in a big room. She spoke Hebrew, Uzbek, and very little Russian. While in Kazakhstan, her knowledge of the latter two languages allowed her to communicate with the locals. On the yacht, she could only communicate with half of the women she was locked up with. She often spoke with one of the women whom they took upstairs almost every night to have sex with. She prayed they would leave her alone. The woman explained that she was lucky to be small and slender. They preferred the larger, well-rounded Russian women.

Lital told Raffi she was very grateful for his offer to pay her way to go back home, but she did not want to return to her family. When Raffi asked where she wanted to go, Lital said she wanted to go to the United States. Raffi explained that would be difficult to arrange. She could not claim to be seeking political asylum. Besides, she could not speak English. Raffi asked if she would like to come to England and live with his family. His two young daughters were fluent in Hebrew, as was his whole family. He was sure he could arrange things so she could stay in England. Lital was ecstatic.

Most of the women wanted to go home as soon as possible. After they had been outfitted with some decent travel clothes, the government of Bermuda made all arrangements for them. Two of them elected to accept Raffi's offer, and returned home on his plane. Clint confirmed that the government had used their connections in the various countries to make sure the families of the women were able to receive them and provide the proper psychological care for them if needed.

J. J. was very concerned about the mental condition of the women who had repeatedly been sexually abused while on the yacht. She did not think it would be wise to let them go home right away. She spoke to Sharleen about her concerns, and the two of them decided to petition the governor to allow these women to stay temporarily in Bermuda. They promised to take them into their homes, so the women wouldn't even need work permits. Sharleen had the larger house with three bedrooms, so she took three women home with her, while J. J. took the other two to her home.

Late during the first night that the women were staying at her house, Sharleen thought she heard a noise downstairs. When she went down to investigate, she found one of the women on a couch in the living room. She was crouched in a corner of the heavy leather couch, her head buried in her elbow, which was resting on the wide armrest. What Sharleen had heard were the woman's sobs. Sharleen went over to the couch, but when the woman saw her approach she pulled away deeper into the corner of the couch. Sharleen hesitated; she wanted to go over and comfort the woman, but the woman clearly wanted to be left alone.

Sharleen went back upstairs and took her very best robe out of the closet. She had only worn it once; it had been a gift from Clint on their first wedding anniversary. She always considered it too nice to just wear around the house. She also grabbed a pair of fuzzy slippers she had just bought. She hurried back downstairs and sat down on the couch, very close to the woman. The woman lifted her head and looked at her. Her large green eyes were like those of a frightened animal. Despite the deep circles under her eyes and the tangled-up condition of her long blond hair, Sharleen admired the woman's beauty. Sharleen held out the robe. The woman stopped sobbing and stared at her. Sharleen encouraged her to take the robe. She was aware the woman did not understand her English.

"Here, honey, just take it. It's chilly in this room, and it will feel nice to wrap yourself in it." Sharleen's gentle urging worked, and the woman reached out and accepted the robe. She put it on and smiled at Sharleen. Sharleen reached down and put the slippers on the woman's feet. She slid close to the woman, and carefully put her arm around her shoulders. The two of them sat that way silently, and Sharleen waited patiently for the woman to place her head against her shoulder.

Softly she said the woman's name, "Nina." She pointed at herself and said, "Sharleen." The woman gave her a big smile and moved closer.

In the morning when Clint came downstairs, he found Sharleen half-asleep on the couch. Nina was fast asleep in her arms. Sharleen motioned for Clint to be quiet. She carefully got up, taking care not to wake Nina. She took a blanket from a nearby chair and covered Nina. Then she pulled Clint into the library.

She closed the door and almost hysterically burst out, "Clint, we have to find the women they auctioned off! Those bastards sold them into slavery! They're being abused sexually! We have to find them and free them!" She was tearing into Clint like it was his fault.

Clint let her carry on for a bit before he quieted her down. "I agree it's horrible, but where do we start? They're spread all over the world."

Sharleen realized she had been unreasonable, yelling at Clint the way she did. "I'm sorry, honey. I know you hate it too. But I have an idea. The authorities have impounded all the records they uncovered on the yacht. Those records will be used to prosecute Kai and his cronies, but they could also be used to find the women and girls they auctioned off in the past. Those people from Interpol are still here in Bermuda, and so are the men from Servans Te. Maybe they have some ideas how we could find them. Do you think you could arrange a meeting so we can discuss this?"

Clint agreed, and immediately started contacting all the people whom he thought could help. He knew he could depend on his friend the prime minister attending, but was pleasantly surprised when the governor promised to come as well. To make sure he would not lose any of the enthusiastic responses he received, he scheduled the meeting for the very next day.

Clint opened the meeting by announcing that he would like to create a group dedicated to hunting down the kidnapped women and prosecuting individuals and organizations that dealt in human trafficking. Antoine and he were willing to put up one million dollars as seed money to get things going.

Anna Boonstra, the head of the Interpol group that had come to Bermuda, was the first to respond.

"I like the idea. As a matter of fact, I like it a lot. But we'll have to raise a lot more than a million dollars to have any impact. This is a big world, and there will be a lot of ground to cover. Unfortunately, the sex trade is a worldwide problem, and most of the time we feel helpless when asked to help locate a missing woman. We just don't have the manpower to assist in all the cases that deserve our attention."

One of the men from Servans Te agreed with Anna. "It would be great if our company could assign some agents to do nothing else but try to locate kidnapped women and girls. Unfortunately, we are only hired when it concerns runaway daughters from well-to-do families. I am not privy to what our company charges, but I guess it is pretty steep. Our management might even take on the project on a pro bono basis. Believe it or not, we do occasionally do some pro bono security work, but the expenses would still be huge. You have to be able to offer worldwide coverage. As Anna already said, that requires a lot of manpower."

An animated discussion followed. Several of the bankers present promised to contact their head offices to see if they could get some funds for the project. The governor promised to solicit through diplomatic channels. The best news came from Raffi Nussbaum. He had been listening in from his office in London on an open phone line. He waited until most of the attendees had spoken before he told Clint he had something to add. His voice came booming from the speaker phone located on the middle of the conference table. "I have two daughters, and this whole thing has been giving me nightmares. I am privileged to be able to afford to have Servans Te guard my family. But I still think, what if some creeps had kidnapped one of my daughters? In my case they would probably ask for ransom money, and against all advice I would pay it to get my daughter back. But what about the families who were not asked for ransom, and their daughters were sold for sex? There should be some agency they could turn to for help. Clint, if you manage to successfully create the group you described to us, I pledge to contribute five million English pounds, and I will raise double that amount from my friends and business associates."

When Raffi finished, the people sitting around the conference table applauded. Raffi responded, "This is the very least I can do. After meeting those lovely girls and women, I have been sick just thinking what would have happened to them if you had not accidentally found them. I agree, if we have access to the records of the auctions, we have a moral obligation to try and find the women and return them to their families."

LI

All five women who temporarily remained in Bermuda spoke Russian. J. J. had recruited Mike Aleksenko to help communicate with them.

Mike was the young American lawyer who had joined Jimmy Garretson's law office to gain experience in international law. His parents had emigrated from Russia to the States before he was born, but the family spoke Russian at home while he was growing up. Mike was a popular figure at the country club, especially among the single women, who were always eager to join the young American hunk in a game of tennis.

Sharleen called Mike and asked if he would be available to escort the women on a shopping spree. She felt it would be good for their morale to take them to the beauty parlor, followed by a trip to a small, exclusive clothes boutique where she and J. J. loved to shop.

Mike was available, and Sharleen called J. J. to tell her of her plan, and ask if she would join, together with the women staying at her house. J. J. said she had planned to take the women to the hotel for a massage; maybe they could do that first.

Sharleen pointed out that would not be a good idea. "Honey, I don't think we should do that. After what these gals have been through, we shouldn't have some stranger's hands all over their bodies rubbing and tugging at them."

"Oops, you're right. What was I thinking? Beauty parlor and nice clothes, a girl's best friend. Let's do it. Did you ask Mike to come along to explain things?"

"Yup. Mike's aboard. He really likes these women. I think he understands what they are emotionally going through. For a single guy, described by many as playboy, he is very gentle with them. I'm going to call Janet at the beauty parlor and ask if she can reserve a separate section for us. And I'll call the boutique and ask them to close the shop while we're there. I don't want people gawking at our girls. I want to spoil them; maybe they'll relax a little. Are you okay with us picking up the tab? I have an account in both places. We can split the bills later."

Mikie had been watching Nina, and he was smart enough to realize that she was in trouble. From the day she arrived at the house he had worried about her.

He asked Sharleen, "Nina not happy, why?" Sharleen explained that people had been mean to her and not treated her well. Mikie said that made him mad. He kept insisting on bringing her food. Especially candy, and his favorite chocolate drink.

Mikie had come along on the outing for the women. On the walk from the parking lot to the boutique he noticed that Nina shied away when men approached in the opposite direction on the sidewalk. After he got Sharleen's okay, he moved over next to Nina and gently offered her his hand. Nina gratefully clamped onto his big hand, and noticeably felt more comfortable walking close to the gentle giant. When the women were browsing in the store, Mr. Collins, the owner, came over to greet them. Mr. Collins was a heavyset man. He was not Asian, but his face had oriental features. When he approached Nina she darted back and quickly went to stand next to Mikie.

Mikie offered her his arm and said in a brotherly way, "It's okay. Mikie here."

For the remainder of the shopping trip, Nina stuck close to Mikie. Even when Sharleen helped her select a nice silk shirt and a matching skirt, Nina made sure Mikie was near. On the way back to the car she seemed less anguished. She was very happy with the clothes Sharleen had helped her select. While chatting happily in Russian with one of the other women, she kept her arm linked with Mikie's.

Later that evening, everybody gathered at Clint and Sharleen's house, so the women could show off their new hairdos and try on their new outfits. Everybody, including Nina, was in a good mood, and it was the first time Sharleen had heard her laugh. Sharleen was delighted with the change in Nina's appearance.

She turned to Clint and said, "I can't get over how beautiful she is. What a difference from the first time we saw her on the yacht."

Clint smiled, "I think she is your favorite, but don't treat her as a kid. She is a grown woman."

Sharleen dropped her voice and whispered, "When I get a chance I'll tell you what that woman went through. It's not pretty!"

Raffi's visit to Bermuda to confer with Antoine on a new project interrupted everything, and delayed Sharleen's telling Clint what she had heard about Nina's capture.

Raffi brought glowing reports about Lital. "My wife is crazy about that girl, and my daughters are delighted to have her as an older sister. Actually, Lital is very unsophisticated, and it is hard to tell who is older, she or my daughters. They take her all around London and introduce her to their friends. Lital loves it. I've spoken to her about eventually going home, but she says that is out of the question. She is convinced her family, especially her father, will never accept her back after she ran away from their marriage arrangement. I contacted her family, and she is right. Her father talks about her as if she is dead. I invited them to come to London to see if we could smooth things over. Her mother said that it was too early for that. She felt that eventually her husband might come around, but now she could not even mention Lital's name."

During Raffi's visit they received great news. Two kidnapped girls had already been located, and

Interpol was in the process of returning them to their families. Both had been "bought" by the owner of a massage parlor in Belgium. The owner was a woman who, in her younger days, had been a prostitute. She and her entire staff had been arrested. The report further stated that one of the girls gave a detailed description of the gang that had kidnapped her, and Interpol was investigating the lead. In addition to the two girls they were looking for, Interpol discovered five teenage French runaways who had been forced into prostitution. These girls were also safely returned to their parents.

LII

J. J. had prepared breakfast for Saskia and Ingrid, the two women staying at her house. Except for Nina and these two, all the other women rescued from the yacht had since left Bermuda.

None of the three women wanted to return to their home countries; J. J. was working on obtaining permission for them to settle in Bermuda. The prospect looked good for the two older women, but Saskia was only seventeen and that created extra difficulties.

J. J. called up the stairs for the women to come down and join her for breakfast. Only Ingrid came down, so J. J. went upstairs to get Saskia.

When she entered Saskia's bedroom she saw the girl lying unconscious on her bed. An empty bottle of diazepam still rested in her out-stretched hand.

J. J. rushed over and reached for Saskia's throat, feeling for any sign of her pulse. She found a slight pulse. J. J.'s heart was pounding in her chest; her hands were shaking so badly she had trouble reaching in her pocket for her cell phone to call emergency. At that moment Mike Aleksenko called up the stairs, asking if J. J. and Saskia were coming down. He had dropped by to see if Ingrid and Saskia wanted to join Nina and him on a tour of the sleepy fishing village of Flatts.

J. J. yelled down the stairs that Saskia was unconscious on the bed. Mike raced up the stairs. He burst into Saskia's bedroom, scooped her up in his arms, and ran down the stairs. With J.J running behind him, he raced for his car.

On the way out he yelled in Russian for the bewildered Ingrid to let him pass. "Out of the way quick! Saskia is dying. We have to get her to the hospital!" J. J. helped him shove Saskia into the back seat and jumped in next to her. While J. J. cradled Saskia in her arms, Mike drove at break-neck speed to the nearest emergency room.

He came to a screeching stop in the area reserved for arriving ambulances and J.J ran inside to get help. Two orderlies responded immediately. They placed Saskia on a gurney and raced into the emergency room. J. J. ran alongside the gurney, tears streaming down her face. Mike threw the car into the nearest parking space and sprinted behind them.

Dr. Ramos, the emergency room physician asked if J. J. or Mike knew what she had taken.

"She had an empty bottle of Diazepan in her hand", J. J. responded. "The doctors prescribed that for her continued anxiety; she's been through a lot."

Mike was completely out of breath but he managed gasp "Doctor do something quickly! You have to save her; she's only seventeen."

The doctor immediately took out a file of flumazenil and injected the full content into Saskia's arm.

By this time J. J. had regained her composure, but she was still crying, "Is she dying doctor? Will she die?"

Doctor Ramos led J.J to a chair and calmly assured her and Mike, "No, she'll be okay." He went on to explain, "Looks like you got her here in time. Although not usually fatal when taken alone, a diazepam overdose is considered a medical emergency. It generally requires the immediate attention of medical personnel. The antidote for an overdose of diazepam, or any other benzodiazepine, is flumazenil. This drug is only used in cases with severe respiratory depression or cardiovascular complications.

"Because flumazenil is a short-acting drug and the effects of diazepam can last for days, several doses of flumazenil may be necessary. Artificial respiration and stabilization of cardiovascular functions may also be necessary. I'll have her brought over to the intensive care unit and we'll keep a close eye on her."

Doctor Ramos cleared the way for J. J. and Mike to go with Saskia to the I.C. unit. On the way J. J. called her home hoping Ingrid would pick-up. When she did Mike told her in Russian that Saskia would be okay. Ingrid explained that she had used sign language to explain to the emergency responders that Saskia had been taken by car to the emergency room.

Next, J. J. called Antoine. After telling him what had happened, she asked him to call Sharleen and the others to tell them. J. J. and Mike stayed with Saskia until she regained consciousness and was well enough to be moved to a regular hospital room.

It was past noon when J. J. left. Mike stayed with Saskia. J. J. and he felt she needed someone to talk to, and he was the only one who could speak Russian with her. Saskia's attempted suicide had affected him even more than J. J. He wanted to stay with her and find out why she would do such a thing. Like most people he had heard of young people attempting suicide, but witnessing it had really shaken him up.

After he had asked Saskia how she was feeling and brought her a cup of water, he started telling her how frightened he and J. J. had been when they found her. Over and over he repeated how happy everyone was that she was recuperating

Finally he carefully broached the subject. "Why did you do it? Don't you like us? What was bothering you? Were you still frightened from being kidnapped and held on the boat?"

Saskia turned away from Mike and lay on her side for a long time, staring at the wall with her back toward Mike. Mike did not push her. He patiently waited for her to respond to his question.

Mike was still carrying on an awkward monologue when J. J. and Sharleen entered the room.

Saskia heard them ask Mike how she was doing and slowly turned over. She sat up against the pillows. Still she did not speak.

Mike spoke, "I think you don't trust us. That makes us feel very bad. We really would like to help you. Give us a chance; let us try."

"Promise to stop them from trying to send me back home?"

Mike grabbed the opening. "Okay, I promise. I'll tell them to stop looking for your parents."

"They won't find them anyway. Because I'm not from Ukraine like I told everybody. I'm from Belarus. If they find me, they will kill me or worse, sell me again to those bastards."

Mike quickly translated for J. J. and Sharleen. He added, "I've no idea where this is going. Do you think that drug the doctor gave her was some sort of hallucinogen? I'll try to get her to tell us more."

But Saskia did not continue.

Mike had to get her to talk. "Your parents sold you?"

All three were astonished when Saskia blurted out in English, "No, of course not. They killed my parents. Nobody will believe what they did."

Still speaking Russian Mike asked, "Who, your parents?"

Again in English, Saskia replied. "No, the government killed them."

J. J. and Sharleen cautioned Mike to stay calm. He needed to gain Saskia's confidence and get her to tell them more.

"Sounds like your English is quite good, but we can continue to speak Russian if you like. Try to trust me. I'm your friend. If you don't want to go back home, we'll help you. I am a lawyer, and J. J. and Sharleen will protect you."

Saskia reverted to Russian. "I've got a headache."

"Doctor Ramos told us you would have a headache for a while. Lie back and relax; that will help. You'll feel better if you tell us more about yourself. If you share your story with us, I swear we'll help you in any way we can. Relax, trust us. We can make sure nobody harms you or makes you do anything against your will. I promise."

Sharleen sat down next to the bed and calmly took Saskia's hand. J. J. stood on the other side and said, "I got to like you a lot, I was so glad you came to stay at my house. You can stay as long as you like. We'll not force you to return home."

Saskia looked at Mike. His boyish good looks were totally disarming; she opened up.

Speaking in English, she haltingly told her story. "I am originally from Belarus. My father was in the government when Belarus gained independence from the Soviet Union. His cousin Sasha Mickewicz was a minister who tried to negotiate closer ties with the European Union. His goal was to get Belarus to eventually join NATO. After a highly contested election, the opposition party came into power and formed a new government. Shortly afterwards, Sasha Mickewitcz died in a single car accident."

Saskia took a sip of water and tightened her grip on Sharleen's hand. She looked at J. J. as if asking for support. J. J. responded by reaching over and taking Saskia's free hand which she gave an encouraging squeeze.

Saskia continued, "My father accused the government of arranging his cousin's death. Despite threats, my father continued his campaign against the government. He played an important part in the next election. When the party in power won with over ninety percent of the vote, my father set out to prove that the election had been rigged. Eventually the threats against my father and our family became so bad that we had to flee to Poland. When we arrived in Poland I only spoke Belarusian and Russian, but in Poland I learned English. I transferred to the International School.

"My father continued his fight against the dictator who headed the government in Belarus. After my father returned from Brussels, where he addressed members of the European Parliament, the threats became more and more severe. One day while we were returning home from a concert in Warsaw, our car was struck by a heavy cement carrier. My father, Mother and my three sisters died instantly. By some miracle, I was thrown clear of our car. I survived with only a few broken bones.

"After I recovered, the government of Belarus sent an official to bring me home. Since I was a minor, I could not object. The government of Poland could do nothing about it. Belarus claimed that Poland did not have jurisdiction over me. I was a citizen of Belarus and a minor. A court in Belarus had claimed jurisdiction over me.

"Before we reached Belarus this so-called government official sold me to a group of Russians who dealt in human trafficking. They, in turn, sold me to the yacht people."

Saskia was interrupted by a nurse coming into the room. "How is she feeling?" She asked.

Saskia answered for herself. "I feel a lot better now. I still have a little bit of a headache, but that is all."

The nurse was surprised, "So you do speak English. That's great! I've come to take your vital signs. If everything looks good, Dr. Herbert will come see you. He'll decide if we can check you out."

Ten minutes later, Dr. Herbert walked in. "Hello. I'm Dr. Herbert. I'm the psychiatrist assigned to your case. You were checked into the hospital for taking an accidental overdose of diazepam. You were unconscious on arrival. That is pretty serious, so I have to ask you how that happened."

Saskia looked at J. J. as if asking permission to talk to the doctor. J. J. nodded okay. "The doctors gave me the pills because I had trouble sleeping. I have nightmares and wake up very scared."

Dr. Herbert looked up from the folder he was looking through. "Yes, the records show they prescribed diazepam. Based on your history that was correct, but they must have warned you not to take more than two tablets per day."

Again, Saskia looked at J.J who encouraged her to answer. All she said was, "I made a mistake."

Dr. Herbert smiled. He did not believe it was a mistake. "Normally I would have to keep you for observation for at least a day or two. But I see in your record that Joanna Jennings, our minister of Public Safety, brought you in. If Madame Minister wants to check you out of the hospital, I'll have to sign the release. But I would prefer keeping you a while here in the hospital, so I can talk to you about this mistake."

J. J. spoke up. "I'm Joanna Jennings. Yes, I brought Saskia to the hospital. The incident happened at my house."

Saskia turned to J. J. a look of bewilderment on her face. "I thought you were Mrs. Johnson, Mister Johnson's wife."

J. J. smiled. "Yes dear, I'm Mister Johnson's wife. We are happily married, but I kept my maiden name"

Saskia was worried, "And you're part of the government? You'll send me back to Belarus when they find me!"

J. J. put a protective arm around Saskia. "Absolutely not! My government is much like the government you told us your uncle and father fought and died for. You are a refugee. I could never be part of a government which wouldn't protect you from the dangers you could face in your home country. You are safe with us."

She gave Saskia a big hug before turning to Doctor Herbert. "I agree with you Doctor, Saskia should stay here so you can spend some time with her. She has been through a lot. Because we thought there was a language problem she has never been seen by a psychiatrist.

Saskia objected, "I'm not staying here by myself."

Before Dr. Herbert could respond, Sharleen jumped in. "No way will I leave you here by yourself. I'll ask the nurse to have another bed brought in. I'm staying with you."

Both J. J. and Mike questioned whether that was necessary.

Sharleen was determined. "Look, I know how it feels after you have been held captive by people who want to harm you. Believe me, you are scared. I was lucky I had someone to be there for me. I want to be there for Saskia. Clint will know why I have to stay."

Mike had no idea what Sharleen was talking about, but J. J. knew. Sharleen had told her all about her escape from the Mafia and her reunion with Clint.

Sharleen got up from her chair and sat on the bed next to Saskia. "This is exciting! Now that I know you speak English I can tell you, how a long time ago, I came to Bermuda to escape from people trying to kill me. And maybe you can tell me about your folks. Sounds like your father was a very brave man. I would love to hear more about him."

Dr. Herbert realized that Saskia was in good hands, and he signaled to the others that it was time to leave the room. Without saying another word, the three of them quietly slipped out of the room.

LIII

In the week after Saskia's hospitalization, she had three sessions with Dr. Herbert. At the end of the week, J. J. and Sharleen met with Doctor Herbert. Since Saskia had no family in Bermuda, J.J. and Sharleen were her de facto guardians. This allowed Dr. Herbert to discuss his diagnosis with them.

"You know her history. You must be aware that this child has been severely traumatized. I recommend that you keep her away from the other women who were on the yacht. Their presence continually reminds her of what she was put through. I also recommend that she be brought in contact with people her own age as soon as possible. I appreciate that the two of you have been trying your best to help her, but unfortunately she does not relate very well to adults. She remains highly suspicious of everyone. She can't get herself to fully trust anyone, especially not men. She finally admitted to me that she is upset that she revealed her true identity to the young man I met in the hospital. I think his name was Mike. He's young, and she feels less threatened by him. But after the sexual abuse she had to endure on the yacht, she is still uncomfortable in the presence of men."

Based on what the doctor had told them, Sharleen took immediate action. Ingrid was moved to her house, and she made plans for Saskia to meet some young people. At the country club, Sharleen had met two young girls, Freda and Marieke Hoeksta. The girls were twins, just about the same age as Saskia. Sharleen thought they would be the perfect young people for Saskia to meet.

Sharleen had made the right choice. Saskia took to the twins immediately, and the three of them started hanging out together. In the meantime, J. J. got to work trying to find some positive identification for Saskia. The girl had no passport or other identification. J. J. contacted the Bermudian Embassy in Poland. She asked that they get copies of the court order used by Belarus to gain jurisdiction over Saskia. The response came quickly. J. J. received copies of the court order, complete with a copy of Saskia's birth certificate. When J. J. showed the birth certificate to Saskia, she refused to admit that it was hers.

With the help of Doctor Herbert, Sharleen and J. J. did their best to convince Saskia that she could trust them, she was safe in Bermuda. J. J. had to repeat over and over again that her government would not allow Belarus to take her back. Saskia finally admitted that the birth certificate was hers. The name on the birth certificate was Katya Navitski. According to the date on the certificate, she was now seventeen years old.

Finding the birth certificate and learning Saskia's name did not solve the real problem: Saskia's shame about what had happened to her on the yacht. She wanted to get away from Bermuda. She no longer felt comfortable in the place where she had been rescued from the yacht. Everybody in Bermuda knew that the women found on the yacht had been rescued from a gang engaged in human trafficking. No one knew the real story, but everyone guessed. The story and all the speculations had repeatedly appeared in the press.

The twins, Freda and Marieke chose to ignore all the rumors, and treated their new friend like any girl who had newly arrived on Bermuda. They did, however, have long discussions with her about her name. Should they call her Saskia or Katya. The three of them finally decided on Saskia, the name she used when they met. Like most of the kids whose parents were not permanent residents of Bermuda, the twins' social life centered around the country club, and they did their best to get Saskia involved in all the activities at the club. Even though Saskia was reluctant, they introduced her to Arjan Wassenberg.

The twins had a huge crush on Arjan; they secretly called him the Dutch Adonis. Arjan's father and mother worked for a Dutch tourist agency and were stationed in Bermuda. To made things exciting for the young girls, Arjan was eighteen and drove a scooter which he was secretly teaching them to ride.

Since they were too young to legally drive the scooter on the open road, the lessons were confined to the country club parking lot. Saskia had driven a moped before and loved racing around the parking lot on Arjan's scooter.

The annual junior awards presentation had been planned to coincide with the big dance held for the younger members of the club. Arjan had won the golf championship and suggested that all three girls come as his date. The twins exploded with excitement. Come hell or high water, they were going to drag Saskia along.

At first things went very well at the dance. Saskia turned out to be a terrific dancer. But when the band started a slow song and Arjan put his hand around her waist, she rudely pushed him away and shouted, "Don't touch me!" She quickly sat down.

Kitty Jaffrey, who had been asked to be one of the chaperones at the dance, noticed what had happened. She was aware of the rumors surrounding Saskia's rescue. She walked over to where Saskia was sitting and asked her to join her for a coke at the bar. Saskia was happy to get away from the others at her table who were asking her, "What happened? What did Arjan do?"

Once seated at the bar, Kitty quickly caught Saskia's attention when she said, "I was raped when I was fourteen. You want to hear about it!"

"You don't mind talking about it!"

"No Saskia. Most people know the story, and I'm not ashamed of it. I'll tell you what happened. Like I said I was almost fifteen years old and walking home from school when this creep grabbed me and pulled me into his car. It took two days for the police to find me. That awful man had kept me in his dirty apartment and raped me repeatedly. For the next month I refused to leave the house. I would not go back to school and refused to see any of my friends. When I finally went back to school I kept to myself, even pushing away my best friend. She tried her best, but I did not want to speak with anyone. This went on for a full semester.

"One day I was walking down the hall, my head down clutching my books to my chest, when a boy came up to me. He asked if he could talk to me. I told him to go away, and leave me alone. He said, 'Is that because everybody makes fun of me?' I told him no. I just wanted to be left alone. He said he was afraid to ask, but would I go with him to the junior prom. I said 'Why me, couldn't you get anyone else to go with you?' He told me maybe but that wasn't why he asked. I wanted him to go away and leave me alone, but I was curious. So I asked why he did ask me. His answer surprised me, and it shook something inside me.

"To this day I remember Vincent's exact words. 'I always used to admire you from a distance. I thought you were so pretty and happy. I used to daydream that you were my girlfriend. Then you came back to school and you were like an injured little bird. I went home and cried all night. Now you, the loveliest girl in school, are not going to the prom, and I can do something about it. Big loser me, the one they make fun of, can do something about it.'

"I rushed to tell him he was not a loser, and he wasn't. Sure he was a real geek, but he was so smart that he got straight A's without cracking a book. It took me a moment to make-up my mind, but I agreed to go with him to the prom. My parents were delighted, and Mom got me the prettiest dress.

"Vincent's father drove us to the school. We were a little late, and when we entered the gym my girlfriend, the only one who knew I was coming, spotted us. She stood up and started applauding and the couples at her table stood up and applauded, and then everybody in the gym started applauding. I held back a little, I was a little embarrassed, but Vincent grinned and whispered into my ear 'Today we are winners.' My girlfriend rushed over, gave me a big hug and led us to her table where she had kept a place for us. Vincent and I had a great time.

"When he brought me home he asked if he could kiss me. I nodded yes, and he kissed me on the cheek. I put both hands behind his head and kissed him hard on the mouth and said, 'Thank you, you're the greatest.' He responded with, 'Today we are both winners.' I rushed inside and told my parents what a great time I had at the dance and that I surprised myself by kissing Vincent on the mouth to thank him. My parents hugged me and my father's eyes were moist when he said 'Welcome back sweetheart. We missed you'."

Saskia had listened very carefully. "Vincent must have been very special. Do you still see him?"

"Oh yes. My husband and I visit with him when he comes to Bermuda for vacation. He was fresh out of college when he started his own company. He had some proprietary software and within a few years sold the company for three hundred million English pounds. He went on to establish a few more companies, which he sold for successfully more money. When he comes to Bermuda he stays in his house. He owns the big mansion right next to Ocean View Hotel. But now it's time for you to create your own welcome back. You look like a winner to me; I know you can do it."

Saskia got up and walked back to the table where she had been sitting. Arjan was talking to Freda. She leaned over the back of his chair and kissed his cheek while she said, "I don't want to interrupt you two but can I have the next dance?"

On the dance floor she put her head on Arjan's shoulder and said, "I'm sorry, truly sorry. You've been a great friend and didn't deserve my stupid behavior."

LIV

Saskia was making rapid progress. She was no longer seeing Dr. Herbert, but she kept telling J. J. that she felt she was living in a fish bowl. Everybody on the Island seemed to know her story. Wherever she went, people stared and pointed at her. J. J. discussed the problem with Sharleen, but they did not have a good answer to the problem

The solution came from an unexpected source. The twins, Freda and Marieke, had become very close to Saskia. They asked their Father if he could help. They wanted Saskia to come to Holland and live with them

Their father, Gerrit Hoekstra, was the manager of the Bermuda office of N.V Verrenigde Bank Holland. He was scheduled to rotate back to the Netherlands in three months.

Gerrit Hoekstra consulted his good friend the Dutch Consul in Bermuda. He found out that Saskia, based on her history, could be admitted into the Netherlands as a refugee. With the help of Jimmy

Garretson, he got the paper work submitted. Saskia's dream became reality. In two months, she would return with the Hoekstra family to the Netherlands, and live with them in their home in Hilversum.

LV

With only Nina and Ingrid staying at her house, Sharleen had only two lost souls to worry about. She hovered over them like a mother hen. Ingrid had started to pick up some English, and after a few lessons from a language teacher, Sharleen placed her in the care of Doctor Herbert. Nina was more of a problem. Mike was the only one who could carry on a conversation with her. Sharleen was happy that he was always willing to spend some time with her.

Sharleen and Clint were having dinner alone when she finally told him what she has heard about Nina. The graphic details of what the woman told her had upset Sharleen to the extent that she woke up several nights in a cold sweat just thinking about it. Sharleen considered herself quite worldly, but this was beyond her realm of imagination. She had trouble verbalizing the details of what the woman had said, so she only gave Clint a general overview of what they did to Nina.

"The only gal in the group who spoke English took me aside and said I should know what Nina had to endure while on the yacht. Unlike all the other women, Nina was on the yacht for about three months. They did not show her at several auctions and kept her hidden away, to be abused by the crew. At least five times a week, they would fetch her from below. Kai would allow several crew members to have their way with her while he watched. He never had sex with her himself, but he got his kicks watching while members of his crew raped her. He encouraged them to try various kinky positions, and often asked two or even three men to try and have sex with her at the same time. During the time that the English-speaking woman was aboard, Kai started forcing Nina to also have sex with some of the women. Nina was mortified when Kai and two of his men made her do all kinds of sexual acts with Saskia, the young girl who was staying at J. J.'s. I am so glad everything turned out so well for that child."

Clint was appalled at what had happened to Nina. "No wonder you've been hovering over her. She must be traumatized. I know all the women saw a psychiatrist when we first brought them ashore, but doesn't she need more help?"

"I checked. Dr. Malloy says she probably needs a lot of help, but the first thing I had to do was gain her confidence. We don't have a Russian-speaking doctor available, and treating her using a translator is not very effective. He told me we could best help her by getting her to trust us and to feel secure here.

We must make her feel she is in a non-threatening environment, surrounded by loving people who really care about her. Dr. Malloy said we might be surprised how resilient she turns out to be. He told me to watch carefully. If I do not see any improvement in the coming weeks, I have to contact him. I think she is already doing a lot better than when she first moved in with us. Lately Mike Aleksenko has been taking Nina and Ingrid on tours of the island and for lunch at the country club. And guess what."

Clint said he had no idea.

"Turns out Nina is a fabulous tennis player. Mike took her out on the courts and was very impressed. He tried to buy her a tennis outfit in the pro shop, but Nina refused to wear shorts. Mike did not push it, and they settled on a nice pair of white slacks. She did accept a pair of good tennis shoes, and the two of them have already played several sets during the past week. And I think we are developing a problem."

Clint did not understand why the two of them playing tennis was not a good thing.

Sharleen explained. "When Mike comes by to ask if she wants to go with him to the club for a game of tennis, Nina readily accepts. She loves tennis, and I think she is starting to get attracted to him."

"Why is that bad?" Clint asked.

"He's just a happy-go-lucky guy, and pretty soon he'll be returning to the States. I'm afraid she'll get hurt."

Clint did not see it as a big problem, "Talk to him about it. He's a great guy. He'll understand. I'm sure he's not the type to lead her on."

The next time Mike came by the house, Sharleen sat him down to talk about it. She was very strict with him. She said he should realize that Nina, after all she had been through, was very vulnerable, and could easily be hurt if she became too attached to him. Mike told Sharleen he was very attracted to Nina. She was one of the most attractive women he had ever met, and the two of them got along so well.

Sharleen said that he had better think this over. "Take a week or two, and date some of your many lady friends. See how you feel about her after that. Let me warn you if you hurt that girl in any way, I'll break your neck!"

Being talked to like that called for an aggressive response, but Mike accepted it. He told Sharleen he would seriously think about his relationship with Nina, and not come by the house for a while.

Exactly two weeks later, Mike was back and asked to speak with Sharleen. "I've thought about it a great deal, and I'm very serious about Nina. I think about her all day, and believe it or not, I've missed her these past two weeks. Yes, I've been out on a few dates, and it's not fair to those gals. I'm thinking about Nina while talking to them. I almost lapsed into Russian while dining with Lilian, and I've gone out with her a lot this past year."

This was not exactly what Sharleen had expected, but she was honest with Mike, and admitted to him that Nina had asked about him all the time. She had lied and said he was away on a business trip. Mike had a sheepish grin on his face when, like a little boy, he asked Sharleen permission to take Nina to the club for a game of tennis, followed by dinner. Just the two of them, without the usual entourage. Sharleen could not help but say yes. It stirred her romantic side when she helped Nina get ready to go out with Mike. Nina and she communicated mostly with sign language, but she could sense Nina's excitement. *Thank God,* Sharleen thought. *She is acting like a normal girl.*

After that, nobody was surprised that a romance developed between Nina and Mike. But it was a surprise to everybody when Mike's parents showed up to meet Nina. It seems Mike had been telling his parents about Nina from the beginning. He never told them much about her release from the yacht. Just that she had been kidnapped in her home country and kept prisoner on the yacht, and that he was one of the few who could speak to her in her native Russian. When Mike begged his parents to come to Bermuda to meet Nina, they realized how serious he was about this girl.

"Finally," his mother said. She had thought he would never settle down, and she was ready to have a daughter-in-law. One who could speak Russian would be a big plus.

It was not hard to like Mike's parents. They were a very active middle-aged couple who enjoyed life. They were proud that they could take on Mike in a game of tennis and hold their own, but were quick to admit that a serious game of doubles against Mike and Nina was a little too much for them. It was obvious that Mike's parents gloated over his accomplishments. He was their all-American son, a Rhodes Scholar, with a law degree from Yale. Sharleen was worried about how they would feel about Nina. She spoke Russian, but as immigrants, would they prefer an American girl for their son?

Sharleen's worries proved to be groundless. Mike's mother instantly fell in love with Nina, and the feeling was obviously mutual. The two of them chatted away all day long. It was Nina who showed Mike's mother the beautiful sights of Bermuda.

The subject of Mike's eventual return to the States could not be avoided. It turned out that Nina longed to go to a place where nobody knew much about her past, and definitely not about the episode on the yacht. She had never even discussed all the details with Mike, although, like everybody else on Bermuda, he knew what Kai and his gang were all about.

Mike, assisted by J. J., had been looking into the possibility of getting immigration papers for Nina. The quota for the eastern bloc was loosening up, but even so, to go through the normal procedure could take years. They delved into Nina's past to find a loophole.

Nina had been a physical education teacher and part-time tennis pro when she was approached by a local modeling agency. The pay was very good, and they promised her that, with her face and body, they could get her promoted to pose for international advertising campaigns. It turned out the agency was a front for a group who dealt in human trafficking. The owner of the agency was a high-ranking party official with strong national government connections. Mike took this bit of information as the basis for Nina's application for political asylum. In any case, he planned to marry Nina, and that also could allow her to stay in the United States.

During the engagement party for Mike and Nina, Lakota and Ehawee questioned Mike about when he and Nina planned to get married. Would they marry while Mike was still working in Bermuda, or would they wait and get married in the United States? Mike had to admit that they had not yet decided what to do. His parents were pushing for a wedding in the States, but the problem would be getting Nina into the United States on an immigration visa. Lakota thought that once they were married, Nina could stay in the States regardless of whether they married in Bermuda or in the United States. Mike explained that it was much more complicated than that. To explain, he took out his computer and Googled "marrying an alien." He found *ALL LAW by Ilona Bray, J.D.*:

> *If you are an undocumented immigrant in the United States (sometimes referred to as an "illegal immigrant"), nothing stops you from marrying a U.S. citizen, or most anyone else you wish to marry. U.S. citizens marry illegal immigrants on a regular basis. (The main limitations on marriage in the U.S. have to do with your age and whether the person you wish to marry is a close relative.)*

> *Whether that marriage will get you a green card (U.S. permanent residence) however, is another matter. In theory, these immigrants are "immediate relatives," and are eligible for a green card through the marriage. But undocumented immigrants face some very high hurdles in claiming this right.*
>
> *Despite the fact that your marriage may be valid, when an illegal immigrant seeks to become a legal resident, various issues come up.*
>
> *Of course, to get a green card based on marriage, you would also have to prove that you meet all the various other eligibility criteria, such as that it is a valid (legally recognized) marriage and that it's "bona fide" (you're not just getting married to get a green card). You'd also have to overcome any other possible grounds of inadmissibility.*

"So, you have not decided what to do?" Lakota asked.

"No." Mike replied. "I'm still trying to figure out how to get Nina into the States. I have discussed it many times with the American consul here in Hamilton, and his staff is trying to help us. The only thing for sure is that Nina and I will get married. And if that means I have to stay here and live in Bermuda for the rest of my life, so be it!"

Ehawee squeezed Lakota's arm and leaned over to whisper in his ear, "Told ya, he's nuts about that girl. You and your, 'that playboy will never settle down' opinion of him. I told ya, you were wrong."

LVI

The excitement surrounding Nina's and Mike's engagement was soon followed by another wave of excitement, caused by the announcement by Ehawee that she was pregnant. Sharleen and J. J. acted as if they were the ones expecting a baby.

Sharleen was so excited about it that Clint asked if she was sorry she never had a child of her own.

Sharleen thought about it for a long time before she answered. "No, I'm not."

"Were you worried we'd have a black baby and the child would never fit in, having one white and one multiracial parent?"

"That's an honest question, since we know it was on your mother's mind. It's a question I should have asked you in high school, but my life went a different way. Having a baby was never a question while I was married to Giovanni. As a matter of fact, I had my tubes tied to prevent having a baby. After we got together so many things happened, in such a short period of time, that there was never really a time I wanted a baby. You never mentioned it, either. It was still possible to have my egg fertilized by your sperm and replanted in me. Would you have wanted that?"

"No. Even during the time with Jada I never wanted children. Don't ask me why. Maybe it was my relationship with my parents. But, they tell me with women it's different. Do you ever feel something in your life is missing?"

"Honestly, no. Anyway, there would not be any time for another child. Ehawee has already chartered J. J. and me for babysitting duties. She asked us to be substitute grandmothers and help her raise the child. Since she grew up on a reservation and was always treated by her tribe as a princess, she feels she will need help giving the child a normal upbringing. J. J. and I are still giddy about the idea that we would know how to be normal."

"You still haven't answered my question. Let me put it this way; do you feel fulfilled? Is your life what you wished it to be?"

"The simple answer is, more than I ever wished for! To start with, I am living my high school dream. I am living my life with my high school sweetheart. The guy I was madly in love with, and still am. And don't forget our very special blessing. We have Mikie; a gift we can only treasure. We might have had a rocky start, but Jada gave us her mantra, 'NEVER TOO LATE' and we have lived by it.

Also by Harold J. Fischel
Taylor, The Journey Home ISBN:0692341811 /
ISBN 13:9780692341810
Anthony ISBN:1494851210 /
ISBN 13:9781494851217

Reviews of *Anthony*

Reviewed By Jack Magnus for Readers' Favorite
Harold J. Fischel's coming of age story, Anthony, is inspiring and heartwarming. Anthony's life is turned upside down by his mother's illness, but the adults he comes in contact with as he grows up help make his life story a triumphant one. Yuni's friend, Aunt Rita, is a marvelous character as are Kay and her parents. Anthony's progression from a withdrawn, small and chubby kid into a confident, caring and ethical young man is wonderful to watch. Fischel's writing style is accomplished and smooth, and I quickly became immersed in this athletic and ethical story of triumph over adversity. Anthony is a marvelous book and is highly recommended reading

Reviewed By Katelyn Hensel for Readers' Favorite
Harold J. Fischel's book Anthony is as meaningful as it is simple. A simple story, with a normal plot, but the depth and the meaning within is so much moreIt's not often that I find a book that truly moves

me, but Anthony may have just been it. Anthony is so real...such a realistic and poignant character. He is bitter, confused, sad, angry, and while his experience is not necessarily the norm of a typical young adult, you can easily relate to him. What a transformation. Anthony goes from a scared and weak child to a fierce, understanding, and competent young man. I loved seeing the way that other people had an effect on him. Usually you see characters change because of events that happen, but Anthony really changed based on his perception of himself vs. the perception that others have of him. Fischel writes with skill and craftsmanship that is a joy to read. I would read anything else he has to offer in a heartbeat.

Reviewed By Lorena Sanqui for Readers' Favorite

Anthony by Harold J. Fischel is a wonderful coming of age novel. I loved the story of Anthony, but it didn't seem to follow one plot line. There were lots of smaller stories crammed in the book, although they all revolved around Anthony. It was okay but everything happened too fast; there was conflict after conflict so that it felt like there was no real climax and the ending seemed abrupt. On the other hand, I welcomed all the surprises and I loved all the characters. Anthony was resilient and strong, even when he was still a kid. Everything he experienced growing up only made him stronger, some of the things that happened to him even made me cry. Aunt Rita was a really nice person who just made some mistakes. Kay was persistent and supportive in all that Anthony does. All the supporting characters also played big roles in Anthony's success. Overall, a good book with great characters.

Reviewed By Mamta Madhavan for Readers' Favorite
The story evokes poignant feelings and it is wonderfully narrated. All the characters have important roles that have been portrayed well. Anthony's growing up and leaving behind a troubled childhood, to finally becoming a responsible husband and father has been developed well. His leaving behind the stigma of being an illegitimate son and then holding down an important job position is true to the times and resonates well with readers. The language is simple as it targets young adults. The story line is fascinating, which will make it difficult for readers to put the book down. On the whole, it is a very interesting book.

Reviewed By Melinda Hills for Readers' Favorite
I truly enjoyed the book and felt that it told a terrific story. You portrayed Anthony's younger years with warmth and compassion and provided him with many opportunities to rise above his circumstances. As he grew up and began the relationship with Rita, it was portrayed naturally and innocently in its own way and, again, provided opportunity for Anthony to grow, mature and understand himself. I really appreciate the way you allow Anthony to restrain himself in so many different situations and not 'go with the flow' – do what everyone else is doing because of

peer pressure. It is also important later in the story as his daughter is intimidated by her fear of how others will react to her, so Anthony's experiences are a good background from which he can provide understanding and guidance.

Made in the USA
Middletown, DE
31 July 2016